THE MASKS OF MANOVALO

THE EIGHTH BOOK OF DUBIOUS MAGIC

RENOIR

To Karl, a different sort of mind to challenge and inspire me!

And, as ever, for my darling bride and Muse.

CONTENTS

1

MORNING INGLORIOUS

"But why *can't* I go out and see Teasy?"

Morton Overbeek sighed. He was sure that if he looked up 'precocious' in an encyclopedia, there would be a picture of Nicola. Sweet, sometimes. Charming, even – sometimes. But definitely precocious.

"When TZ is in the workshop, he's there to work, and not be disturbed."

"*Feh!* I would not disturb him!"

"Little contessa, you cannot *not* disturb him. Or me. Or anyone else, I'm afraid!"

Nicola planted her fists on her slim hips, or where her hips would be in a few short years, and pouted. As good-hearted as she really was, it was an expression that came easily to her.

"I think you are jealous of me, Blob. I think you are afraid Teasy will like me better than you," the girl said, not quite seriously.

Morton sighed again. They'd had this conversation, or something like it, a number of times. He wasn't sure that Nicola truly grasped the fact that, even had her charms been more fully developed, she was fundamentally not the type that his partner (business and romantic) was interested in. Or perhaps she did, and considered it a challenge.

"Nicola, you know you're always welcome here in the store. And when the workshop door is open, you're welcome there too. But when that door is closed, it means one or other of us is in there working, and we need to concentrate. You live with an artist – you understand that."

"*Feh!* Giancarlo can work when I am around. Often he does – he says I am an inspiration to him."

"Hmm, perhaps so. Crafting music is probably different to creating jewellery."

Both Morton and Tadeusz Zybysko were makers of fine jewellery. Overbeek cut, polished and set gems with studied elegance. His Eastern European partner was a creative silversmith whose work combined flair with delicacy. Young Nicola shared a house with Giancarlo LaGrigio, a mostly reclusive composer, who was known to be a master of a wide range of instruments. The American-born jeweller had met the musician on a few occasions, thanks to Nicola, and appreciated the quality of his work.

"If you're bored, little contessa, you can help me put together a new window display. I'd like it done before the morning's tourists are out on the street," he offered, with a smile.

"Oh, could I? Thank you, Blob!"

She skipped to his side and hugged his ample frame. Her nickname for the American was a little unfair – Morton was overweight, but scarcely obese. He carried his weight badly, though, rarely dressing in clothes that flattered, or even disguised, his shape. He accepted her name for him with good grace, as did 'Teasy', whose title was simply Nicola's version of Overbeek's usual pronunciation of his initials. The two men privately quite liked the collective name of "Teasy and the Blob" – it made them think of comic books, or something from American television. It was silly, but somehow more interesting than "Tad and Morty", as Overbeek's mother persisted in calling them.

Man and girl were busily removing the current display from the picture window, so typical of the small stores in Venice – a narrow frontage for a deep cavern of wares and workshop that looked out upon a small *riello* that was a spur of one of Venice's larger canals. There was little activity on the *Fondamenta Margherita* – the walkway outside the shop, at this hour, so movement caught their attention. Both tensed, and Morton Overbeek paled.

Quickly they withdrew from the window, Morton propelling Nicola into a place of some cover – not behind the counter, too obvious, but among a small stack of boxes and crates, several of which were open.

Three figures were striding purposefully toward the jewellery store. Even a casual observer, had there been any, would have reached some immediate realizations. The three men were related to each other (brothers, in fact); they were brawny men well-used to physical work; they had a definite objective, not just a morning stroll for exercise; and that objective was trouble.

Morton made no attempt to lock the door. That would have only led to more damage being done. He rapped quickly on the workshop door, gave an urgent warning cry of "The fishmen!", and hoped that would be enough for his partner to somehow prepare himself. Then he stood behind his counter, his hands pressed against its top, waiting for the storm to hit.

The door was thrown open. The glass shook in its frame, but miraculously didn't break, perhaps to the disappointment of the burly figure who'd shoved it. The brothers strode in in single file – no two of them would have fitted through shoulder to shoulder. All three filled much of the space in front of the counter, and all looked around belligerently. They were swarthy, heavy of brow, large of body and thick of stubble. They might have modelled for the cavemen illustrated in some children's books.

"We want the smith," growled the one whose stubble came closest to resembling a beard, its edges having apparently been shaved into shape.

Morton held up his hands and spread them helplessly, about to claim ignorance of his partner's whereabouts. The brother with the largest nose and the most receding hairline reached over the counter, grabbed the front of the jeweller's shirt and lifted him onto his toes.

"Don't bother to lie, American. Duilio, Luigino, in there!" He nodded towards the workshop door. Clearly, they knew the layout of the shop from past experience.

"*Si*, Ugo," replied Luigino, the surly one who'd growled first.

Ugo held Overbeek helpless while his two brothers lumbered to the back, Luigino pulling a coiled length of plastic rope from a deep pocket as he walked. Tadeusz may or may not have answered had they knocked at the workshop door. The point was moot, as Duilio kicked the door off its hinges as soon as he was close enough to do so.

The two brothers didn't break stride as they entered the room. From the front counter, Overbeek could hear crashes, thuds, and incoherent cries of pain that clearly came from the silversmith, not his 'visitors'. In remarkably short order, the brothers came back out of the workshop. TZ had been tied quickly – arms pinned to his sides, wrists behind his back, ankles tightly bound. He was slung face-up over Duilio's broad shoulder, so his own back was bent painfully as the thug walked.

Ugo frowned at the upside-down face of the smith. "You were told that Il Duce wanted that figurine."

"The... the silver cat was already bought and paid for by Signor Abbondanza... in Rome..." the bound man stammered.

The attempt at an explanation only earned him a slap across the face from Ugo, briefly releasing one hand from Morton's shirt before replying, "That man is in Roma. Il Duce is here. You were told – he *wanted* it. What he wants, he gets."

"I can make another, just for him!" suggested the silversmith through pained gasps.

"But it will not be the first," was the answer. There was more than a suggestion that these weren't Ugo's own words, but a recitation of something he'd had clearly explained to him. He snapped his fingers then returned his grip to the jeweller.

"To... to his own design!" cried Zybysko, squirming frantically.

That didn't even elicit a reply. Luigino held open the shop door as Duilio marched out, his protesting burden still draped over one shoulder. If there was anyone else out on the fondamenta, they made themselves scarce. Ugo had hauled Overbeek from behind the counter and was propelling him backwards out after the others.

Nicola rose up from her hiding place, a look of rage on her dark young face. She looked likely to dive out and bite Ugo from behind on the leg, like a small but savage guard dog. Morton saw her, and frantically signalled for her to stay away. He knew that there wasn't a shred of conscience between these three men, and any interference would only get her hurt, probably badly. The girl knew that too, but it wasn't her own fear that made her pause. It was the fear in Morton Overbeek's eyes. Fear of having her pain, or worse, on his own conscience. In that moment of hesitation, all five men were out of the shop. Nicola's dark eyes glittered, and her mouth was set in a grim, hard line. It wasn't a look that suited her pretty features.

With Duilio grasping his shoulders and Luigino clutching his feet, TZ was swung twice before being pitched off the fondamenta, over the guardrail and into the riello. The brothers ignored the water that splashed onto their clothes, although Luigino quickly produced a ragged handkerchief to wipe his hair. Ugo still held Morton as they all watched the smith's awkward, desperate efforts to keep his head above water. Duilio took a rapid series of photos with his mobile phone.

Shrugging at the realization that Zybysko seemed unlikely to sink immediately, Ugo tossed the jeweller to the ground. "You upset Il Duce Grosso again, and the next time he will go into the water tied to something heavy, eh? Like you, perhaps." He punctuated that last threat with a sharp kick to Morton's calf.

With neither another word nor a backwards glance, the three strode away, as instinctively in step as three soldiers. Now a couple of neighbouring shopkeepers ventured to appear. None proved remotely useful, although to be fair, the well-deserved reputation of the three brothers had everyone genuinely frightened.

It was Nicola who darted from the jewellery store, clutching a sharp implement she'd grabbed from the workshop, and dived into the riello. Tadeusz had enough presence of mind to stop struggling as she sawed at the plastic rope around his arms, then wrists. By the time she got through his ankle bonds, he was bobbing in the water like an exhausted seal. Finally, some arms were extended to help the pair back up onto the walkway. Immediately the cold late-January air on wet clothes and skin set them both shivering.

Towels materialised, and both Tadeusz and Nicola were wrapped first in one of these, then each in a massively relieved arm of Morton 'Blob' Overbeek. From somewhere, a restorative glass of grappa was produced and refilled as required. No one objected when Nicola grabbed it and swigged her own share.

The matronly woman who owned the little handbag store two doors down shook her head, sympathetically enough, but with a resigned, accusatory tone said to Tadeusz, "You should know better, signore, than to cross the brothers Culatello."

Even she shrank slightly from the withering glare that Nicola gave in response. "*Feh*," the girl said under her breath.

.ooo.

2

THE LOVERS

On the face of it, they were simply a happy, if more than usually lucky, couple. JB and Q, they affectionately called each other. Met while working as Public Servants in the Australian capital, Canberra. Fell in love. Each independently came into a substantial amount of money. Now they were taking the opportunity to 'live the dream', travelling the world together, her with a notion of writing a book, he contentedly going along and enjoying life.

There was, of course, a great deal more to it than that. Those basic facts were true. Elizabeth McKew (formerly Elizabeth Dance, until her recent divorce from a passive-aggressive misery of a man) *had* been a very efficient administrative officer in a major government department. Subsequent to her separation she realised she'd fallen for one of the business analysts in her team, the seemingly unprepossessing if eccentric John B. Stewart, and was delighted to find that the feeling was mutual. They *had* both become unexpectedly financially secure, and discovered a mutual love of travel which they indulged while she worked on her first manuscript.

But there was nothing simple about them, or their lives together.

John B. Stewart remembered nothing of his life before the age of ten, when he was found wandering the streets of Brisbane in ragged jeans and a too-small purple t-shirt with "John B." written on the collar. He'd then been adopted out of a good orphanage, well-raised, and made his way through University with a flair for history and languages, but a low threshold for boredom and too great a fondness for single malt scotch. After a few jobs he'd drifted into the Public Service mostly from a chronic lack of ambition, and had been on a career path that had flat-lined early.

Then, one drunken evening, he'd run his head forcefully into a poker machine in a misguided and futile attempt to produce a decent payout. The impact had triggered something he described as a faint buzzing, deep within his brain. Thereafter, in strange, unpredictable, often unreliable ways, John B.'s spoken wishes came true. He was a wizard.

Elizabeth had been one of the overwhelming majority of Stewart's friends and acquaintances to dismiss his claims as, at best, 'eccentricity'. But she'd been quietly struck by his evident sincerity, and intrigued by his avowed determination not to "wish for anything too grand" – a combination of not wanting to 'burn out' the strange power, and a lack of greed that matched his lack of ambition.

The downside of John B.'s dubious magical power was that he'd found himself drawn into a succession of weird and dangerous situations, in conflict with an assortment of what he described as "whackos, freaks and nutjobs". It had started with a mad sorceress, somehow connected with a covert US military base, who'd sought to summon an immensely powerful demon from what she'd called "the Outer Dark" and somehow take over what would be left of the world.

Elizabeth didn't know, or quite understand, the whole story, because John B. didn't himself. The 'dark arts' had never interested him. The final battle with the sorceress had somehow turned upon his new-found magic proving a suitable 'power source' for the right counter-spell, fortuitously known by another former work colleague who *was* a student of the occult.

Since then the unlikely wizard had been caught up in the machinations of a variety of villains, mystics and extremists of different faiths and types. Among them had been a rogue ex-Soviet scientist, a psychic researcher determined to forcibly extract the secret of John B. Stewart's power. That attempt had gone fatally wrong (just in time), but had left the intended victim the sole beneficiary of a very substantial Swiss bank account, since vaguely described as "the inheritance" to anyone who wondered how he'd been able to give up work.

It had been Elizabeth's interference that had been key to JB's survival, and her first realisation that there really was something to his 'magic'. She didn't understand it, and in truth, neither did he. The power's origin was as unknown as his own.

At least she knew something of her own parentage, she thought, although she had no recollection of the father who'd abandoned his family. She had his name, and understood he came from the islands north of Scotland, and that was about it. Her mother had been bitter and resentful. Elizabeth never thought that unreasonable, but she did eventually recognise and chafe at her mother's wheedling, possessive, controlling nature. She'd realised too late that the same behaviours were the hallmarks of her husband Sonny, and it said a lot for the strength of her own character that she'd finally thrown off the influence of both, and vehemently claimed her independence. Peculiarly to some observers, her almost immediate relationship with John B. was actually an assertion of that independence. She'd realised that she felt respected, valued, truly loved – for the first time in her life, and that was something to be embraced.

It was worth the whirlwind and occasional madness, not to mention the danger they'd shared. They'd braved fires, fights and perils at sea together. In Norway she'd miraculously survived being shot in the back. Perhaps not miraculously, she thought. More correct to say 'magically'. John B.'s own escape from a watery grave had seemed little less extraordinary. The travails had only made their bond, their love, stronger.

Q's financial windfall had been only marginally less improbable than that of her beau. While in Scotland researching local lore and old family history as source material for the novel she'd decided to write, Elizabeth found clues to a forgotten 15th Century colony in what was much later the US State of Maine, established by an ancestor from the Orkneys. Following that trail had led to the New England coast and the substantial treasure of Henry, the White Prince of almost forgotten local legend. It also led to encounters with modern day pirates and a sea serpent.

Their lives together were proving *unusual*.

At least recent weeks had been for the most part blessedly peaceful. They'd driven down from Maine to New York in a rented BMW SUV, randomly nicknamed Yvette. Packed securely in the back of the vehicle had been a sturdy, World War Two-vintage ammunition box.

Its worn exterior belied its contents, for all that they'd been very much older. It held Elizabeth's treasure. Gems, jewellery, ornaments and coins, the youngest more than six hundred years old, some very considerably more. It had been the legacy of the self-styled 'Prince', Henry St. Clair, intended as foundation of the treasury of the new empire he'd sailed across the world to establish, funded by his own family's wealth and the largesse of some Venetian backers. When he'd returned to the Orkneys to replenish provisions, weapons and new colonists, Henry had fallen victim to German mercenaries in the employ of the English throne.

Bereft of his leadership, those remaining in North America vanished without leaving a trace in the history books. Nearly a century later, Columbus knew nothing of them. Almost stillborn, the European settlement disappeared. Some of its members must have succumbed to disease or disaster. Others intermarried with the native population they seemed to have co-existed amicably with. More than amicably, if you consider linguistic traces of Gaelic and startling incidences of red hair and blue eyes among a couple of indigenous tribes.

The most precious pieces of Henry's treasure had been preserved for the promised and prophesised return of the Prince, or his descendants. Secured in the custody of remnants of one strange ancient tribe, themselves bordering on the legendary. Hidden for centuries, it took the combination of John B.'s magic and some unique distinguishing spark of Q's own mysterious bloodline to bring the small hoard back into the light.

A paragon of organisational skill, while they were still in Maine Elizabeth had established that the best, most reputable and reliable brokers for her newfound inheritance were to be found in New York. There may have been individual dealers and potential buyers in different parts of the world who might offer a better deal on certain types of item, but the Big Apple held a concentration of businesses which would doubtless connect with those options anyway.

Besides, Christmas in New York had a reputation for being something special. It would be their first Christmas and New Year together as A Couple, and they'd wanted to celebrate the romance of the occasion. They hadn't been disappointed.

Nor had the gem traders and antiquities brokers let them down. Over the course of a few weeks, Elizabeth had gradually parlayed most of that boxful of valuables into a Swiss account of her own. Some eyebrows were raised in auction-houses and markets across the world at the quality and rarity of some pieces that suddenly came up for sale, and the prices gained were a fair reflection.

Not everything of 'Prince' Henry's heritage was sold. Some items had been given as gifts to folks in Maine who'd provided help in its acquisition. Life-saving help, in some instances. Two particular stones, an amethyst and a turquoise, had been kept aside by Q and John B. as presents for each other. And a considerable cache of old Venetian coins had not joined the many Spanish, English, Scottish, Roman and even Persian currency that had fetched tidy sums at specialist auctions.

While in Maine the couple had befriended a reclusive authoress named Dorothy Duncum – 'Texas Dorothy' to the locals. In some ways a strange and mysterious character herself, Dorothy had recommended to them the owner of a particular small museum in Venice. It had seemed almost a reluctant recommendation. They were not to expect anything like a good price for the coins, but the museum owner, Marina DeNucci, might be the best possible source of information about the coins' history, which may have some relevance to the family story. Such details meant more to Elizabeth the aspiring writer than the potential commercial value, especially when there were so many other riches now in her possession.

So, after revelling in the seasonal celebrations, learning to ice-skate in Central Park, exploring galleries, enjoying shows on- and off-Broadway, and haunting a few excellent jazz clubs around Chelsea and Greenwich Village, the pair had finally set off for Venice. Enthusiasm and energy restored by the break, Elizabeth was looking forward to learning more about her ancestor, a figure seemingly lost to conventional history.

John B. had absolute faith in the organizational skills of his beloved as she spent a busy day or two on-line, making travel and accommodation arrangements. He'd have made it up as they went along, but recognised the wisdom of her more ordered approach. They said "good-bye" to trusty Yvette at New York airport. Despite the considerable mileage they'd chalked up, there were no administrative hassles with the hire company, much to everyone's satisfaction. The direct flight to London was long, but comfortable.

They chose to travel business class. While they could certainly afford even better, JB and especially Q were ill at ease with seeming 'ostentatious'. Each had been raised in what had been, at best, a working-class environment. 'Showing off' had been something that other people did, and a source of resentment more than envy. Business class on their international flight offered comfort, legroom, decent if not fine food, and as satisfactory a drinks menu as could be found on an aeroplane. They both appreciated good wine and good whisky, although John B. rarely found the excellent single malts he favoured 39,000 feet above the ground.

They dozed intermittently, unconsciously taking turns to sleep with head resting on the other's shoulder. Flight attendants smiled at the way the loose curls of their long hair mingled – hers brunette and neat, his shades lighter and better described as shaggy. It looked somehow symbolic of a romance.

There was only a small delay in London before their flight to Venice. Strictly speaking, the flight was to Marco Polo Airport on the

Italian mainland north-east of Venice. The city itself was built on over 120 islands, many of them small, connected by more than four hundred bridges, known locally as *ponti*.

Marco Polo Airport provided the first and only inconvenience of their journey. Typically efficient Elizabeth had ensured that they had appropriate documented approval to bring an unusual amount of currency into the country (albeit very *old* currency). The ancient coins were secured in a locked, lined leather case inside an antique post-man's satchel Stewart had found in a Manhattan second-hand store, and immediately chosen as his new hand luggage. It was a fitting companion for the old khaki duffel bag that was John B.'s usual luggage, packed with the jeans and myriad purple shirts that consti-tuted most of his wardrobe.

The metal mesh lining of the case, as well as being resistant to the slash of a thieving blade, made the contents unrecognizable to the airport scanners. That was intentional. Not every Customs officer in the world was scrupulously honest, and while the Australians were willing to display the contents and prove they matched the documen-tation, Elizabeth wanted nobody else opening the case.

That wasn't the problem for the vexatious man at Marco Polo, though. He took umbrage at the *weight* of Stewart's hand luggage. He didn't care that the matter had been addressed, and resolved, in both New York and London (with some bureaucratic wrangling and addi-tional payment changing hands). Perhaps that was the issue – his own palm hadn't been greased.

The man had imperiously berated them with much finger-pointing and hand-waving, brandishing several pages of *regole* which he'd extracted from a large ring binder on his desk. Even the glare of Elizabeth's green eyes – a shade of rare colour and brilliance, hadn't shaken his bluster, perhaps because he didn't make eye contact with the irksome foreigners.

Frustrated, John B. had growled, "I wish you'd get some snappy treatment of your own, mate."

Oblivious to the comment, the official had unthinkingly slapped a hand down on the binder. The rings sprang shut, one of the metal hoops stabbing right through the webbing between thumb and fore-finger. The officer yelped loudly and shook his hand frantically, the binder still attached, pages of *regole* fluttering to the floor. Blood spurted across the desk. Another uniformed officer rushed over to assist. Noting swiftly that the Australians' paperwork was in order she waved them through while she tried to settle her colleague enough to release his hand.

"I hope that's the one he writes with," said Q unsympathetically.

Without a backward glance they made their way out to catch a waterbus, the leisurely mode of transport which would take them over to Venice itself.

.ooo.

3

BUONGIORNO VENEZIA

Fifty or so minutes later, the waterbus had deposited Elizabeth and John B. at the Piazzo San Marco. From there they boarded a *vaporetto* – one of the large, open-decked ferries that constituted most of Venice's public transport system. Elizabeth had made thorough notes while doing her on-line research, and ensured she had the correct route number to take them to the stop in Giardini, from where they could walk to the apartment she'd booked.

Already they fancied that they felt Venice changing their own internal rhythms, physical and emotional. It wasn't just pace, although vaporetti certainly moved at a slower speed than most buses or trains. It was more subtle than that, and might have been missed by folks less aware of their environment and their own place in it. Travel by water instead of by road had a different feel to it, moving *in* the route rather than *on* it.

Their new temporary home, a month's rent already paid based entirely on instinct, a detailed description, and a few photos on a website, was a fully self-contained two-bedroom unit remodelled and refurbished out of the second storey of an old building on one of the narrow passageways that branched like little blood vessels off the main artery that was the Via Garibaldi. It was in a small district called Manovalo. Not on the 'tourist trail', the area had been for many generations home to workers and labourers in Venice, and remained one of the few places in the city where locals lived. By far the greater number now lived on the mainland, and commuted daily to their work, most of which was in the tourist trade that was really all that sustained the former global trading hub.

The address given for the apartment - Manovalo 219 – was characteristic of the peculiar Venetian manner, but fortunately the website had also included detailed directions of how to get there. Without difficulty they found 'their' lane, Viale di Tavola.

The name indicated that it had once been a place of table-makers, but now most of the buildings down the short, narrow way appeared to be residential. A hand-painted sign that read *Lavanderia e ferro* near the end of the cul-de-sac indicated that they could have their washing and ironing done for them if required (although John B. openly admitted that the only iron he was familiar with was a golf club). More interestingly though, the first building on the right of the viale had been converted to a pasticerria.

It produced only pastries and cakes – bread was the specialty of a panetteria – but the display cabinets on the ground floor held a simply mouth-watering array of choices. There were several ovens toward the back, away from the main street, and more up on the first floor along with the preparation area. The Australians realised quickly that the aroma of baking would fill the viale every morning, and it was a delight they looked forward to.

Reluctantly tearing themselves away from the various sweet and crisp options, John B. and Q made their way along the lane. Elizabeth quickly found the bright blue painted door described on the instructions . Those notes also included the code for the little locked box mounted beside the door. She dialled up the six-figure combination, and the lid popped open to reveal two sets of three keys, each on their own ring.

She took them out, admiring them as she held them out for John B. to choose a set.

"Nice touch," she observed, indicating the small tags on each ring. "The owner must be a Star Wars fan." The decorations were small enamelled likenesses of R2D2 and Chewbacca respectively.

John B. selected the furry face of the Wookie. "You're much better with technology than I am, sweetheart. And I do kind of aspire to the big fella's facial hair."

"Don't aspire too hard please, babe. I'm fond of your face, and I'd like to still be able to see most of it."

They both laughed and kissed. Both were growing their hair long, he from persistent habit, she because her ex-husband had for all of their time together Not Wanted her to. Elizabeth's brunette loose curls were still tidy, but John B. it seemed could never be anything but shaggy. Despite his proclaimed Wookie-esque ambitions, his efforts at beard growing continued to disappoint. When it did eventually get past the point of rough stubble, the hair tended to grow in all different directions, defying all attempts to comb it into any sort of neatness.

As expected, one of the three keys unlocked the blue door, which opened into a vestibule slightly bigger than a phone booth. A closed door on their left presumably led into the ground floor apartment. The back of the tiny chamber was the steep staircase that led up to their own rooms.

The largest of the three keys opened their apartment door, painted in the same blue as the downstairs portal. They stepped inside, and both grinned broadly. Manovalo 219 was an old building, quite drab when seen from the outside, but this interior was a delight.

It was shiny, white and modern, but not soulless as so many such places can look. They'd walked straight into the living area, large enough to function as both lounge and dining room, and separated from the spacious kitchen only by a long bench. No chance of a cook missing out on conversation with any guests! The two bedrooms opened directly off the living space, with the door to what they correctly assumed was the bathroom between them.

The main bedroom overlooked the laneway, which was narrow

enough that they could have easily conversed with neighbours across the viale, had they wished. It was easy to imagine washing lines strung between facing buildings in times past. Indeed, when they looked properly they realised that such arrangements were still in place all along Viale di Tavola. Probably some of these homes had been in the same families for generations, with old relationships (and probably rivalries too) still maintained. That could be explored soon enough.

While the main bedroom was generously-proportioned enough to comfortably fit a queen-sized bed, the other barely had room for the two single beds it contained.

"Reminds me of Islay," Stewart remarked, prompting an affectionate hug from his beloved.

The first night they'd spent together was in a guest house on that Hebridean island, in a room even tinier than this. At least the Venetian room had a built-in wardrobe at one end. Their Scottish quarters had barely space for their bags at the foot of each bed. Aglow with new romance, they hadn't minded at all at the time, but admitted now that the bigger bedroom was a much more appealing prospect. This room would be a place to keep their luggage. It had no window, but natural light came in from a skylight in the ceiling. There was such a fitting in each of the rooms, even the bathroom, they discovered.

Checking the wardrobe in the small bedroom revealed one useful bonus – the reason for the third key on their sets. It was a fire safe, securely fixed to both wall and floor. It was conveniently large enough to hold passports, Q's modest jewellery box and her laptop computer, and with only a little squeezing, the leather case of antique coins.

Resisting the temptation to flop onto the big bed, the couple settled into the living room to get themselves organised. While Elizabeth spread the low coffee table with maps and brochures they'd picked up at the airport and vaporetto station, John B. explored the kitchen.

There were plenty of utensils and electrical kitchen devices, but almost no groceries in any of the cupboards. A solitary tin of tomato paste, and another of white kidney beans. Traces of rust around the top of the latter suggested that it had been there for a long time.

At least the owner, or perhaps the previous occupants, had left in the fridge a few drinks. Two bottles of a local dark beer, and two of pre-mixed Bellini, the popular cocktail of sparkling wine and peach nectar first created in Venice's famous Harry's Bar in 1948.

They both enjoyed one of each (although the premix was a little too sweet for both palates) while they leisurely read through the pile of brochures.

"No mention of this Musee Barche that Texas Dorothy told us about. Maybe they don't advertise," said Elizabeth, eventually.

"Hopefully a friendly local can point us to it. I wish we could find someone like that," said her beau with a smile.

At which point there was suddenly a terrible howl from the laneway outside their window.

.ooo.

4

———

THE BEAST

There had been enough drama and death in their lives together that both had leapt from the couch and dived for the window in one movement. The heavy curtains had been pulled back so they had a clear view of the viale below.

Nothing untoward was visible. There was nobody to be seen in the lane. It occurred to the Australians as they looked up and down that no one else seemed to have reacted to the sound. No heads poked from doorways or windows. No evident twitching of curtains.

Then the noise came again, echoing up to them as it bounced off the old brick walls. John B. nudged his sweetheart and pointed. Sitting in the middle of the lane, right opposite their downstairs door, was a cat. Scruffy, mostly black with a smear of white just visible on its chest. It looked up, directly at them it seemed, appearing to squint with one eye, and howled again.

It was not a conventional feline sound. There was an almost human quality to it, but not quite a scream, on reflection. More like an operatic soprano warming up pre-performance with a bit of yodelling.

The pair looked at each other. Q giggled and John B. burst out laughing.

"Well, *that's* a relief!" they both said in unison, and laughed again.

"I suppose I should go check that he or she is okay," suggested the wizard. He was fond of animals, starting with his own late and still-lamented white Persian Kat, and had previously shown a remarkable bond with animals as diverse as horses, a ghost dog and a sea serpent.

Elizabeth squeezed his hand. "Okay babe. We've got to get some groceries in anyway. We can go and be tourists, the coins have waited six hundred years or more to come home, they can wait some more. Let's go explore the neighbourhood, and see if the cat's still there when we get downstairs."

The animal had again been staring up at them as she spoke, and then sat quietly as they put shoes on, gathered up keys and a shopping bag that folded to pocket sized, and made sure they had their credit cards. Each card was sustained by its owner's own Swiss account, and neither was in any danger of being 'maxxed out' in the foreseeable future. They'd already changed out of the clothes they'd travelled in, Q now in black tights and a long-sleeved white t-shirt, over which she wore a zippered coat the catalogue inaccurately described as 'peacock blue'.

John B. had changed jeans and purple t-shirt, opting for one from his rock concert souvenir collection: this time Rick Wakeman's *Journey To The Centre Of The Earth* tour. His concession to the cool air outside was to put on the purple tartan waistcoat his sweetheart had had made for him, although he didn't so much as button it.

Neither was especially surprised to find the cat still apparently waiting for them when they emerged onto the viale. It made another noise at their approach – a much quieter sound something like *uurgh*.

Elizabeth was a little hesitant. She'd heard and read stories of unpleasant diseases carried and spread by ferals and street cats across Europe. If her beau had read them though, he gave them no heed as he knelt to pat the creature.

It stood and rubbed against his outstretched hand. As it turned under his affectionate touch it was revealed to be a tom, although somewhat to their surprise, neutered. Maybe it wasn't a feral? He was fairly light, but not emaciated, there was no collar, and his fur, while dusty, couldn't be called filthy. The irregular white smear on his chest was all that relieved him from 100% blackness.

Apart from his voice, what was odd about the cat was his face. It seemed almost lopsided. On a human you might have thought he'd had a stroke. The right eye was half closed, and a patch of dampness on one side of the chin suggested an unfortunate tendency to drool. And the whiskers on that side – there were only half the number of those on the left, and even those were mostly quite short, only two matching the length of those opposite.

"He seems placid enough now," said Q without surprise.

The *urgh* noise had changed again, into something reminiscent of a child gargling.

"I think that's his purr," said John B. with a grin. "Come on, little mate. We're going shopping. You want to tag along?"

The cat continued its peculiar purr, and seemed content to pad along at their heels as they strolled out onto the Via Garibaldi. Knowing they hadn't passed any especially useful shops on their way in, they turned in the opposite direction to how they'd arrived. The street wasn't quite empty, but it was quiet. Manovalo wasn't an area frequented by tourists, and many of the residents would be working at this hour.

Watching the reactions on faces, it struck Elizabeth that some people weren't so much surprised to see a cat ambling along beside them like a well-trained Labrador, as they were to see it was *this* particular cat.

He even waited patiently outside while they entered a small *salumeria*, a deli where they presumed he'd be unwelcome. Having made her own choices, Elizabeth was watching through the front window while John B. selected a few specific meats he wanted to try. She noticed a few people, presumably local, who acknowledged the cat. A few even bent to briefly stroke it. But the animal made no move to follow any of them, nor to wander away on its own. The same thing happened when they went into a small supermarket.

Satisfied with the modest amount of groceries that they'd acquired, the couple decided to treat themselves to coffee. They sat at a small table outside a coffee bar, the cat quiet and seemingly content by JB's feet, showing no interest in the bag of shopping near him. They considered their options.

"You're not having a latte?" asked Q in some surprise.

"From what I've read, you can only get *caffellatte* at breakfast in Italy. We're a bit beyond that. Even cappuccino is for mornings only. I've no idea why – maybe the milk used to go off by lunchtime," explained the wizard.

With a sceptical eyebrow raised, Elizabeth pointed to an item on the menu.

"What they're calling a latte is very likely just a glass of milk. If you just order *caffe* you'll get a shot of espresso," John B. explained.

'He's been reading a tourists' guide on the plane,' Q thought to herself. "So, what are these different options?"

"*Americano* – what we'd call a long black. *Doppio* – long, strong and black, *ristretto* – super strong. *Macchiato*, strong but with a dash of milk. And then there are various liqueur options. Sorry, I don't see *te* on their menu."

"Hmm, thanks. A macchiato, I think. Thanks babe. And something to nibble on, please?"

As the wizard stood up, the cat shifted slightly to park himself close by Elizabeth's feet. Shrugging, John B. ambled inside, to the service counter of the bar. There he was served by a frankly beautiful, olive-skinned young woman whose nametag proclaimed her to be named "Mac".

"You don't look Scottish," said John B. with a grin.

He got a pretty smile in return. "It is short for Immaculata, signore. A very... old fashioned name. I would not change it, but..."

"I understand." He changed the subject as Mac wrote down his order. "That's a beautiful piece of music," he said, indicating the sound system on a shelf behind the counter, from which emanated a silky arrangement of guitar and keyboards.

"*Grazie*. It is called *Toccare di luna*, recorded by Leonardo Delocchio, an important local man. He is very successful."

John B. spotted the note of local pride in Mac's voice. Given the quality of the music, he didn't blame her. He gave a small bow of gratitude and strolled back to rejoin his beloved outside. The cat promptly shifted again to settle at his feet.

"Seems as though you've been adopted, babe."

"It looks that way, doesn't it? I wonder..."

The wizard pulled his chair further out from the table, and patted his leg. As if he'd been waiting for the invitation, the dusty black animal jumped up onto his lap and curled up, purring in its own peculiar way.

It didn't take long for their order to be delivered. Two macchiatos, a glass of latte on the side, and a selection of biscotti on a white plate. Mac brought the tray out herself, and showed only a little surprise at the feline presence.

"The feral is a regular visitor?" asked Elizabeth.

"Si, *signorina*, although I haven't seen him on a stranger's lap before. But he is no feral. A *gatto felice*, a happy cat. He wanders much around here, but has a home with Signore LaGrigio. That place, over there."

She indicated a faded orange-and-white building on a corner back up the street. A little larger than its neighbours, it gave the impression of having once been grander than its currently reduced station. They realised that, by its evident size, some part of it must just about back onto their own modest apartment, although the entry points of the two were well apart, on different streets.

"The signore is a most excellent maker of the musical instruments," Mac continued.

That explained the modest violin-shaped sign hanging from the wall beside the front window, too small to be read at that distance. The curtains were drawn, so whatever wares might have been on display were hidden.

"Doesn't look open yet. I didn't think it was very early," said Elizabeth.

"Oh, Signore LaGrigio does not keep... regular hours. He opens only when he feels like it, I think." The smiling Mac gave a little curtsey and went back inside.

John B. patted the slightly misshapen black head. "I hope you're not just being kept as a source of future violin strings, little mate," he said.

Elizabeth looked up in some concern, then saw the gleam in her beau's eye and realized he'd been joking. Still, it was an unpleasant thought.

"He does seem quite well looked after, I suppose," she said.

The cat sniffed at a fragment of biscotti he was offered, but put his head back down and closed his eyes, still purring.

"Not starving, at any rate," observed John B.

They chatted casually about plans for the rest of the day, which amounted to taking the groceries home, then going for a stroll up to, and along, the Grand Canal that wove its way through Venice.

Suddenly the cat lifted his head and gave a loud yowl. He made no move to get off John B.'s lap, but sat up and yowled again.

"What - ?" Elizabeth began, while Stewart shrugged in puzzlement.

At the sound of the distinctive feline voice, a girl who'd been striding along the Via Garibaldi looked up from her angry introspections and broke into a run towards the bar. The expression on her face lightened as if a switch had been thrown inside her head.

She arrived at the Australian couple's table and, ignoring them both, began to tousle the black fur on the lean cat's head.

"B'giorno, Toscanini, *tesoro mio!*"

The Australians waited to see if they'd receive any acknowledgement. The girl was slim and dark, in the early years of being a teenager, they guessed. Straight dark brown hair fell past her shoulders. It looked damp, as if she'd not long stepped from the shower, but Elizabeth noticed the girl's dark blue jumper looked similarly damp. Had it been raining while they'd been indoors? She hadn't noticed any other evidence of it.

Still apparently heedless of their presence, the girl knelt and continued to fuss over the cat, who tilted his head and stretched his neck appropriately to let her scratch at wherever he wanted.

"Toscanini, you are so *edonistico!*" the girl chided gently.

"Well, now we know his name. Good morning Toscanini," said John B., delicately scratching a point on the bridge of the hedonistic cat's nose, right between his eyes.

The girl was about to protest, but abruptly realised that the cat was very evidently enjoying that particular attention.

"He doesn't like being touched near his eye," she said, puzzled. "Not usually..."

Now she actually paid some attention to the man upon whose lap Toscanini had settled. He had skin much paler than her own; long, shaggy brown hair, again much lighter in tone than hers; kind eyes that she immediately liked; clearly hadn't shaved recently; solid but not overweight; purple t-shirt bearing the name...

"Rick Wakeman! Oh, bellisimo! His music is excellent!"

John B. laughed. "You'll get no argument from me, signorina. I'm surprised though, I must admit. I'd have thought he'd be a bit before your time."

"*Feh* – my Giancarlo plays his music. It's very interesting, very good."

"Well, bravo to your Giancarlo then." Stewart held out the hand that had been scratching the cat. "I'm John B. Stewart. This is my darling Elizabeth McKew."

"Hello there," added the darling, a little more reserved than her beau.

Standing, the girl appeared to notice Elizabeth for the first time. Pretty brunette; long wavy hair, almost but not quite curly; and wow, really *interesting* green eyes.

"Hello. My name is Nicola," she replied, shaking John B.'s hand then reaching out to offer the same greeting to Elizabeth.

As the two females clasped hands, they looked into each other's eyes, both with the same expression of careful assessment. They both smiled cautiously.

Nicola looked back to the shaggy man and said with a hint of surprise, "Toscanini likes you."

The man grinned in response. "He seems a friendly little guy."

The girl's expression seemed to suggest that, while this was true, he wasn't usually quite *this* friendly, especially with strangers.

Intrigued, Elizabeth asked, "What happened to his face?"

Nicola's own features darkened into a scowl. "He was kicked, hard. One of the *stronzi* Culatelli."

"What's a Culatelli?" the brunette replied. She'd worked out just by the tone of voice that *stronzi* was a pretty potent term of abuse.

"Three brothers. Stupid, bad, vicious men. I do not like them. I *really* do not like them."

'Clearly!' thought both Australians. Even as he felt an instinctive deep dislike flare within himself, John B. decided that a swift change of subject was in order.

"So, what Rick Wakeman albums does your Giancarlo have?" he asked casually.

"Al-bums?"

"CDs. Recordings."

"Oh! Oh, Giancarlo does not play recordings. He plays the music. He is teaching me. I have learned to play *Catherine of Aragon*, *The Forest at the Centre of the Earth*, and some of *The Court of King Ferdinand*."

John B. was impressed. "That's quite a list!" he said.

The praise brought the smile back to Nicola's face. "Oh, there is much more he teaches me. The jazz, the blues, the rock music, even the classical. I do not like that so much, but Giancarlo tells me it is good for my technique." There was a mischievous glint in her eyes as she said, "I have the good fingering."

Only barely did Elizabeth contain a reaction to what sounded a lot like a deliberate double entendre. How old was this girl? 'Don't rise to the bait,' she told herself. She watched John B.'s face. If the wizard had caught it, he wasn't showing it.

"You like music – you should come so we can play for you!" exclaimed Nicola. "Maybe even play together, hey?"

Again, Elizabeth bit her tongue. Having spotted one possible double meaning, was she now finding more in perfectly innocent remarks?

"Flattering to be asked, but I doubt I'm enough of a musician to be of a standard with you and Giancarlo," laughed John B.

"Likewise, I'm afraid," added Q, relaxing a little.

Nicola smiled. "Ah, but the fun is in the playing." She looked at the black cat and continued, "I think Toscanini would like for you to visit, too."

That elicited another of the cat's strange sounds from his most un-feline vocabulary.

"Well, my thanks to you both," replied John B. graciously. "But we've literally just arrived in Venice. It'd be good to just find our way around for a day or two. But very soon, okay?"

"What will your parents think of your inviting strangers home?" Elizabeth wondered aloud.

In return she got a look so cold that she felt her blood start to freeze. Eventually the youngster seemed to give herself a shake.

"Parents, *feh*, I live with my Giancarlo. He will not mind when I tell him we will have visitors. Especially one who likes Signore Wakeman's music. We live over there, in the *villa arancione*."

"Ah, the orange building. Your Giancarlo is the son of the violin maker?" guessed John B.

"Giancarlo makes many instruments. All sorts. Come tomorrow, late in the afternoon before dinner. You will see."

JB and Q exchanged doubtful looks. The cat Toscanini uncurled, stretched, looked up at Stewart, and with a noise like *ee-oo* jumped off his lap and padded over to Nicola.

"See you, too, I guess," said the wizard, addressing his new feline friend.

The girl waved but didn't look back as she strode across the street towards her home, the black cat trotting at her side.

"Well, we did say that we wanted to find a friendly local, didn't we?" John B. asked cautiously.

"Hmm," was Elizabeth's dubious response as she scrunched her napkin and dabbed a biscotti crumb from the corner of her mouth.

.ooo.

5

———

STREET SCENES

Elizabeth's mood required some lightening as the couple took their shopping back to the apartment and unpacked it. She wasn't jealous *as such*, she told herself, but she was conscious of how pretty the waitress had been, and especially aware of how precocious young Nicola had seemed. It wasn't that she didn't trust her beau. More that she didn't trust other women. Some of them.

Then she remembered Ariane, a young woman in Maine who she knew was close to John B. She'd seen first-hand just how close their friendship was, and realised it was just that. A close friendship, and nothing more. She wondered about her own insecurity. Paranoia, even?

Her father had abandoned his wife and child very early. The two people closest to her in her earlier life, mother and ex-husband, had both been possessive and manipulative. She realised in a startling moment of clarity that her lack of faith wasn't in John B. Stewart, but in herself. Suddenly putting down the packet of crispbread that she'd been holding, she grabbed a handful of purple t-shirt and pulled her beau into an embrace.

"Sorry I'm tetchy, babe," she whispered.

"I hadn't noticed," he replied. "Maybe I'm dense. Would a stroll up to the main part of town cheer you up?"

"That sounds good."

Soon they were wandering hand in hand along the *Riva degli Schiavoni*, the walkway on the northern bank of the great *Canale di San Marco*. The air was still brisk, but it was a clear day. They stopped frequently, often to watch boats, from gondolas and humble dinghies, to massive ocean liners carrying thousands of passengers to and from the tourist haunts of Venice.

"We should try one of them someday," mused Elizabeth. "Maybe a good opportunity to focus on finishing my novel, once I've got a bit more detail from this museum. Wherever it is."

"Sure," agreed John B. equably. "As long as we're together, I don't mind how we travel. Certainly, the idea of someone else doing all our cooking and cleaning for a little while is appealing!"

Their stroll took them to, and across, the Piazza San Marco, the great square outside St. Mark's basilica. It was late morning, and the place was typically full of tourists from all over the world. The babel of voices, in different languages and accents shouting to be heard over each other, were an assault on the ears. The crowding and the jostling were almost as uncomfortable on their bodies.

"Wow! Even New York wasn't as bad as this!" Elizabeth said, craning to call directly into her beau's ear.

"At least this'll thin out a bit mid-afternoon, from what I've read. A few thousand of this lot will cram back onto their cruise ships and be gone," he shouted in reply.

Suddenly the wizard felt a sharp tug from the area of his left hip. He looked down, and saw a slim black chain extending taut from a belt loop of his jeans. The other end of the chain was firmly connected to his wallet, currently clutched in the hand of a dark-eyed young man in a striped shirt. John B. grabbed the would-be pickpocket's wrist before there was time for the denim anchor to be torn – fortunately they were tough, good quality jeans.

The young man squirmed in Stewart's grasp, letting go of his loot.

John B. released his captive in order to catch the wallet, but the pair had a fleeting moment of eye contact.

"I wish you'd give up your thieving ways, mate," said the Australian, in a low even voice.

It's doubtful whether the young man even heard the words, far less understood them. He just ducked and ran, losing himself in the crowd again. It had all occurred so quickly that Elizabeth missed it, and was puzzled when they'd stopped short in their stroll, still holding her beau's other hand.

"What happened?" she asked.

"Just a good reminder of why we bought a couple of things to deter thieves," was the reply, as the wallet was returned to the pocket it had been slipped from.

Elizabeth squeezed John B.'s hand and pressed a little closer to his side as they walked.

Already a hundred metres or more away, the youth in the striped shirt, though shaken, picked another target. Luck was against him again, though. The press of bodies that gave cover to his activities happened to move just the wrong way, and he jostled the side of the man whose pocket was being dipped into at that precise moment. The man was a professional footballer. His wallet was fat, but he wasn't, and his reflexes were sharp. Instantly realising what was happening he spun and planted his fist in the middle of the pick-pocket's face. Shoving his wallet firmly back down into his pocket, the footballer strode away, leaving the would-be thief sitting on the ground with a streamer of blood and snot decorating his striped shirt.

Cautiously wiping his bloodied nose on the back of his arm, the young man resolved to make one more attempt. It wasn't that he needed the money, but there was a thrill in every successful 'lift', and it had always been so easy, ever since he was a kid... He watched the tourists milling about, ignoring him as he got to his feet. He stood slightly crouched, ready to move quickly and lightly. There! A woman, obviously a tourist, obviously not too clever, the large bag over her shoulder left invitingly open. Easy to lift a purse out of that!

He trailed his target for a few paces, then closed in quickly as the woman looked toward an alluring shop window. His hand darted into the capacious carrier, but his fingers were immediately entangled in a layer of crumpled, sticky, used tissues. Instinctively he jerked his hand back. The movement alerted the woman who swiftly turned, pulling her bag tightly to her midriff.

"*Socorro! Policia! Me han robado!*" shouted the visitor from Madrid.

The pickpocket didn't need to speak Spanish to realise she was shouting for help from the police, and although she hadn't actually been successfully robbed, as she was shrieking, he knew enough to make a hasty retreat into the anonymous shelter of the densest part of the crowd, thronging about the front of St. Mark's Basilica. But in that haste, he stumbled and fell, landing awkwardly on all fours.

Looking up at the Basilica's ornamentation rather than down at the pavement, an overweight tourist trod on the young man's hand. Two of the fingers, so deft at slipping into other folks' pockets, were fractured. Moaning and whimpering, the thief half rolled, half crawled to shelter against a wall. He looked up at the mosaic of Christ In Glory and the Last Judgement .

"I get it, I get it!" he said to himself. "From now on I'll stick to fixing boat engines. The money is good, and it's a lot safer."

Now well beyond the square, the man who'd uttered the magic words was oblivious to the life-changing moment transpiring in his wake. He'd have been very pleased had he known, but no longer felt any need to check on the outcome of every wish. He may not know how or why the magic worked, but he knew it did, and that as long as he was careful, it usually worked out for the best.

He and his beloved had ambled from the grand piazza into the area called the Mercerie. Once the domain of haberdashers and fabric sellers, its narrow, jumbled streets were now home to a great variety of different wares. It was arguably the busiest shopping precinct in Venice, and the many shop windows offered plenty of distractions to the wandering tourists.

John B. was admiring the range on view in one of the many little mask shops. Carnivale was imminent, he realised, and the best and brightest of masks were on display. Like many such stores, the masks were mostly variants of the few traditional shapes and styles, but distinguished by their extravagant colours and ornamentation. The words *Artigiano Veneziano* were prominently displayed on a sign in the window, signifying that at least some of the masks were made by a craftsman on site.

While the wizard pondered options, Elizabeth was two store windows away, fascinated by a display of exquisite glassware. Not something she was normally attracted to, and probably not a sensible purchase while they were enjoying their present nomadic lifestyle, but the beauty of some of the pieces was undeniably attractive.

As she was bent forward examining an elegant small bottle in subtle shades of green, she felt a firm hand grasp her left butt cheek. John B. was affectionate, and often demonstrably so, but he was also respectful of time and place, so Elizabeth didn't think twice about spinning quickly on her toes and delivering a hard slap to the owner of the errant hand.

She struck the side of his jaw, with enough force to knock him backwards if not quite to the ground. As he staggered, his two equally ugly companions, his brothers if she read their looks correctly, laughed uproariously. As they laughed at him, the embarrassed one gave them a 'Go to hell!' gesture, touching his thumb to his tongue. It only increased their mirth.

At a table outside a small restaurant directly opposite, a very over-weight man sat watching the scene. He laughed heartily, and unsym-pathetically, at the brother whose unwelcome grope had earned the sharp response.

"Luigino, you're such a fool," the fat man chortled through a mouthful of spaghetti marinara. "Surprisingly good taste, though. And she's a spirited little wench. Nice."

If the red-haired woman sitting alongside the portly fellow had any reaction to his apparent interest in the 'spirited wench', she didn't show it. She continued patiently coiling the pasta noodles around a fork, ensuring a good coating of the thick sauce, then feeding him when he opened his mouth like a baby bird.

Noticing the small commotion, John B. was immediately at the side of his beloved.

"Everything okay, sweetheart?" he asked.

"No worries, babe. Nothing I couldn't handle – nothing of any importance."

She looked straight at her assailant as she spoke, further increasing his chagrin, as well as the mirth of his brothers. Other passers-by, who hadn't seen the incident itself, found themselves chuckling along with the two brothers, and the man laughing loudly out front of the restaurant. Luigino didn't have the complexion for a bright red blush, but his face definitely darkened.

With an arm around Elizabeth's shoulders, John B. headed deeper into the Mercerie, softly asking, "What happened?"

"Some low-life, too free with his hands. Maybe he's used to meek submissive women – he didn't like it when I slapped him. His equally ugly mates thought it was funny, though."

"Hunh, that would have hurt even more. He's lost face."

"Did you see him? It's a face he should be glad of losing."

Arm in arm they lost themselves in a retail reverie, the incident dismissed as casually as the earlier encounter with the would-be pickpocket.

Luigino Culatello was less sanguine though. His mood lifted a little when the portly Il Duce Grosso waved the three brothers over to the restaurant, and bade them go and help themselves to a round of drinks, on his account.

"You are more generous than they deserve, *ciccino mio*," the redhead said softly, after the three had gone inside.

"They're an investment, Squila. They save me from getting my hands dirty," the fat man replied.

"I understand," she answered, as she napkinned away a trace of mussel from one of his chins.

Unobserved at another table, a figure dressed all in black nodded thoughtfully.

.ooo.

6

LOCAL COLOUR

Much of what the Australian couple spent the remainder of the afternoon and early evening on could best be described as 'window shopping'. Some potential purchases appealed to either or both of them, but they knew that Venice has a multitude of shopping opportunities, and there were other districts beside the Mercerie to visit. Likely cheaper ones, which does matter, even when money isn't a problem. No-one likes to feel ripped off, and both came from backgrounds where value meant more than impulse buying.

A few small items were bought, mostly as gifts to be sent back to Australia or elsewhere. Hand-crafted things that they felt were unique. Other shops may offer something similar, but not quite as beautiful, well-made or cleverly designed.

They snacked on slices of fresh pizza in the mid-afternoon, sitting under a shady tree in one of the smaller piazzas. More shopping followed, and an hour or two lost in a small art gallery that seemed crammed with paintings all from around the time of Elizabeth's ancestor, the self-proclaimed 'Prince' Henry.

There was a noticeable chill in the air by the time they started to be aware of their appetites again. Having turned down Nicola's implied offer of a home-cooked meal that evening, they somehow felt reluctant to go back to the flat in Viale di Tavola and make their own dinner. Neither was dressed for a five-star restaurant, but there were plenty of welcoming trattorias on their ambling way back to Manovalo. There was also a shop from which John B. bought his beloved's choice of a fine-spun woollen shawl in soft shades of white, aqua and green. Much as she loved and appreciated his bare arm around her shoulders, the wool did help insulate against the breeze that carried the cold of the waters surrounding them.

And in the fullness of time, Manovalo 219 proved to be satisfactorily warm and snug. Elizabeth and John B. happily contributed to the warmth in the apartment, enjoying the frisson of excitement that usually accompanies the first night in a new bed. And eventually they fell asleep wrapped contentedly in each other's arms.

As they'd guessed, the morning was enriched by the aroma of fresh baking that had drifted up from the pasticerria. The mouth-watering scents had filled the narrow street and been captured by the apartment's air-conditioning unit, so they woke to a room redolent of sweet temptations. Which they completely failed to resist, of course.

John B. was down the stairs and back up again in surprisingly quick time for a man not noted for the speed of his movements. He prepared coffee while his beloved rather reluctantly dragged herself out of bed. The apartment was sufficiently warm that she didn't feel the need to add much to her overnight attire (nothing), beyond draping her new shawl over her bare shoulders.

Clearly it was a morning for temptations, and less than half of the fresh coffee was consumed before the mugs, and most of the pastries, were temporarily abandoned. They'd be lightly reheated and enjoyed later.

It was a little beyond mid-morning by the time the couple made their way back out onto the Via Garibaldi and turned towards the Grand Canal.

A few coins from Prince Henry's hoard were in a zippered pocket of Elizabeth's purse. In similar manner to her beau's wallet, this was secured by a chain to a toggle inside her coat pocket. The rest of the coins were secure in the small safe. There was no point in carrying them around until their fate had been properly determined.

They'd still found no reference in any tourist material to the Musee Barche that Texas Dorothy had directed them to.

"I reckon we go back to the earlier thought, sweetheart. We should ask a local," suggested John B. as they strolled.

"We've just got to find the right one, hey babe?" Elizabeth agreed.

"I wish we find just the right person to take us to the museum. There, my love. That ought to do it."

"Perhaps specifying *which* museum?"

"Ah. Bugger – didn't think of that. Sorry."

"It's okay, babe. A museum crawl around Venice could be fun, if it comes to that," she replied with a laugh.

Walking as usual with an arm around each other's waist, they tightened the embrace momentarily. Some of their previous work colleagues would have been surprised to see their interaction. There'd been a general suspicion, even an expectation among a few, that "it'd never last".

Elizabeth McKew was "too good for him", she had class, was supremely organised, and while she was good company, was more business-like than a social butterfly.

John B. Stewart was an amiable drunk for whom work was a means of paying his bar tab – untidy, unambitious, genial but eccentric. Give it a few weeks, let her get over the rebound of her (completely unforeseen by these folks) split from Sonny Dance, and they'd both realise how completely incompatible they were.

It hadn't worked out that way. Yes, they were very different individuals, but the differences were part of what made the relationship work. Each had traits that the other knew (privately, if not openly) they lacked in themselves, and they were simply better together. Neither wanted to change the other, but the longer they were together, the more they each subtly changed themselves.

John B. had added a few variations to his routine wardrobe of purple t-shirts – his travelling ensemble now included options of a Hawaiian shirt, tartan vest and a satin dress shirt, although all were admittedly still in shades of purple. He drank considerably less than had been the case a year earlier. Not by direction, but because he now had other pleasures to devote time and effort to. And while he was no more ambitious in a 'conventional' sense than he'd ever been, he'd discovered in himself an impulse to make a positive difference in the world. He didn't understand his magic – its origin or how it worked – but he was determined to use it for something more than personal gain.

As for Elizabeth, she was more relaxed than she'd been for most of her life (and not just the adult years). It wasn't just that her new partner wasn't compulsively controlling like her ex, and her mother before him, although that helped. But she was developing a new self-esteem. No-one at work had thought of her as lacking self-confidence. She was far too good at her job. But there's a difference between knowing and trusting your abilities, and *liking* yourself. At last Elizabeth was exploring what she enjoyed and was interested in. It was a journey that had brought some danger, but a great deal more delight and *that* was what she focussed on.

It was mid-morning when their perambulations took them to the district around the imposing square called the Campo San Stefano, home to bullfights two hundred years earlier. Now the area housed an eclectic mix of up-market boutiques and traditional shops (including a parlour selling traditional rich Venetian ice-cream – notwithstanding the weather it was an irresistible treat) nestling amongst a cluster of churches and palaces dating back to the 16th century.

Again they found themselves among jostling crowds of tourists, their enjoyment of the city being tempered by sharing it with quite so many other visitors. They'd quickly come to recognise the real pleasure of being able to retreat to Manovalo. Even during the day, that part of the city was much less crowded. They resolved to do their sight-seeing in the mornings, as early as possible, then escape the crush to linger in the gardens that gave the Giardini district its name, or in their own cosy place on the fringe of that district.

Ice cream finished, the couple stood looking at the iron bridge over the canal to Venice's largest museum, the Museo dell' Accademia, wondering whether to brave the throng. Information about the Musee Barche was continuing to prove elusive.

"I guess it would make sense to ask at one museum about where to find another. They don't really *compete*, as such, do they?" said Elizabeth, thoughtfully.

"There's only so many tourist euros to go around, sweetheart, but the idea seems sound. Or... wait... there's another option." John B. pointed across the canal. "If you want to know anything in London, they reckon you should ask a cabbie. We're in Venice. I reckon we should ask a gondolier."

On the other side of the Ponte dell 'Accademia (a 1985 reconstruction of the 1854 iron bridge which Mussolini inexplicably had demolished) they could see several gondolas lined up at a small jetty, and a queue of hopeful passengers waiting to board. More would-be passengers than boats, by the look of it.

"Well babe, it certainly looks like the local equivalent of a cab rank."

"I just wish we don't have to wait long to get the right gondolier to help us," said the wizard.

As the two Australians walked arm-in-arm over the bridge, they could see a small fracas breaking out amongst the folks in the queue. Some of the people who'd been standing patiently had objected to a newly-arrived foursome who evidently believed that 'waiting in line' was something other people did, and had barrelled their way to the front.

Most of the gondoliers kept themselves away from the trouble, staying on their boats, some of which were pushed away from the jetty just in case. Two, however, clambered up ashore and got involved. One was a small wiry fellow who shouted loudly as he tried to stand between two larger men who'd been trying to twist each other's collars. The other gondolier, a much larger man, wrapped an arm around the shoulders of one of the newcomers and shepherded him away from the slim youth who'd objected to being cut in front of.

The two female companions of the belligerent one flung themselves onto the gondolier's arm, shouting shrilly in German. One started kicking at his ankles. The girlfriend of the youth whimpered and shrank back, even as her boy wrestled with the impulse to hit one of the harpies. Others weren't so restrained, and grabbed at the frauleins' shoulders.

A substantial number of people in the queue decided that discretion was the better part of valour, or perhaps remembered that they'd left something important in the museum, and beat a hasty retreat from the melee.

John B., on the other hand, accelerated his progress over the bridge. Elizabeth followed only slightly behind. The wizard didn't break into a run, and wasn't looking for a fight *as such*, but he had an instinct that someone might need assistance. And right enough, as he got close he saw that the smaller boatman was struggling. The German had an arm around his throat from behind, having dispatched his original opponent with a thumb to the eye.

Suddenly attacking from behind, with simultaneous movements Stewart reached over and grabbed the wrist of the bigger man's strangling arm, and drove his own knee into the back of the fellow's leg. As the leg buckled, the choke hold reflexively loosened. In that moment John B. raised and twisted the seized wrist in a fluid sharp action. There was a guttural yelp as the shoulder popped out of joint.

As the smaller gondolier staggered free, trying to draw ragged breath, his companion took a pace forward and spread his brawny arms wide, knocking assailants off balance.

"*Abbastanza! Genug!* Enough!" he shouted in a booming voice.

The effect was akin to a bucket of ice water being thrown over proceedings. There was just something in the timbre of that voice that commanded attention. All action stopped – well, all aggressive action. The man with the dislocated shoulder was staggering about as he moaned. John B. grabbed his arm again, and with a sharp jerk popped the joint back into place before the fellow could resist.

The German fellow blanched and gulped out an uncertain, "*Danke...*" He seemed unaware that he'd just been assisted by the same man who'd done the damage in the first place. His own victim was rubbing at his abused throat and glaring.

In moments the crowd had dispersed, as if by magic. Some had gotten themselves onto gondolas still attended by their oarsmen, others departing on foot over the bridge with a definite air of "nothing to see here". Led by the women, the German foursome were among that number.

As the tall gondolier dusted down his wirier colleague he smiled at the purple-shirted visitor who'd so willingly assisted, and said, "*Grazie.*"

"*Prego,*" came the reply.

Elizabeth ran her eyes over the man. He was charismatic, no doubt about that. Gondoliers' work naturally developed upper body strength, and this fellow's showed in his broad shoulders and barrel chest. Sparkling blue eyes that looked genial enough, but hinted at depths that hid old, cold steel when required. She might guess his age at mid-thirties. A ruggedly handsome face was topped by a thatch of thick black hair, rather eccentrically styled to hang long on the left side, like he'd grown his own beret.

"*Piacere, signorina, mi chiamo Mario,*" the man said, and held out a hand.

Following John B.'s usual lead, Elizabeth had tried to quickly learn enough of the local language to be polite. She recognised, "Pleased to meet you, miss, my name is Mario," and responded in kind, introducing herself and her *caro* – although her pronunciation of 'beloved' came out sounding like the word for a foot-race.

The gondolier grinned at her accent, not unkindly, and said, "My English is good, if you'd prefer?" He briefly turned his attention back to the older boatman, and having reassured himself that the man was recovered, quietly indicated that he should take the last couple in the former queue onto his craft. Then he spread his arms wide to the two Australians. "Where can I take you, on this fine morning? May I suggest a leisurely, romantic tour of the Grand Canal? There is no time of day that the canal is not romantic!"

"Well, we do have a destination in mind, sort of, but when you put it like that, we're really not in any hurry, are we babe?" Elizabeth answered, slipping an arm around John B.'s waist.

"No argument from me, pretty lady," was her beau's reply.

As they made their way onto the gondola, Elizabeth reached for her purse while John B. struggled to haul his wallet from a pocket of his jeans. "What will the fare be?" she asked.

The man who'd introduced himself as Mario bowed and said, "No fare for you two. Consider it a courtesy."

Stewart looked up sharply and met the gondolier's gaze. The wizard knew the look in those eyes, even if the eyes themselves were different. "A courtesy," the Australian repeated, thoughtfully.

"*Si, signore.* Just as you say."

Elizabeth hadn't been with John B. on the golfing trip to Hawaii, so she was unaware of what had suddenly struck him. He explained later, as best he could, after a phone call to a friend on the Big Island brought the surprising, but not-quite-surprising news about the big charismatic fellow called Courtesy.

There had been much distress locally when the popular local had paddled out from his surfboard hire business on a kayak seemingly too small for his ample frame, and disappeared. Swept out to sea, it was presumed, though no trace of man nor kayak was ever found. For a man known in some quarters as 'The Navigator', it seemed an unlikely end.

But that revelation was several hours away for John B. as the gondola was propelled out into the canal.

"My apologies for that – *incident* at San Stefano," said Mario as he worked. "Our city is a little more frenetic than usual today. It is the first day of Carnivale, and the spirit can be a little infectious."

"The party spirit, you mean?" asked Elizabeth.

"*Si.* That, and more. It is the Saturnalia. The time for breaking rules and celebrating the doing so. For ten days we pretend there is no difference between rich and poor, aristocrats, artisans, workers and mendicants."

"Rich man, poor man, beggar man, thief, eh?" quipped John B.

"Ah yes. We have many of all of those, I fear. But this is a time for enjoyment. In ten days, Lent will be upon us, and meat is forbidden to the faithful. *Carnum levare* in the Latin, and alas some people have traditionally frowned upon most forms of fun in that period of abstention, not just good meat. And so the celebration beforehand assumes great importance as an opportunity to fit in as much self-indulgence as possible before discipline is imposed."

"I hadn't realised the religious significance," admitted Elizabeth.

"*Signorina*, this is Italy, even if the city still maintains a deep sense of independence. For many Venetians there is a religious significance to almost everything."

As he steered the gondola Mario pointed out several buildings as they glided past, often giving insights to their history pertaining to rich men, poor men, beggars and rogues whilst doing so. Some were sites which he recommended as worth visiting, others as worth avoiding.

"But my best advice to you, my friends, is to walk lost. Look about. Read. Ask. Learn. Explore. The joy is in the journey, not the destination."

The wizard grinned. "Good advice, mate. We have been working on that principle, as much as possible!"

"Ah, but we do have a destination, babe," pointed out his beloved. "After which we can happily go back to wandering lost. Mario, do you know a place called the Musee Barche?"

The gondolier smiled broadly. "There would be few of my *amici* who do not know the Museum of Small Boats, but yes, I know it probably better than most."

'Why am I not surprised?' thought John B. to himself.

The gondolier looked closely at his two passengers. "You have business with Marina – Signorina DeNucci." It wasn't a question. "Let us not delay, then."

The Australians were both sufficiently alert to pick up a subtle shift in the boatman's manner. He was as jovial and garrulous as before, but they both recognised a small shadow of reserve. Notwithstanding that, Mario guided the craft down a couple of narrow canals – *rio menuo* – before easing it in alongside a little landing platform. He pointed to an adjacent building, its old plaster-work painted bright blue, the bricks a much paler shade.

"Should we tell Ms DeNucci you sent us?" asked Elizabeth, smiling.

Mario looked thoughtful before replying, "Yes. Yes, it will do no harm for her to know I am still thinking of her." The gondolier helped his passengers disembark. "Travel safely, my friends. Look for me if you need me," he added, a hand on John B.'s arm for a moment longer than necessary to support him.

"Thanks. We will, though I don't expect it will come to that. Still, expect the unexpected, eh?" replied the wizard.

"As you say."

The boatman gave a final cheery wave as he headed his craft back to the main waterways.

"Nice guy," observed Elizabeth. "You two seemed to know each other, sort of."

"Sort of is about it, sweetheart. Something familiar – he reminds me of someone I met, over in Hawaii. Which makes no sense at all, I know. Never mind. Let's go see this Ms DeNucci, and hope she's helpful."

The two Australians arrived at the Musee Barche just as the museum's only other visitors, a family from the Italian mainland, were leaving. The children were happily clutching small wooden model boats that they'd just been bought, and the adults wore the slightly glazed expressions of parents who've just spent an hour or so fielding the seemingly endless stream of questions that young minds can conjure.

Behind the counter just inside the front door stood a woman, perhaps just on the younger side of middle age. An inch or two less tall than Elizabeth, she might have been described as statuesque, but she had an air about her that was more formidable than fetching.

Dark penetrating eyes sat above an aquiline nose and under thick but impeccably shaped black eyebrows – the same colour as the mass of black curls heaped in picturesque disorder atop the woman's head.

Automatically she went to extend a welcoming hand to her new visitors, but stopped dead when she looked at John B. Stewart's face.

"Oh!" she said. "It's you!"

.ooo.

7

MEETING MARINA

John B.'s response was a blank look.

"Um... pardon? Sorry – have we met?" he asked.

The woman's lips pursed momentarily before she replied, "A long time ago. Of course, you would not... remember."

Elizabeth wasn't oblivious to the awkwardness of the moment, although she understood it no more than her beau appeared to. Still, she stepped into the breach, taking a pace forward and holding out her hand.

"Elizabeth McKew. Am I correct in assuming you're Marina DeNucci? A pleasure to meet you."

Some force of habitual politeness pulled Marina's gaze away from Stewart's face, the curator turning to the brunette. Her expression, however, was studiedly neutral rather than welcoming.

"Yes. Yes, I am DeNucci." She paused for a moment, as if assessing the new arrivals. "Welcome to the Musee Barche."

That sentence sounded more practiced than sincere, but such was often the case in tourist establishments, both Australians knew from experience. Still, that unexpected first reaction had jarred. The curator was aware of this, and while unapologetic, she seemed determined to move on quickly.

"Have you an interest in boats?" she asked. "I have a fine collection of small vessels and their accoutrements. Gondolas, *scialuppe* – lifeboats, remnants of early *vaporetti*. Nothing military – if that is your interest I would direct you to the Naval Museum – but here, you will find much of the maritime history of Venice. And beyond."

As she spoke, she'd ushered the pair into the museum. The downstairs area was as 'open plan' as you could imagine, although liberally supplied with thick posts supporting the upper floors. A variety of boats were visible, interspersed with glass cabinets, and mannequins dressed in costumes from across at least a couple of centuries. Panels of text provided explanations in several languages – a courtesy not often extended in Italian museums, John B. noted to himself.

"I'm noticing that Venice has quite a lot of very... specialised museums. Furniture, fabric, glassware. It's like displaying the individual pieces of a jigsaw, rather than the completed picture," observed Elizabeth as she looked around.

Marina pressed her fingertips together unconsciously. "Indeed. To truly appreciate the whole of a thing, one should appreciate the intricacy of its parts. To know if the whole is indeed greater than the sum of its parts, one must understand the value of those parts."

"And your preferred parts are boats? Interesting choice, though it makes sense in this city, I suppose," said the brunette.

"Maritime transport has been the most significant, crucial element in the history of civilisation," stated the curator.

The words themselves smacked of zealotry or obsession, but they were delivered in the perfectly even tone of a schoolteacher conveying an everyday basic fact to a group of children, like 'the sky is a long way up' or 'water is wet'.

"It's an impressive collection," John B. said. "There's a lot of work has gone into it. All on your own?" he mused aloud, considering what some of the boats must weigh, bereft of the buoyant support of the canals.

"Predominantly," replied the curator. "For some time, I had valuable help from my dear Mario."

Elizabeth had spotted a small photograph of a familiar figure in a striped shirt, unobtrusively displayed amongst the exhibit of gondola paraphernalia. "Oh yes – we met him! He brought us here, in fact. Said to say 'hello' from him."

Marina DeNucci's voice in response was cold enough to chill fresh coffee. "I am... recently bereaved. That man is not *my* Mario."

"I'm sorry," said John B. genuinely. "I'm sure it's a common name, even among gondoliers."

The intensity of Marina's reaction was disconcerting, and he thought it wisest not to pursue the matter. Elizabeth was similarly diplomatic, although she peered at the photograph intently for a moment longer. There was certainly a strong resemblance, although not the same eccentric hairstyle. Wait – yes, the eyes were somehow different.

"Yes, my apologies too," she said, turning to their host. "Actually, there was someone else who directed us to you. A lady in America. She thought you might be interested in something I've inherited."

"In America?"

"Yes. Charming woman – a writer, named Dorothy Duncum," said Elizabeth.

"She is a collector of other peoples' stories," replied Marina.

It wasn't mere pedantry. It seemed that the distinction was very important to the curator. It was to be clearly understood that in *her* view, there was nothing 'creative' about Dorothy Duncum. Mentally noting that, but also automatically defending the woman they'd befriended in Maine, John B. mused that it was not unlike collecting other people's boats instead of building them.

"Yes, so she told us," Elizabeth said casually. "Anyway, when she saw these she suggested we bring them here."

As she spoke she'd been reaching into her purse to liberate the antiquities she'd been carrying. Like a croupier, in one fluid move-ment she laid out a line of coins across a convenient countertop. Two gold, four silver, none less than six hundred years old.

Marina examined them carefully. She wouldn't make a very successful poker player, John B. observed. Whilst she was now wearing an expression of no more than professional interest, there had been a definite flash of excitement in the dark eyes when the coins first appeared.

"Coins are not normally my specialty," Marina began thoughtfully. "I do, however, recognise the age and origin of these…"

"Venetian, fourteenth century. Yes. That's why we're here," said John B.

"You inherited these, young lady? Ms McKew," she added, as if to confirm she'd been listening when the couple first arrived.

Elizabeth gave a heavily edited and condensed version of the story of her ancestor, the self-styled Prince Henry, and his journey from the Orkneys via Venice to establish a colony on the distant coast of what is now Maine. The details of how the hoard had come into her possession, particularly the role of a crew of pirates and a possibly prehistoric sea monster, were omitted.

"I've got quite a few more of these," she understated, "if you're interested."

Marina looked thoughtful. "I have some awareness of Henry St. Clair. Much of what is known of his exploits has come from the writings of the Venetian Antonio Zeno…"

"Yes, his letters home after he joined Henry's expedition. Joined and helped to finance," Elizabeth said, having spent much of the last few months studying her ancestor's history, with her beau's assiduous help.

"The merchants of Venice have a long history of interest and investment in expanding opportunities, right Marina?" added that beau.

The curator couldn't hide her intrigue at the provenance of the six coins.

"As I indicated, I am not a collector of coins. But I recognise the rarity of these. The gold *ducats*, yes, but perhaps surprisingly I think the silver *grossi* even more so. There has always been an impulse to hoard gold. But the provenance of these, the link to Venetian history and the brothers Zeno, they are certainly of interest…"

Her voice trailed off for a moment, presumably as she contemplated that history.

"Interested as I may be, I am not in a position to make an offer that would match that of certain individuals – collectors or investors. I could make enquiries locally, if you wish."

"The monetary value isn't of primary importance, believe it or not," said Elizabeth. "I'm actually more interested in the story behind the coins. Oh, getting a good price would be nice, sure, but that's not why we came here. I'm trying to learn all I can about my ancestor. His connection to Venice, and those letters you mentioned, may fill in some details for me. It's not the commercial value that matters to me, but the history, hence our seeing you."

Marina's vanity was stroked, as Q had been sure it would be.

"Have you read the Zeno letters?" enquired the curator.

"A few extracts, that's all I've been able to get hold of."

"Hmm... I may be able to do better than that," replied DeNucci in a quiet voice that carried a clear implication that of *course* she could.

With a wry smile John B. said, "Information is currency. It can be worth more than euros, can't it? Knowledge is power, so I'm told."

His casual quip seemed to strike a nerve. The museum owner's back stiffened slightly, and her expression hardened again. 'Is she always this touchy?' Stewart wondered, 'Or is it me? Us?'

Q continued her diplomatic efforts. "I'd be very grateful for whatever help you can offer. Transcriptions, translations – I'm afraid my Italian is minimal – they'd be much appreciated. And if there are pieces of the collection that would add something to the history you've collected and displayed here, well, that would be fair exchange, I think. We can bring the rest of the coins for you to examine and make a selection from. In the meantime, keep these half-dozen as a show of good faith. A temporary exhibit, if you like."

There was no eye contact in response. The curator's attention seemed fixed on the handful of gold and silver. John B. noticed a small, apparently unconscious movement of her fingers, as if their tips were rifling through the contents of a filing cabinet or a box of cards. With a small shake of her dark hair Marina brought her attention back.

"Yes. Yes, that would be satisfactory." She recovered her diplomatic equilibrium. "More than satisfactory, thank you. It is a generous offer, and I appreciate it. I have little of note from the period. Such items as were preserved tend to be on a grander scale, more suited to other collections. Coins such as these, while not strictly maritime themselves, were integral to the trade which drove the city-state."

Elizabeth held out her hand. "Shall we call it a deal, then?"

The two women exchanged a stiff, formal handshake. John B. made a move to copy the gesture, but Marina's response was to turn away. She seemed determined to *not* have any physical contact with him. More puzzled than perturbed, the wizard shrugged.

If Elizabeth noticed, she made no comment, saying only, "We'll bring the rest of the collection tomorrow, if that suits?"

There was a moment's pause, during which the curator appeared to compose herself and her thoughts.

"Yes. Yes, that would be fine. Although, perhaps if you were to wait a day or two, I might be able to contact some of the coin specialists I mentioned. I'm sorry – I have been... rude. As I said, I have not long ago lost someone dear to me, and I fear that I am being more... sensitive than usual. Your offer is extremely generous, and I do appreciate it."

Apology accepted, the two Australians bid their *arrivederci* and exited the Musee Barche. Now armed with a small simple map, they were able to make their way back toward the centre of Venice on foot. They'd have had no objection to another gondola journey, but the little dock was deserted when they emerged. The air was brisk, but clear, so a walk wasn't unwelcome.

"Interesting woman," observed Q casually as they walked arm-in-arm. "I know she wasn't at her best, but somehow I can't imagine her and Texas Dorothy as friends in any case."

"No, neither can I. Although Dorothy didn't actually say that they were. I think they've known each other for a long time though," replied John B.

"Mm. Again, never actually said, but I got that impression too. I got the impression she knew you too – which now I think of it, was true of Dorothy as well."

The wizard shrugged. "I know – that was the first thing she said to us, remember, but I've got nothing, sweetheart. It's not like I've been here before, or to Maine. But you're right, there's a sense of... recognition, that I can't pin down."

"Theirs, or yours, babe?"

"Mostly theirs. Nothing more than a faint buzz for me, I'm afraid."

They strolled in thoughtful silence for a bit, before Q asked, "Is it like the buzz in your head you reckon you've had since the magic first happened?"

"Yes and no. Like the difference between a mozzie bite and a sandfly bite, maybe. Both itch, but not exactly the same. And thinking about it, there have been others. You met Auld Wullie Bromleigh, back on Islay. And that seamstress in Norway."

"Hannah Aldoy. You're right. Even the fellow on the gondola, Mario. He seemed to know you. Not mutual?"

"That's an odd one," admitted John B. "I'd be willing to swear I've never met him before, but there's a resemblance to someone I met in Hawaii. Not a physical resemblance, but – I dunno, I've never given much credence to auras..."

They enjoyed a long, slow, meandering stroll, with stops for window shopping, view appreciation, pizza and wine. As Mario had suggested, 'walking lost'. There were also occasional detours to avoid knotty crowds. Eventually they were walking along the Via Garibaldi, back in the district that was their temporary home.

As they neared their apartment, a distinctive sound came from a shop doorway – the peculiar yowl of the black cat Toscanini. The animal bounded into view, rubbed himself against Q's ankles, then wound himself around John B.'s lower legs in a way that might best be described as 'trip hazard'. Obliged to stand still for a few moments, the wizard was an easy target for Nicola when she ran from the same doorway and leapt to wrap her arms around him.

"Nice to see you, too," John B. said with a grin.

Elizabeth's expression was rather less cheery. "Hello," she managed, not quite through gritted teeth.

The girl disentangled herself from John B. and wrapped the brunette in an unexpected hug.

"'Buongiorno, Lizbetta," she said with a smile to melt any frost. "Is good to see you! Are you ready to come to dinner?"

"Um, a little early, I think?" replied Elizabeth.

"*Feh.* To eat, maybe. Not too early to visit."

"Tell you what," said John B. "It's been a bit of a busy day. Give us time to shower and change, unwind a little, and we'll see you at your place in about an hour. Okay?"

Nicola looked at him slightly quizzically, as if uncertain of why a shower could be necessary, or if it was, why it might take an hour. But she shrugged.

"Okay. See you soon. Come on, Toscanini." She skipped away, the cat trotting behind her.

"You know, just for a moment I thought she was going to offer to come home and have a shower with us. One of us, at least," observed Elizabeth.

"It's hard to know what to expect," admitted John B. "It'll be interesting to find out what this violin maker is like."

.ooo.

8

____

THE MUSICIAN

I t was slightly more than an hour later when the two Australians arrived at the door of *G. LaGrigio* – a whitewashed wooden thing, stark against the orange wall. Overhead hung the small violin-shaped sign.

Q had been insistent that they share their shower. Not aggressively insistent, but quietly determined, and John B. had very readily agreed. He knew that his beloved was making a non-verbal statement. He knew that, as far as he was concerned, there was nothing for her to be concerned about, but he also knew that the most effective way to manage her insecurities was to hold her and love her, just as tenderly and passionately as she wanted.

So, as they'd approached the building that was home to the unusual girl and even more unusual cat, the arms they had around each other's waists were probably held just a little tighter than usual.

Just as John B. raised his hand to knock, they heard from the other side of the door the sound of an amateur soprano warming up badly.

"That'll be Toscanini announcing our arrival," John B. predicted accurately.

The door swung open, apparently by magic, although in fact

under the effort of young Nicola. She stepped out from behind the portal, and greeted her guests with a surprising formal bow.

"Buongiorno, *mi amici*," she said with a smile that suggested 'Look at me, I'm on my best behaviour!'.

"Hello, my friend," replied John B., returning the greeting and the bow.

Q couldn't help but grin, and followed her beau's lead. The smile she got in return from the girl was warm and genuine.

They were ushered in through a small entrance hall to a surprisingly large open plan room. There were no windows, but several doors that evidently opened onto smaller rooms and presumably one or more staircases. It was very clear, though, what the primary purpose of the room was.

A grand piano stood in the centre of the room. Near it was an electric piano, on the other side a drum kit. On racks and on tables about the room were various other instruments: acoustic and electric guitars, a mandolin, saxophone, flute, violin , harmonicas of different sizes – even, to John B.'s delight, a pair of kazoos. A mixing desk stood against the far wall, and a half dozen speakers were mounted on the walls in what could be presumed to be carefully planned positions.

Seating was less considered. A handful of chairs, no two alike, dotted the room, along with two beanbags and several large cushions which bore the signs of having been sat upon for many long sessions. Clearly the most comfortable option was a large well-stuffed armchair. It looked to be a close cousin of John B.'s own favourite chair in the loungeroom of the Waramanga cottage he shared with his housemate Darren. ('Must call Darren!' the wizard thought to himself when he first noticed the chair.)

Toscanini was perched on the arm of the chair, and gave another yowl as the Australians walked into the room.

"Yes, thank you, my friend. I know they're there."

The speaker waved a friendly hand from his comfortable position, sunk in the ample chair. The other hand clutched part of the project he was currently working on, that was otherwise cluttering his lap – a deconstructed violin.

"Welcome!" he continued. "Pleased you could come. Nicola has told me about you, as has my other companion here."

The cat exclaimed something like *nyeek* as the couple approached. Their host was clearly not in a position to stand and greet them just at present, although he did extend his hand.

"Giancarlo LaGrigio. You must be Signorina Elizabeth, and you of course are John B. Stewart."

"Indeed. At your service," replied the wizard with a grin and a bow. He'd taken an instant liking to the fellow.

"Good afternoon, Signore LaGrigio," said Elizabeth pleasantly as she cast a curious eye over the instrument-maker.

He was clearly not a young man – the hair on his scalp was thinning, although his beard was thick and neatly trimmed. Both were a rich shade of silver. The laughter lines which were the only creases on his face, ran deep in ruddy skin. He wasn't especially fat, although an earnest young doctor would probably have advised him to lose a bit of weight.

Nicola skipped across the room, pushed the violin pieces out of her way and deposited herself on Giancarlo's lap, throwing her arms about his neck for good measure.

"My Giancarlo is the finest musician in all of Venice, and probably the world!" she enthused.

"Thankyou, widget, although I think you're a little biased."

The girl jumped back to her feet and scampered over to an old, nicely carved cupboard.

"Drinks!" she announced, rather than asked.

"We managed to rustle up a decent Australian red," said John B., proffering the bottle.

Giancarlo eyed the label as he started to struggle out of his chair. "Rutherglen – excellent choice, thank you. Better with food, later, I think. Spirits for now? Let me just put this away…"

Nicola had succeeded in tangling the strings and other pieces of the instrument LaGrigio had been working on. As he picked it up, it hung limply like musical roadkill.

"Poor violin – it may yet be a fiddle, I fear. You know the difference, I think," he said with a small wink.

John B. grinned. "Nobody minds if you spill beer on a fiddle."

"Or wine, or anything with alcohol in it. Yes," agreed the silver man.

Nicola had extracted several bottles from the cupboard. A honeyed bourbon and a Speyside single malt Scotch were amongst them, enthusiastically selected by Elizabeth and her beau respectively. A good English gin was Giancarlo's own choice. To Elizabeth's surprise young Nicola poured a small shot of an aniseed liqueur for herself.

The girl handed around the glasses, and accompanied Giancarlo's with an affectionate hug that broadened the silver-haired man's smile. Elizabeth had never had a grandfather that she'd known, but if she had she was pretty sure she'd never embrace him quite like that. Freeing himself, perhaps reluctantly, Giancarlo gestured around the room.

"Nicola and I don't stand on ceremony here…"

"No – we sit on the floor!"

"Indeed. Please, make yourselves comfortable wherever appeals."

Given first choice, Elizabeth opted for a big old wicker chair, padded with cushions in peacock-feather satin. It was a little more straight-backed than might have been expected. The others drew their seating choices around her, like circling the wagons. A leopard-print fuzzy bean bag for John B., a pair of large, square and well-stuffed cushions in Moorish fabric for the two hosts.

The cat padded around them, sniffing at each one (and their glass) in turn. Rather than selecting a particular lap to occupy, he sashayed over to the television cabinet against a wall and jumped up to settle on top of the set. It was an old picture-tube model, that John B. rightly suspected hadn't been used for a very long time.

"I never got around to getting rid of it," Giancarlo explained. "Had an idea of repairing it at one point, or at least recycling the speaker components. Then when the cat moved in, it was one of his first choices as a perch, so I've just kept it there."

"It's part of how Tosca got his name," said Nicola proudly.

Blank looks from the visitors prompted Giancarlo to explain. "One of the claims to fame of the great Arturo Toscanini was that he was probably the first conductor to regularly be on television. A series of live concerts from 1948 to '52. Add to that, our little friend's unusual voice sometimes has... operatic overtones, and a rather peculiar rhythmic pattern that reminds me of Arturo's metronomic rigidity."

"And he doesn't eat fish," added the girl.

"Indeed. The conductor had a lifelong aversion to seafood of any find, and our Toscanini is similarly unwilling to eat fish – unusual in a cat. Put all that together and, well, the name seemed obvious."

'To anyone knowing the minutiae of early-20th century operatic conductors,' thought Elizabeth.

"How did you find him?" she asked. "Or did he find you?"

"A little of both. I'd been at a recording session with a... man I know, and as I left the studio I almost tripped over a little black shape huddled in the darkness. I apologised, the kitten made a strange noise back which I took to also be an apology, he followed me home, and proceeded to follow me back and forth ever since. He wanders quite indiscriminately now, I think, but this is where he always comes back to."

"He knows where he's well looked after, I'd say," said Elizabeth.

"Indeed. Where he's loved." Giancarlo's smile was the very picture of benign. It was easy to imagine any waif or stray being drawn to that countenance.

There was some pleasant conversation exchanged about cats – Elizabeth's brief childhood time with a tabby kitten before her mother decided it was all too much trouble, and taking up too much of her daughter's affection. John B. talked about his late much-lamented Kat. The big white Persian had been, in his way, Stewart's best friend, and had been an important part of some of his first experiences in magic (although the wizard didn't recount things in quite that way).

There were stories of Toscanini's interactions on the streets of

Venice, including his painful encounter with the Culatello brothers. Their casual cruelty towards the small cat they found waiting patiently outside the recording studio was one of the reasons that Giancarlo never returned to that particular place. No, they weren't musicians, but they were known to work for the owner of the studio.

Looking about the room Elizabeth remarked, "So, I'm not surprised - you don't just make instruments, you play as well. Any one in particular? Nicola mentioned you were teaching her keyboards."

"There is nothing my Giancarlo cannot play!" announced the girl proudly.

The silver man smiled, but Elizabeth quietly noted that he didn't deny or correct her. He merely said, "I have some preference for stringed instruments, although I've tried never to limit myself."

With very little prompting, Giancarlo agreed to "play something for them". Nicola scampered to fetch the lute he indicated with a nod, and then, as he tightened a string, settled herself behind an electric piano.

The duo proceeded to produce a playful little piece. The form was almost light classical or even medieval, but as they took turns playing little solos over the other's rhythmic underpinnings there were moments of jazz and even something like 'hillbilly' music. Unlikely from the combination of instruments, but so well played that it worked.

As soon as they finished, Giancarlo smiled proudly at his protégé as their visitors applauded enthusiastically.

"Wow!" was Elizabeth's response. "I never expected that... sorry, that sounds awful – it's just... that was... superb."

"I told you my Giancarlo could play anything," the girl said with pride.

"And I have an excellent student," replied her mentor, equally proudly.

John B. was shaking his head in admiration. "There were so many elements woven into that," he said. "It has to be original, but I'm sure there were bits I almost recognised. One fragment from a band I used to love years ago, probably never big in Venice. The Ozark Mountain Daredevils, they were called – great name, great outfit."

Giancarlo smiled broadly and called Nicola over. He whispered something in her ear. Moments later she handed him a violin (intact, this time), and took up a guitar for herself. The silver man drew the bow across the strings a few times, then launched into a fluid tune, while the girl played a chord progression underneath. As he recognised the music John B. found himself tapping a gentle rhythm on his knee, then eyes closed, began to sing.

Q sat and gazed in surprise, and ultimately admiration. She didn't know the song, but she'd never heard her beau really sing before. (What he did on aeroplanes with the headphones on didn't really count.) It wasn't a great voice, even with the bias of her love she'd have admitted that, but it worked for this song. And LaGrigio's violin swept beautifully across the tune, adding the right layer of emotion. It was finished too soon, as far as she was concerned. She hugged her beau, and thanked Giancarlo with shining eyes.

"I haven't even heard *Giving It All To The Wind* for years," admitted John B. "Thank you! I'm amazed I managed to pull up most of the lyrics from wherever they were buried!"

"Ah my friend, music is a better key to memory than almost anything, I've always found," replied their host as he handed his violin to Nicola. "Is anyone else hungry?" he asked.

"Now you mention it, yes," answered Elizabeth, with some surprise, as if the music had prompted an appetite she hadn't previously noticed.

"Widget, would you do the honours of preparing dinner?" Giancarlo asked.

Nicola grinned and nodded enthusiastically. She helped her mentor stand and the two conferred quietly for a few minutes. Q snuggled against her beau.

"Babe, that was really lovely. I haven't heard you sing like that before."

"Not something I do much of, I'm afraid. Mum always said, 'there's nae money in it', right back from when I was a kid first living with her. I suspect she'd dissuaded Dad from a career in music, and I probably let that put me off something I really enjoyed."

"Mothers can do that," replied Q with some bitterness.

"Sometimes well-intentioned, sweetheart. They're just... passing along their own baggage. Eventually, it's up to us whether we carry it on."

Elizabeth leaned over and kissed him. "I think you're kinder than my mother deserves – I don't know about yours. But thank you."

"Come, my friends," said Giancarlo warmly, having politely waited for them to finish their quiet conversation. "While Nicola slaves in the kitchen, shall I show you around our humble home?"

While the 'music room' dominated the downstairs area, there were other rooms off of it, some of which took advantage of light from large windows. One of these might have been the showroom that fronted the main street, if the heavy curtains were to be drawn back. A layer of dust suggested this hadn't happened for some time. There were two small rooms full of books and papers, much of it sheet music, little more than alcoves really. What was revealed to be Giancarlo's bedroom wasn't much bigger. It accommodated a rumpled double bed and a desk, both littered with notebooks. Two staircases at opposite sides of the large main room led to the upper storey.

"I don't do stairs much anymore when I can avoid it," admitted Giancarlo. "My knees. My workshop is up there, but there's a lot I do down here. The first floor is store rooms. Guest rooms if we're entertaining. Sometimes a music night may go much later than anticipated. Nicola's room."

Elizabeth was quietly relieved to hear that the girl had her own room. She'd still harboured some quiet reservations about the relationship between her hosts. Without thinking she remarked, "I'm glad she has that space to herself."

Smiling, Giancarlo replied, "Well of course. I often keep... unusual hours. Writing, playing – creating. It doesn't always work to a timetable. Sometimes Nicola is the same, but she is young and I know she needs her sleep."

Elizabeth raised an eyebrow. "Is Nicola your niece, or..."

"Grand-daughter? No, no offence taken – there is, as you've noted, a substantial difference in our ages," Giancarlo said with a self-deprecating smile. "No, we're not related. Nicola's own family were – possibly still are – dysfunctional would be too mild a word. When I met her, she'd had a difficult past, was enduring an awful present, and faced a truly terrible future."

"Abusive parents? What about her school? Don't the authorities here take any interest in such things?" asked Elizabeth.

"Perhaps, but even then, the options are limited. Parents are regarded as a child's best option, even when they obviously aren't. Schooling had ceased for Nicola at a very early age. Conventional schooling, at any rate. She was being schooled in... other things. That said, her parents made no public objections when she left them. I suspect they had... other options available to them."

"Sounds grim," said John B. quietly.

"Indeed. Unfortunately, we can't save everyone every time, my friend. But I sensed Nicola's talent and was able to get her away from what would have been, as a poet wrote, a short and brutish life."

"You don't just teach her music, do you?" Elizabeth's suspicions had flared again. They hadn't actually seen evidence that Nicola *occupied* what was explained as 'her' room. There was still a note of accusation in her voice, and something like righteous indignation.

"Nicola was what I think you might call *worldly* when I first met her. Her family had not been kind. I have tried to teach her that not all the world is demanding, cruel and violent – not easy when that is the tone of so many early memories. And when those characteristics *are* revealed to exist in the world. But as I say, I hope I'm teaching her that they're not universal, or even 'normal'. At least, they do not have to be *her* normal. No, Elizabeth, I don't just teach her music. Or literacy. I try to teach her kindness, gentleness, and compassion."

John B. discreetly squeezed his beloved's hand, hoping to reassure her. He had an altogether too clear idea of what Nicola's future would otherwise have been.

"There's a saying I heard when we were with the tribes in Maine, sweetheart. Prepare the child for the path, not the path for the child," he said.

"Mmm. I'm sorry, Giancarlo. I'm probably sounding terribly prudish, not to mention suspicious..."

"You have the girl's best interests at heart and mind. No need for apology. I can only ask that you accept I share those precise sentiments."

For a few long moments they looked deeply into each other's eyes. Not many people met Elizabeth McKew's unflinching gaze without difficulty, but Giancarlo LaGrigio seemed undisturbed. Finally, they both nodded, as if satisfied with each other.

Having maintained a diplomatic silence, John B. took the nod as a gesture of closure and suggested, "Shall we check in with the chef?"

The small galley kitchen was another of the rooms tucked off of the big music room. When they entered, immediately making the room awkwardly crowded, an open window was allowing the steam from a cast iron saucepan to escape to the street. Nonetheless, the aroma of the food filled the room delightfully.

"Smells fabulous!" enthused Elizabeth. "What is it?"

"It is called *rixi e bixi* – one of my favourites!" came the reply. "Just about ready."

"Well timed, then," said Giancarlo, taking four bowls and spoons from a narrow cupboard by the door.

The meal was served up almost immediately, and they returned to their places in the music room, eating from bowls perched on their laps. Glasses of the Aussie red sat on the floor around them. Nicola shared in the wine, this was Italy and presumably traditional, but her share was smaller than the others.

Rixi e bixi proved to be a very moist risotto, well endowed with chopped pancetta and fresh peas in a delicious broth.

"Seriously beautiful," said Elizabeth, carefully spooning up the last fragments of rice and peas from her bowl.

"Too right. Thank you, Nicola," agreed John B., savouring the last of his pancetta.

Toscanini had had a serve of the meal put in his own plate by the kitchen door, and had evidently enjoyed it as much as his two-legged friends. Certainly, the plate was licked clean. He now sat companionably among the four, making his own strange variant of a purr.

It eased into a relaxed and relaxing evening of conversation. Much of it was about music, not surprisingly. Nicola had a few questions about Australia and other places where the visitors had travelled, but less than the Australians perhaps anticipated based on past experience. It wasn't that the girl wasn't interested. More that she had a pleasant casual, not eager, anticipation that she'd experience and find out things for herself in the fullness of time.

The Australians were surprised by the lateness of the hour when, yawning and stretching, they finally offered their farewells. After hugs all round, the couple made their way back out onto the Via Garibaldi.

The night air was more than brisk, and Q snuggled into her beau's embrace as they took their short walk home. Typically, he seemed oblivious to the chill, but was very happy to share body warmth. A few other folks were on the street, and a good sprinkling of lighted windows suggested that plenty of locals were night owls. As they walked, they could just hear the sound of music coming from behind them. Evidently Nicola had left a window open.

Inside their apartment, as they deposited their clothes in the spare bedroom they realised that they could just make out the sound of the piano and guitar through the wall. This must be where the buildings adjoined, and the reverberation of the music must be travelling up from the floor below. They smiled and sat on the bed together, savouring the sound for a few minutes longer. Then Q squeezed her beau's hand, blew in his ear, and led him to their room.

.ooo.

9

———

PRIVATE LIVES

Whilst the Giardini district, of which Manovalo was a part, was home to most of the Venetians who actually still lived in the city, it didn't house them all. A few private dwellings were scattered in other parts of the city.

One of these was a substantial building in what had been the old Jewish quarter – the Ghetto it had been called, before the name had quite so many negative connotations – on a northern island of the city. The building was grander, or at least larger, than most of its neighbours. Not by coincidence, it stood within a short distance of the Campo San Leonardo. Its owner called it the Palazzo Grossi, with the same sense of self-aggrandizement that had led him to coin his own nickname.

Leonardo Delocchio, self-styled *Il Duce Grosso* - by his usage, 'the Silver Duke', referencing his passion for that particular precious metal. He was not oblivious to the alternative connotations, particularly in English. It was another of 'his little jokes'. He described himself sometimes as "amply built", but in truth was at least three times the weight that would have been healthy for a man of his height and thirty-odd years.

He was still quite capable of walking, but it was an indicator of his innate laziness that he often chose to travel the streets of Venice on a heavily reinforced modified three-wheeled electric scooter. The modifications allowed the little vehicle to travel at considerably more than the 8kph it had been originally designed to achieve. Even with the load of Leonardo's bulk, and the less-than-aerodynamic canopy that was another modification – bedecked in heavy waterproof silver brocade and extravagantly coloured tassels. Although it was quite unlike anything Oscar Hammerstein might have envisaged, it was called, "My little surrey with the fringe on top," by Il Duce.

He was self-indulgent in the same way that Randolph Hearst had been rich. He could afford to be. Delocchio had quite quickly and suddenly achieved fame as a composer and musician, mostly in his own recording studio. Then he'd parlayed that income into the buying and selling of artwork at considerable profit.

His successful sales included his own pencil drawings, marketed on the prestige of his name rather than particular artistic merit. His drawing style looked like it hadn't progressed much after his twelfth birthday.

But he was a well-known local figure and commanded a degree of respect. 'Commanded' was an operative word. Despite his sometimes genial and generous façade, some Venetians had learned, to their sorrow, that Il Duce Grosso was not a man to be crossed. What he wanted, he got.

For those times when he wanted company, or at least, an audience, he had other occupants in the Palazzo who would promptly abandon whatever they were doing and pay court to the big man when required. None of them fitted well in regular society, and that was not coincidental. Leonardo Delocchio's forceful personality was at its most dominating when he surrounded himself with folks who lacked 'people' skills.

The three Culatello brothers were among that number, although on this particular day, like many others, they weren't at home. Il Duce didn't mind. They were obedient, but hardly stimulating intellectual company for Leonardo. (Meaning, none of them were bright enough to 'get' most of his little jokes.) Far more useful that they be out on the streets of Venice, being seen, and seeing things for themselves. While not clever, they were cunning like rats and knew the sort of opportunities that their employer took advantage of.

Not surprisingly, the kitchen of the Palazzo Grossi was one of the most extensive and best-equipped rooms in the house. It was in here that a young woman pushed a sweat-soaked strand of red hair from a high cheek bone. Pasqualina was tending to a simmering pot of *all'amatriciana* sauce, to be applied to that evening's tagliatelle. The traditional pigs' cheek and lard – Leonardo's favourite ingredients – were supplemented by her own blend of spices and herbs. Their addition, beyond the usual tomato, chilli and sheep's cheese, were what elevated her rendition of the standard dish into something exceptional. And that, of course, was what Il Duce required.

Content that the sauce was as it should be, the red-haired woman retired to the comfortable chair she'd set up in a corner of the kitchen. From a bookcase beside the chair she extracted one of a large collection of old and dusty tomes and settled down to read. Most of the volumes in the case could be considered recipe books of one form or another. Not all of them pertained to food. Pasqualina was not a patient woman by nature, but had willed herself to become so. Self-discipline ran deep in her.

In another room, a tall thin Englishman frowned at the canvas he was working on. He applied a few more long strokes of black oil paint to one side of the picture, then stepped back from the easel, leaning on his heavy cane. He tilted his head to consider the effect. He nodded in some satisfaction, although the frown barely wavered. The asymmetry was better. Closer to what had been directed, if not particularly to his own taste.

Septimus Smith, he'd been christened. Leonardo preferred to call him 'Sceptred' Smith, his own little joke, alluding to the 'sceptred isle' of Smith's origin. The Englishman accepted the jest with his usual bleak equanimity. He didn't especially like his employer, but he didn't really like anyone. Not even himself, if it came right down to it. But the fat man paid well, which would one day finance the expensive self-contained one-man motor yacht he dreamed of. The means of spending a solitary life at sea.

There would be no impediment to that from the "gammy leg" which was the justification for his collection of canes and walking sticks. The original injury to his knee, the result of a bike accident, had long since healed, but Septimus had noticed that people in the street gave a wider berth to someone who walked with an aid. The more distance between himself and Them, the better, so the sticks had become as much habit as affectation.

Meanwhile, at least he was mostly left to work in uninterrupted solitude in his own room where he could usually paint and sleep to his own timetable, so long as the job was finished by the ordered date. Having set a task, Delocchio let him work without supervision. It wasn't required. Smith was a perfectionist. Obsessively so, to Leonardo's delight. To his further pleasure, the Englishman had no interest in fame or recognition. He derived his satisfaction from what he considered a job well done, and (even if he didn't look it) was happiest when left alone with his art.

Time with the heavy-handed wit of his employer was tolerable. At least he wasn't expected to contribute much to their conversations beyond snippets of agreement and flattery. Anything resembling 'chat' was the purview of the red-haired woman. Strange one, that, and hard to quite fathom the relationship between her and the duke. Sometimes acerbic, other times quite affectionate. Usually polite to him though, and she was a damn fine cook. The other three were barely worth mentioning, with all the artistic sense of the bottom-feeding fish they'd apparently caught in their youth. Altogether, worth enduring for the sake of the money, and the fact of most of his time being spent with paints, inks and crayons on the execution of his art. Well, strictly speaking, not *his*. He worked to Leonardo's quite specific instruction regarding style and content. But the finished product was always impeccable, and that quality was very definitely his.

The most well-appointed of the Palazzo's rooms, even more expensively if less opulently equipped than the dining room, was what Leonardo called his Performance Room. Insulated to be acoustically perfect, it was a spacious recording studio. Its layout bore a resemblance to Giancarlo LaGrigio's music room, with a piano at the centre, ringed by a variety of other instruments. There was even a comfortable armchair in a similar position to Giancarlo's favourite seat.

It was into this chair that the Silver Duke was presently sunk. For once he neither required nor wanted an audience. He was recording his own 'backing track'. The guitar sat almost horizontally across his belly, so he played it much like a country and western steel guitar. The style of the music was very different though. There was a classical influence, a hint of Beethoven and a slice of sweetness. With lush production, lots of orchestration, it wouldn't be out of place in the elevator of a big department store, but this background was comparatively spare. The percussion of a drum machine, and a few layers of keyboard synthesizer set for different effects and tones. Against this, the tune being played on a solitary guitar was quite appealing.

Leonardo's pudgy fingers were surprisingly nimble on the strings. Some improvisation in performance would be fine, but the fundamental structure had to be tight. The piece was to be publicly debuted on the final day of the Carnivale, and Il Duce wanted it to be better than just satisfactory. This was for the sake of his own substantial ego. It wasn't as if he expected anyone in the crowd would be likely to find fault, any more than the man who'd really composed most of it was expected to complain. No one crossed Il Duce Grosso.

BY CHANCE, Leonardo Delocchio was the subject of a rather fawning interview in a Tourist magazine that Elizabeth read over a slice of pizza that was serving as her lunch. She pointed out to the wizard a passing reference to Giancarlo LaGrigio as one of the 'sidemen' who'd appeared on Leonardo's recordings, all of whose contributions were glossed over by both the interviewer and interviewee.

The Australian couple had spent the morning walking some of the fringe of Venice, pausing often to look out toward some of the outlying islands. They had vague plans to visit Murano at least, and possibly Lido and Burano. This day though, they were content to consider them from a distance. Wherever possible they walked along the *rive, viali,* and *fondamenta* that overlooked the canal and lagoon that surrounded the city. Where, over the years (centuries, even), buildings had been built right to the waterfront, the pair detoured down narrow *stretti* admiring the architecture. Walking lost, as the gondolier Mario had recommended, they happened on quirky little plazas, pretty churches, and exotic Byzantine decorations adorning otherwise plain small buildings.

The weather took some gloss off the excursion. There was a blustery wind, with intermittent cold gusts further punctuated by showers of rain that was almost but not quite sleet. It was a measure of how much the temperature had dropped that John B. Stewart wore his tartan vest over a long-sleeved t-shirt that he'd bought at a souvenir stall. Purple, of course, emblazoned with stylised Carnevale masks in black, white and gold. Elizabeth was sensibly wrapped up in a waterproof jacket over a woollen jumper and her own long-sleeved t-shirt. The wool of her skirt and tights was considerably warmer than the worn denim of her beau's jeans.

At least neither was fazed by the puddles that were appearing on the pavements and street surfaces. While in New York they'd both bought excellent waterproof walking boots – good leather, lined with lambs' wool. Their feet were satisfactorily cosy.

When the rain was too aggravating they'd ducked into a convenient shop or bar, or sheltered in a deeply recessed doorway where they kept each other warm and distracted until conditions improved.

Even so, by the time they got back to the welcome central heating of Manovalo 219, they were weary and damp. A hot shower was a relief for both of them.

As he towelled his beloved's back afterwards, John B. asked, "Could I interest milady in a massage?"

Q slipped into the faux Southern Belle cartoon voice she knew he loved. "Why, sir! Ah would be purely dee-lighted to accept yoah kind offer!"

In the spare room a beach towel was laid out to protect one of the bedspreads from oil and any other post-shower wetness. Elizabeth stretched out comfortably, her arms slipped beneath the pillow upon which she rested her chin.

John B. said that he'd learned the techniques of massage from an old Aboriginal healer in Central Australia – the same guy who'd helped save Q's life after the shooting in Norway, thanks to the modern miracle of video calling. However, his brunette lover had a firm conviction that he had a natural talent of his own.

He rubbed a generous quantity of olive oil into his hands and set to work on her shoulders and upper back.

Suddenly they were aware of music echoing softly through the wall. Giancarlo was playing a gentle tune on the harpsichord. Nicola accompanied him on a guitar, picking out a simple melody. It was an ideal background to John B.'s tender ministrations.

The masseur took his time, working his way slowly down her body. His thumbs gently manipulated the small joints between ribs and vertebrae, while his fingertips gently caressed her sides. The sensation prompted a surprising and uncomfortable thought in Elizabeth.

"JB... babe... with all this fabulous pasta and pastries and suchlike we've been enjoying... would you mind if I put a bit of weight on?"

His movements never skipped a beat. "Mind? Why on earth would I? Sweetheart, it's *your* body."

"Well, yes, but you visit it a lot."

They both chuckled before the brunette continued, concern in her voice. "Sonny was always such a control freak. I was never to be anything more than a size 10. I passed up on a couple of lovely Asian outfits because their sizing was so small I'd have had to buy something labelled a 12, or even an L, to fit me, and he just wouldn't have that. Mum was the same, in her own way. Always insisting that I look my best, with her own very clear idea of what that meant."

"Sounds unfair," John B. said softly as he made smooth waves in the muscles of her lower back.

"It's what I was used to. I suppose it framed my own idea of what a 'professional image' looked like too, while I tried to live up to that. Other people's opinions..."

"Listen, pretty lady - it's you I love, not what you look like. I mean, I love that too, but that's not the main thing, far less the only thing. I really appreciate that you care about your appearance, but what matters most to me is that you're happy. If you were constantly finding fault with yourself I'd wind up either arguing with you, or agreeing with you. Neither are good options."

There was a faint note of bitter experience in his voice, and Q wondered again about his past. She knew that she wasn't the first woman in his life, and that there'd been a fiancée at one stage, mentioned once or twice only as being part of the price of his drinking habit. A habit he now controlled, to her quiet pride.

"Thank you, babe. Mmm... I love you too..."

She almost purred with pleasure as his hands worked over her hips and the gluteus maximus he so admired. Relaxing and exciting in equal measure.

They slipped into a silence of mutual contentment for a little while.

A little more oil on his hands, he kneaded the muscles of her calves with long, slow movements.

Q arched her back slightly, eyes closed, and with a blissful smile on her face said, "Mmm – where were you when I was playing hockey? I'd have loved this after a game. Not that I'm not loving it now!"

"Rough game, hockey. Football with weaponry," John B. observed. "Good way to break a shin, I always thought."

"I never broke my shin playing hockey," Q said, with transparent innocence.

"Ah, but did you break anyone else's?"

"Nobody who didn't deserve it."

Stewart smiled as he drew the palms of his hands down the front of his beloved's legs, saying, "I'm glad I'm on your side."

Q opened one mischievous eye. "Oh, there were some deserving cases who were supposedly on my side. Accidents happen."

"Karma's a bitch, especially when she's wielding a hockey stick. Now relax and forget all about those deserving cases." His thumbs worked circles on the balls of her feet.

The filtered sound of the harpsichord and guitar slipped into the silence.

Just for a moment, John B.'s brow creased. One particular passage of music was familiar, but he couldn't immediately place where from. Snap! The radio, on more than one occasion in recent days. *Toccare di Luna*. Had Giancarlo been involved in that recording? JB listened to the easy familiarity with which the harpsichord played the complex piece, and the little twists and 'ad libs' being added.

He smiled his realisation. This Leonardo Delocchio bloke may be getting the credit, but the wizard suddenly knew who was really responsible for 'The Touch of the Moon'.

Any further musings on the matter, such as whether Delocchio may be the sort of 'deserving case' his beloved had referred to, were dismissed as the lady in question rolled over onto her back. Wordlessly she spread her arms, inviting John B. into her embrace.

Well, of course he accepted!

.ooo.

10

GREY DAY

Another morning at Manovalo 219. Another breakfast of fresh coffee and exquisite pastries. The brief excursion to the pasticerria indicated that the weather was shaping up to be more of the same as the day before. Gusts of wind drove drizzle down the little viale, so John B.'s jeans and purple 'Snoopy' t-shirt were damp by the time he made it back up to the apartment. Q solicitously helped him to remove them.

They reheated the coffee a little while later.

Looking out the window at rain dripping from the washing lines strung between the buildings of Viale di Tavola, Q wondered aloud if this was a day best spent at home. Let the tourists clamouring to extract every moment of Carnevale brave the elements. She'd welcome the opportunity to do some more work on her book, feeling that the project had been a bit neglected in recent times.

There was no argument from John B. There were books for him to read, including one on the history of Venice that looked to be more interesting than those intended for the tourist market. From its days as a haven for refugees fleeing Attila's Huns, first hiding then slowly thriving on guile and improvisation among the mud and the islets. The days of mercantile empire, when the *doges* who ruled the city were the most powerful political figures in Europe. The tactical error of trying to leverage commercial strength to military supremacy, draining the coffers and ruining the Venetian reputation, culminating in what amounted to a brief 'Holy War'. The forces of the Holy Roman Empire, the Vatican, France, Spain, Hungary, Milan and Savoy had all briefly united in their opprobrium towards the city-state, before inevitably falling out with each other. Venice recovered economically, for the most part, but never regained her dominance.

During a break in the weather he put down his book and left Q to her work while he did some shopping out on the Via Garibaldi. While he was buying a small haunch of lamb, intended for a slow-cooked dinner, he was suddenly seized from behind in an enthusiastic embrace.

The accompanying yowl from at his heels confirmed his immediate suspicion.

"Buongiorno, Nicola. Buongiorno, Toscanini," he said cheerily.

The embrace tightened in a squeeze. "Buongiorno, caro mio," came the reply.

'Probably a good thing that Q isn't here,' Stewart thought to himself as he turned in Nicola's grasp. He put his free arm around her to return the hug.

"*Calma, dolcezza,*" he said, carefully extracting himself. Leaving the store, lamb firmly gripped in one hand, he dropped to a knee to scratch at the cat's battered head. He was rewarded with the Toscanini equivalent of a purr – a sound like marbles rolling down corrugated iron, and the return of Nicola's embrace, this time around his neck.

"Is good to see you, Jonbi," she said. "I was going to come look for you, and here you are. You must have known I wanted you, hey?"

Thought: 'Definitely glad Q's not here.' Aloud: "Good to see you too, sweetness. What were you looking for me for? Anything in particular?"

"Oh, *si*. My Giancarlo invites you and Lizbetta to come to the casa tomorrow. We are having a... session of jam? Some friends, to play the music together. To play, to listen, to enjoy."

"Sounds... *bellisimo*. What time?"

The girl released her grip to wave a vague hand. "Afternoon. We play into the night. Giancarlo and I will have big pot of *canederli* on stove for anyone hungry."

"Dumplings, eh? Sounds good. I'm not much of a musician, little darling, but I'd – *we*'d love to come and listen."

"*Feh* – I heard you sing. Giancarlo says you have a musical soul."

"Does he indeed? That's a nice thing to hear. Okay, we'll be there."

"*Brillante!*" the girl cried, and dived to plant a firm kiss on John B.'s lips.

At the same time, Toscanini pushed his head firmly up into the wizard's outstretched hand in his own show of affection. Just as suddenly, the embrace was gone and Nicola skipped back a pace, her face still aglow with a smile.

"See you tomorrow, Jonbi!" she said merrily, and skipped down the street like any excited little girl, the cat at her heels.

Stewart shook his head. 'Strange, kind of wonderful, and more than a bit dangerous,' he mused to himself. 'I do get why Q finds her disconcerting.'

He wandered into the well-stocked nearby *alimentari* and bought a few more grocery items for lunch and dinner. He chose some rice as a leaner option than pasta, perhaps conscious (or not) of his beloved's implied concern about her weight, but certainly aware of his own waistline.

Happily ignoring another squall of cold rain, he ambled back to their apartment. Thoughts of music in his head, he whistled as he strolled. If there was any significance to the tune – the Beatles' *I've Just Seen A Face* – it wasn't conscious.

He was still whistling as he climbed the stairs to their blue door. Inside, he deposited an affectionate kiss on Q's cheek as she worked, and handed her another exercise book that he'd just bought along with the groceries.

"Figured that one was getting full," he said.

She smiled gratefully. "I probably should work straight to the computer," she said, "I find it helps sort my thoughts though, if I write on paper first, then edit as I transcribe later."

"Whatever works for you, pretty lady. I just read 'em. I dunno what makes 'em work."

She grasped his hand, and pulled him into a lingering kiss.

It was some minutes before Stewart was busy in the kitchen. He had the lamb in a large pot, covered in water with a very un-Italian blend of spices and herbs. With the exception of the tin of tomato paste, the recipe owed more to Morocco than Milan. 'A change from Italian cuisine,' was his thought. In a similar vein, he'd bought the makings of a welsh rarebit to be prepared for lunch later.

As he stirred the stock mixture he mentioned bumping into Nicola, and the invitation for the next afternoon. He was pleased, and perhaps a little relieved, that Q's reaction was so positive. Whatever her reservations about the relationship between Giancarlo and Nicola, they were good hosts, and the music was excellent. Silently she hoped to hear her beau sing again – that had been an unexpected pleasure, a side of him she hadn't seen before and really appreciated. More than he did himself, she suspected.

Satisfied that the pot was simmering gently, John B. made coffee for them both, then settled into a chair with his book, contentedly listening to his beloved's pen scratching and occasional bursts of activity on her laptop.

With interludes for food, drink, and expressions of affection, it was a very easy, relaxing way to spend a damp day and a cold evening.

THE COLD AND the rain made it an unpleasant day for tourists, even with the delights of Carnevale to entertain them. Staying warm and dry indoors was definitely the best options, and most Venetians will-ingly did so, contributing to the local economy.

Ugo, Duilio and Luigino Culatello weren't much bothered by the weather. They were natives of Burano. While the island is best known across the world as a home of exquisite lace, it has also been home to fishermen since Roman times. The Culatello family probably went back to that time, their forebears amongst those who'd fled the barbarian invasions and settled on the muddy flats in the north-east of the lagoon. While the brothers had never liked the hard work of their father's small boat, fishing in whatever weather, they were well used to water.

Duilio in particular liked water, but for all the wrong reasons. Just as he'd taken the lead in throwing Tadeusz Zybysko into the canal, he'd similarly derived fiendish pleasure from propelling their sister into a canal or the lagoon at any opportunity. All three of the brothers had bullied young Antonella, but Duilio had been the one whose torment of choice had been immersion.

Hardly surprisingly, Antonella had fled home in her early teens. She'd made her way to France and, ironically, made a successful career for herself as a Channel swimmer. Now known by a different name, her brothers were oblivious to what had become of her. Not that they cared.

So, while the three men were annoyed by the intermittent rain, they'd spent most of their lives being annoyed by one thing or another. It didn't matter much to their general disposition. Today was like many other days for them, rain or shine. It was spent pacing Venice as well-recognised (if officially Unofficial) envoys of Il Duce Grosso. Delocchio was an acquisitive man, but one of definite and specific tastes. His passion for silver was most famous, but he had an interest in other *objets d'art* – so long as they were unique. The Culatelli weren't bright, but they'd been well trained in what to look for. Price was no object, because one way or another the Silver Duke wouldn't pay whatever was being asked.

This day's perambulations took the trio into the district that was home to the Musee Barche. The museum itself was seldom of any interest to them. Quite the opposite, in fact, specialising as it did in exactly the sort of boats that they'd left behind. The two younger brothers didn't even spare a glance. Ugo was more efficient on their employer's behalf, casting cursory eyes over the display window that Marina had just redecorated.

Those eyes suddenly widened. He was no expert, but even without the curator's little explanatory sign he would have recognised the quality of the silver coins. And he knew enough to realise that the dates made them even more special.

With a gruff bark he called his brothers back to his side. At Ugo's direction, Duilio turned his phone to take pictures of the array of coins, and of the little sign that sat beside them. Luigino's lips moved as he read Marina's thumbnail description of the coins and their place in the city's history.

Ugo wiped at his large nose. It tended to drip in wet weather, which might have annoyed a man more concerned about his appearance. It was only the vague tickle at the end of his nostrils that irked the oldest of the brothers.

"I think these will interest Il Duce," he said. "Interest him a lot."

"It's a museum," observed Luigino, the youngest. "I didn't think they sell things."

"You don't think, Lui. That is not your job. It's my job. Your job is to do what I tell you. And I think Il Duce will want to know about these coins. And if he wants to have them, then he will have them. It doesn't matter what a museum wants, or does."

The three strode away, again in the lockstep they naturally displayed, as the rain intensified.

Scarcely a few minutes behind them was a tall, lean man, dressed in a long black coat. The rainwater ran in a thin stream off the wide brim of the black hat worn pulled down hard. He'd angled it enough that the water did not obscure his vision. He examined the window display. Then he looked in the direction the Culatello brothers had taken. At a measured pace, he followed them, making notes in his head, to be transferred later to the notebook tucked, safe and dry, in an inside pocket of his coat.

.ooo.

11

———

THE COIN COLLECTOR

The weather improved somewhat overnight. The sky was blue. It was still cold. The wind, however, had settled to be moderate but consistent, and the rain had cleared.

After a leisurely breakfast, the Australians took Q's cache from the firebox, and spread the coins across the table for a final examination.

"Are you sure you don't want to keep any of them, pretty lady?"

Elizabeth picked over the hoard. She selected out a couple, turning them over in her fingers as she examined them.

"There are no dates on them. I thought maybe – oh, it's silly – something like an anniversary of last year, when you and I first..."

John B. reached out and held her hands. "Doesn't sound silly at all, pretty lady. Sounds beautiful, actually. But no, the only way to date these is by the name of the *doge* on one side. This one – Francesco Dandolo – he was around in the 1330s, according to what I've read. But if you want to keep a few souvenirs of Henry's hoard...?"

Q pondered a moment before replying, "No. No, I don't think so, babe. We've got that couple of stones we chose. We've still got a lot of world to see, and we don't need a whole lot of stuff to tote around with us."

"Fair enough. Tell you what, though – I wouldn't mind picking a couple out to send back to Darren. I know he's not as much into his role-playing games as he used to be, but I reckon he's still got a soft spot for antiquities."

With a smile Elizabeth thought of John B.'s housemate back in Canberra. The young man had a surprising collection of old weaponry from around the world, some reproductions, but several genuine antiques. There were swords of various types, spears, even a morning-star that he'd used to good effect when necessary. He may look gangly, but Darren Bond had spent a lot of time practising.

"You can't fight with coins, you know" she said.

Her beau laughed. "No, but let's give him some credit. His interests and knowledge have... diversified. He's grown up a lot since he moved to Canberra."

"Quite a bit of that's due to you, I think."

The wizard shrugged and selected four coins, two each of gold and silver. Gift-wrapped and securely bundled, the package was marked only as 'Souvenirs'. He'd write only an extremely modest estimate on the Customs declaration, and do so with a clear conscience. After all, they'd never yet had an actual valuation, so all he could do was guess. He patted the parcel.

"I wish that these get to Darren safely, with no problems. There, that ought to do it."

The ducats and grossi were repacked, and the old satchel slung over Stewart's shoulder.

"By land or by sea, fair lady?" he asked with an extravagant bow.

"The canals would be quicker, and easier on your shoulder, babe. Let's head up to the big canal. Start walking, and then see if we can pick up a convenient gondola, if they're not all busy up around the tourist traps."

As it happened, a stroll of about twenty minutes brought them to a spot where a gondola was tied up beside one of the city's 400+ bridges. As they looked down at it hopefully, a voice hailed them from behind.

It was the wiry old gondolier they'd met fighting alongside Mario

Vespucci. He was just finishing a coffee, and rushed over to them. He threw an arm around each in turn, kissed both on the cheek, and spoke so rapidly that neither Australian could make any sense of the Gatling-gun torrent of words.

"*Puoi parlare piu lentamente, per favore?*" asked John B., with a help-less spread of his hands.

The older man looked surprised at being asked to speak more slowly. "*Parli italiano?*" he asked.

"*Parlo un po,*" Stewart answered, with a gesture to reinforce that he only spoke a little of the language.

"Sorry, *signore*. I thought you and Mario were old *amici* - friends. *Grazie* for your help that day."

The wizard smiled and gave a small bow of acknowledgement. "Could you take us to Musee Barche, *per favore?*" he asked.

The gondolier nodded enthusiastically. Mario had been right in saying there wasn't a waterman in Venice who didn't know the Museum of Small Boats. John B. reached for his wallet, but the old bloke waved the gesture away.

"*E gratuito,*" he said.

Elizabeth wondered to herself if the free ride was in appreciation of John B.'s help in the scuffle, or something to do with the apparent bond with Mario that this fellow had also noticed. There were still mysteries about the man she loved.

The trip to the museum was much quicker and more direct than the rambling journey that they'd enjoyed the previous time. But then, that had been an introduction to the watery 'streets' of Venice, whereas this was simply a matter of getting to a destination.

As they alighted at the museum's little dock, the boatman doffed his black hat and said, "*A piu tardi, signore e signorina. Grazie.*"

"*Prego,*" replied John B. "And yes, I hope we see you later. Take care!"

The couple waved as the gondola set off back down the narrow little canal. Hand in hand, they strolled over to the museum, and stopped to admire the new window display.

"Nicely done. Good explanation, in a few languages – I always appreciate that," said John B.

"You know, it hadn't occurred to me who the characters on the coin were. The *doge*, getting his authority to rule from St. Mark."

"The patron of Venice, yep. And on the other side, Christ on a throne. Every coin a little piece of propaganda for the 'rightful ruler'. Well, it's not like there were newspapers."

They entered the museum. Several people were wandering around inside.

Leaning close to the curator and speaking softly, Elizabeth offered, "We can come back later, if you'd prefer."

"I appreciate the kind thought, Signorina McKew, but no – I confess I have been looking forward to seeing the rest of your inheritance."

Carefully not mentioning the sundry other valuable items that had been part of said inheritance, mostly all valued, sold, and the proceeds banked, John B. laid the satchel on a counter top. With care not to make too much noise and attract attention, he started to lay the contents out in rows. The morning light caught some of the silver, and reflections glittered on the curator's face as she bent to examine them closely.

"Given the date of my ancestor's travels, in the last years of the 1300s, I admit I was surprised at the age of some of these," Elizabeth said.

"The Zeno family had a tradition of being successful merchants, for many years," Marina said, by way of explanation.

"Old money, in more ways than one, eh?" chuckled John B.

Both women ignored the joke. Marina examined the inscriptions on the coins, already mentally cross-referencing and cataloguing. From under a counter she pulled out a few type-written pages and handed them to Elizabeth.

"I have prepared some notes that may help with your research. History is my forte, and I do appreciate your offer of some of your collection for display here in the Musee."

There was a stiff formality to both the voice and the gesture.

Mentally, John B. told himself that had more to do with unfamiliarity than reluctance. Nonetheless, it was generous, and the brunette thanked the curator sincerely as she slipped the notes into her large purse.

Marina returned her attention to the coins, saying, "Many of the doges between 1340 and 1370 issued very few, or indeed no grossi at all, due to the rise in the cost of silver. The Zeno family, like other Venetian traders, would have retained their old currency as a reserve. The fact that so much – and this would have represented a substantial sum in 1390 – was taken away gives evidence of just how wealthy the family was. It does perhaps also explain the proportion of silver over gold."

"Mm. Heading into an unknown environment, no idea who you might be trading with, or for what – don't take your most valuable stock first up. We know Henry came back for 'supplies'. A supply of gold coins may have been part of what he'd intended," mused the Prince's descendent.

A strange mechanical rumbling made them all turn towards the entrance. An obese man had just squeezed his ornately-decorated mobility scooter through the doorway, and was trundling toward them. In his wake were two heavy-set swarthy men and a red-haired woman.

Elizabeth didn't recognise the man she'd walloped for his unwelcome groping – he hadn't been important enough for her to have paid much attention. Luigino Culatello recognised her, though. As they approached his body tensed and he snarled softly. Ugo glanced at him, and elbowed him sharply. They were here at Il Duce's command, not to indulge in anything personal. Yet.

The unattractive face had registered on John B.'s memory, though, and he watched the dark man carefully, paying less attention than he otherwise might have to the rest of the entourage as they approached.

The front wheel of the scooter bumped against the counter as it was brought to a sudden stop. The driver stretched out a lugubrious hand.

"Signora DeNucci. I am Leonardo Delocchio. I understand you

have some excellent old pieces on display, and here I see considerably more laid out. Ah, it seems my nose for *il argento bello* has once again proved unerring."

It occurred to Elizabeth that the big man's smile would not have been out of place on a snake oil salesman in Dodge City. Alarm bells were going off in her head.

The museum's curator maintained a cautious reserve.

"Signore Delocchio," she acknowledged as she shook the proffered hand, with as much evident pleasure as if grasping an eel. "I know of you, of course. Ms McKew, Mr. Stewart, this is one of the potential investors I had in mind for the sale of some of your collection."

There was a note in Marina's voice that suggested that if she were indeed to have mentioned Delocchio on such a list, he would be at the bottom of it. If the Silver Duke noticed, however, he gave no indication of it.

"Buongiorno, signore," said Stewart, shaking the big man's hand briefly (then checking no fingers had been stolen).

"Buongiorno," echoed Elizabeth.

Leonardo held onto her hand longer than politeness required, and gave her a disarming smile. Dark as his reputation was in some parts of Venice, in most other circles Leonardo Delocchio was esteemed for his charm and ready wit. It was only when you got to know him that the real character became apparent.

"What a delightful set of treasures you have!" enthused the self-proclaimed Duke. If pressed, he would have said that, "of course he meant the coins", but his gaze was firmly fixed on Elizabeth – and not on her green eyes.

"Yes, and I put a high value on them," she replied evenly, perhaps even throwing her chest out a little, although she noted with silent gratitude the sensation of John B.'s hand resting on her waist.

"Signore Delocchio..." began the youngest brother in an angry undertone.

"Hush, Luigino. In the unlikely event that I want your opinion, I'll be sure to ask for it. Now, signorina, that sounded like an Australian accent, yes?"

Il Duce's own English was as faultless as if it were his native tongue, although there was no discernible accent to suggest an origin.

At Elizabeth's cautious nod, Leonardo continued. "The *grosso* is an interesting piece of Venetian history. Largely unchanged for over a hundred and fifty years, and quite significant in coin design across Europe. You see that circlet of little beads around the edge of the coins? A clever security measure, to dissuade the practice of shaving the silver from the outside of the coin. Their design is, ultimately, of Byzantine origin ."

"Interesting word, that," said John B., interrupting Leonardo's showing off of his knowledge to do some of his own. "First referring to the empire that spread from what's now Constantinople – the eastern part of the Roman Empire, in effect. Then applied to the design and architecture that emerged from there, and that occurs a lot here in Venice. Then ultimately becoming a synonym for something intricate, devious or even surreptitious. Things that aren't what they seem."

Delocchio's smile never slipped as he gave a gesture of agreement. "Just as you say. Now, I take it from Signora DeNucci's comment that you are looking to sell these items. Let me say, you will not receive a better price in Venice than what I will offer you."

"Hmm, that may well turn out to be true, Mr. Delocchio, but I'd be a lousy businesswoman if I didn't test the market for myself. I'm not a lousy businesswoman."

Under his breath, John B. muttered, "I wish you'd push off, mate."

Leonardo's charming smile didn't slip. "Of course you're not. You're not local to Venice, so you've no reason to take me at my word. However, I do assure you that..."

"Delocchio? Delocchio? Oh, you're that musician! How wonderful to meet you in person! Look, Bernina – it's Leonardo Delocchio!"

The shrill voice came from one of the museum's other visitors, who'd wandered close enough to hear Elizabeth address the Silver Duke by name. A tall woman with a bouffant hairstyle held in place by enough spray to constitute a fire hazard, she'd grasped her companion by the arm and was charging towards the scooter like a giraffe spotting an especially tender bunch of shoots on a tree that the other giraffes hadn't seen yet.

Ugo and Luigino moved to intercept her, but were in the wrong position to get there in time. Pasqualina stepped forward to block the fan, but was barely noticed and pushed aside.

Leonardo Delocchio, for all his presentment of bonhomie, was an intensely private man. He was also a man with great regard for his own personal space, although he was no respecter of others'. This was uncommon in Venice, whose residents and workers are notoriously tactile, even by Italian standards, and accounted for his limited public appearances in places he didn't have some control over. Having his hand grabbed and pumped like a hydraulic car jack was almost enough to make him shriek. It was only a shred of awareness of the importance of his Public Image that kept a rictus smile on his face as the giraffe woman babbled a stream of enthusiasm at him. To his horror, more of the museum's visitors were being attracted, and were coming over to Meet the Celebrity.

With difficulty, Leonardo extracted his hand.

"Yes, yes, thank you. I appreciate that, thank you. Yes..." He briefly turned back to his previous conversation. "I'll be in touch – you can count on that."

Still wearing the fixed smile, he gunned the motor of his scooter and headed for the exit, one hand fending off any of the public who were too near. He could touch them, but *not* vice-versa! The Culatello brothers made a two-man 'flying wedge' to clear a path - although Delocchio wouldn't have hesitated to run over anyone in his way, they weren't sure that the 'surrey' wouldn't overbalance going over a person-shaped bump. Pasqualina was still seething at the rudeness of the bouffant-haired woman, and before departing in the scooter's wake made a small surreptitious gesture. With that, she muttered something that would have been incomprehensible to more than 99% of most populations.

The woman clutched at her head in momentary alarm at a

strange hot sensation that swept over her scalp, distracting her long enough for her idol's departure. When she next washed her hair, she would be mortified to find that something must have been wrong with her latest can of spray, for the strands were so brittle that they snapped like fine glass, and she was left looking as though a hedgehog had taken up lodging on her head.

As they watched the little crowd disperse back to the various displays around the museum, Elizabeth asked Marina, "There *are* other potential buyers, aren't there?"

"Oh yes," she was assured.

"Let's investigate them, please. I don't think I want that bloke getting his hands on *anything* of mine."

"Amen to that, pretty lady," agreed John B. as he slipped his arm around her.

Marina watched the doorway. "I understand completely. Although, I should warn you that Signore Delocchio is likely to be persistent. He has a reputation for getting what he wants."

With a final exchange of handshakes, the Australians consigned Prince Henry's legacy to the curator, been handed back the old satchel (John B. had quickly developed a fondness for it), and headed for a gondola to take them back to the Giardini district – a walk in the gardens seemed suddenly very appealing.

Marina started to pack the coins away, engrossed in mentally cataloguing each one as she did so. It startled her when a gravelly voice asked, "May I see those, please?"

She looked up to see a man dressed in black clothes, including an old-fashioned long overcoat, standing at the counter. A wide-brimmed back hat was pulled down to shadow his face, but she had a glimpse of small glittering eyes and a long chin.

"Are you a collector?" she asked.

"I am... interested in investments," replied the dark man.

They had a brief conversation about the potential value of the collection. Another new arrival momentarily drew Marina's attention, and when she turned back the man was gone, as swiftly and silently as he'd appeared. Worried, she checked the coins. Yes, all still present. She pondered the offer of keeping some of them for the museum's collection. Notwithstanding their historical significance, if they were going to attract this sort of attention, would they be worth it?

Making good speed back towards the Palazzo Grosso, the brothers and Pasqualina were all grumbling to themselves. She was still put out by the rudeness of the giraffe woman, and though she'd taken a measure of revenge she fantasised about having done something more instantly dramatic. One day she damn well wouldn't keep a low profile! One day...

The brothers were simply their usual bad-tempered selves. They knew their role when in public alongside Signore Delocchio was simply to look intimidating. They were good at that, and enjoyed it well enough, but Luigino especially had really wanted to hit someone, and that Australian girl had been the particular someone. But no, Leonardo's public image had to be maintained, didn't it? And he couldn't be seen to be obviously complicit in assault, could he? Damn it.

Il Duce Grosso was also deep in thought, but not, as might be expected, about his thwarted efforts to obtain the hoard of coins. They could be acquired at any time. That green-eyed Australian girl, though – it was obvious what had attracted Luigino. Equally obvious why she'd spurned his clumsy advance so impressively. Yes, spirit to go with her good looks. Just what he liked. And wanted.

.ooo.

12
—————

IN A JAM, NOT A PICKLE

As they'd hoped, strolling through the lush but well-maintained gardens was good for the spirits of Elizabeth and John B. There had been something disconcerting about the encounter with Il Duce Grosso, for all that the big man hadn't said or done anything overtly threatening.

His choice of companions hadn't helped either. With John B.'s prompting, Q had recalled her previous experience of the younger of the swarthy men, and while she'd laughingly gotten the better of that first encounter, meeting him again was hardly cause for pleasure. Especially when his demeanour indicated that he carried a grudge.

Thus, it was more than usually pleasant to spend a couple of hours among the greenery and the scents of the winter flowers. The wind had eased, and although the air was still seasonably chilly, the sun was bright. For much of the time they strolled in companionable silence. When they did speak, it was to chat about this or that plant with reference to other gardens they'd seen, together or individually, or to mention friends from work or their travels who'd come to mind.

Prompted by those thoughts, postcards were bought from a little souvenir stand. The two sat comfortably on the grass in a sunny spot and shared the writing of chatty notes to friends in different corners of the world. The three old sisters on Islay, who'd all appreciate being remembered, and appreciate even more whatever snippets of news and information were included – different for each of course, so they'd have to converse with each other to get a full picture. Cowley and Lanny in Maine, who'd been crucial in locating the Prince's treasure. The girls Glexie and Ariane had been even more vital, but they were somewhere in Hawaii now, or so it was assumed, and yet to be located. The Mapleton family in Norway, with cards for each of the two kids as well as their parents. Tinkerbell Hardman and Jenny Farmer in their old workplace. John B.'s house-mate Darren, of course. A card to go to Alice Springs in Central Australia, now home to former co-worker (and unlikely authority on many things mystical) Scarlet Burke. To the same city went a card for Scarlet's surprising boyfriend, the biker boss Murph, and his genial Mob.

A card was sent to the address of their best friend, Wilko, in Canberra, but they weren't sure when he might receive it. He'd last been heard of on Islay with his beloved Jazz. The intention had been to linger there awhile before setting off for Africa, where engineer Jazz had her next contract. The Tasmanian man's mobile phone wasn't answering, but that might mean anything – from being out of range somewhere in Africa, to him being unwilling to pay the cost of international calls back in Canberra. John B. was confident that if there was a real problem he would somehow know, so a cheery missive on the back of a picture of carnival masks was despatched without concern.

There was no correspondence for kin for either of them. They didn't have any. Friends were their family of choice.

Cards written and posted, the pair sat with their backs against a big tree. Q rested her head on her beau's shoulder and slipped into a light slumber. He, in turn, laid the side of his face amongst her curls, and allowed himself to doze for a while.

Nobody disturbed them. Few of the crowding tourists made it to this part of Venice, and so the beggars and thieves likewise stayed where the pickings were richer. The locals who frequented the park appreciated the tranquillity, and so weren't inclined to disturb two people so clearly at peace.

It was mid-afternoon when Elizabeth drifted lazily back into consciousness. Her stirring roused John B., who'd been deep in a dream himself. Waking suddenly, his mind held a fleeting image of a great stone city, and of being part of a small group gathered in front of an important assembly. Something about a mission...? No. It was gone, completely.

Q checked the time on her phone. It was mid-afternoon. They'd slept rather longer than expected, or intended.

They stood, and wiped grass clippings and bark fragments off each other's back, lingering flirtatiously on the lower regions.

"I'd like to change before we go to Giancarlo's, okay babe?"

"Oh no! Don't change! I love you the way you are!" he protested with mock seriousness.

She laughed and threw her arms around him. The embrace was returned, and they stood sharing an affectionate kiss for some time.

Eventually, though, they did make their way back to Manovalo 219. There, with only a little mutual interruption, they changed clothes. He into darker jeans and a Daffy Duck t-shirt ("Funniest comedian ever," he'd aver), she into long boots, black satin tights and a long but low-cut belted green top that emphasised her curves. She may not have consciously been preparing to compete with the flirtatious Nicola, but her 'grown-up' charms were obvious. And appreciated.

They arrived at the instrument maker's home armed with enthusiasm and two bottles of wine. John B. would have dearly loved to have a bottle of good single malt, but there were none to be found locally, and he wasn't willing to buy an ordinary blend. Such a compromise might be made out of politeness if a glass was offered, but he hadn't bought a bottle like that since his teenaged years. He'd have to remind himself to search thoroughly in the main part of the city.

The Australians were first to arrive, but Giancarlo assured them that there would be more company coming soon. Meanwhile, the four relaxed on comfortable options around the floor of the music room. Well, the three older ones did – Nicola very soon sat down at the electric piano and began to show off one of the Rick Wakeman pieces they'd discussed when they first met.

The girl was good, no doubt about that. *Journey To The Centre Of The Earth* was a challenging composition, and her rendition of *The Forest* did more than reprise the original. The little flourishes Giancarlo had taught (or were they her own?), weren't out of place. They enhanced, but didn't dominate.

Accepting the warm applause as if it was her due, which it truly was, the girl then launched into *Catherine of Aragon*.

Smiling broadly, eyes closed in enjoyment of the music, John B. idly toyed with the silver pendant he now wore on a simple silver chain.

"I've been admiring that," remarked Giancarlo. "It's a beautiful thing."

"A present from a beautiful woman," John B. answered with a smile. "Bought when we were in Norway."

"It's modelled on an old Viking charm. A protective symbol," Elizabeth explained as she got up from her cushion. Planting a kiss on her beau's forehead she asked, "Can I refill anyone else's glass?"

There were enthusiastic nods all round, including from behind the keyboard. Elizabeth gathered the glasses and went into the kitchen, where a bottle of excellent Venetian pinot grigio was in the refrigerator.

In her absence, John B. looked down at his pendant and mused aloud, "I wonder if we can find the silversmith who made this? He was in Tallinn, I was told. Be nice to get rings made to match it." He had in mind the amethyst and turquoise he and Q had kept for themselves out of Prince Henry's hoard.

"Tallinn?" Giancarlo peered more closely at the Viking symbol. "I believe I know the man you mean."

Coincidence now played so prominent a part in John B.'s life that he realised he wasn't overly surprised by that remark.

However, he was surprised when the musician added, "There is a man near here who was trained by him. His work is comparable."

"You mean Teasy?" asked Nicola.

"Yes. Dear widget, would you please introduce John B. to Signore Zybysko sometime soon?"

"Of course!" the girl replied, happy at the prospect.

"Discreetly! I'd like to make it a surprise, and this'd be easier than a trip to Estonia."

"Just tell me when, Jonbi!" she said enthusiastically, then as Elizabeth re-entered the room bent earnestly over her keyboard to pick out a variation on a Chopin nocturne.

Her mentor had just sat down at the grand piano and started to play a counterpoint when there was a knock at the door. No ordinary knock, this rapped out an interesting complex rhythm.

"I'll get it – you play on!" said John B.

He opened the door to a dishevelled but broadly grinning man with long blonde hair hanging from under a hat that looked like it had been used as a cleaning cloth.

"Ullo dere," said the man, and stuck out the hand that wasn't clutching a guitar case that possibly outweighed him.

He was about as tall as Wilko, which is to say, not very, and thin. Not emaciated, he radiated an exuberant vitality that suggested that this was a healthy skinniness.

"Call me Robi – that's what Nicola does. No fixed abode," he continued amiably as the wizard shook the outstretched hand. "You must be the new friend she was talking about."

"Probably. And you're one of the assembling musos, obviously. John B. Stewart. Theoretically of Canberra, presently of Manovalo and these days it seems no more fixed address than your good self."

"Ah, always a pleasure to meet another itinerant!"

Just as Stewart stepped back to allow Robi to enter, another figure arrived. Closer to John B.'s height and build, but some years older, this man walked with a slight but discernible stoop. As he'd approached, the wizard had noticed the fellow's gaze rarely moved up from a spot just in front of his feet.

Even now, his eyes barely flickered up in acknowledgement as he said, "Buongiorno, signore. I am here for the music, si?" as he sidled his way into Casa LaGrigio.

His guitar case bumped against John B. as he entered, but there was a definite movement to avoid any physical contact. The wizard mentally shrugged as he followed the two new arrivals into the music room.

Nicola squealed delighted greeting to both men, but didn't interrupt her playing. Only when the piece was completed did she jump up and rush over to embrace Robi, complicating his efforts to plug his bass guitar into one of the room's several amplifiers. She took a step towards the other man, but then stopped short as if correcting herself. She smiled and gave a formal bow.

"Buongiorno, Christos!" she said.

"Buongiorno, contessa," he replied, a small smile indicating his appreciation of her restraint.

Giancarlo made the introductions. Robi was, as he'd described himself, itinerant and cheerfully so. He supported himself with a variety of odd jobs around Venice and beyond. Later he mentioned he may well have picked the very grapes that produced the wine they were enjoying. He could, he admitted, play most 'things with strings', but had a particular affinity for the bass guitar.

The taciturn man was Christos. He'd briefly been a gondolier, but found the public contact harrowing. He'd found work as a clerk in an import business, where he was delighted to have his own small office all to himself. He was good with book-keeping, but his true delight was in playing and writing music.

As he tuned his bass, Robi nodded towards the unattended drum kit. "Stefano's not here yet. Not like him to be late."

Giancarlo shrugged. "Alas, he won't be joining us. Trouble with his sisters."

"*Feh*, they are always trouble, fighting with each other," was Nicola's contribution. "One is wrapped too tight, the other is too loose."

Elizabeth raised an internal eyebrow at that particular assessment coming from Nicola, but confined herself to saying, "No wonder the two don't get along, then."

"I'm hoping John B. will fill the breach," said Giancarlo.

"You're a musician, then?" asked Robi.

"Hmm – drummers are not always regarded as such by other musicians," observed Christos, but the hint of a smile suggested this may be as close as he came to jest.

"Unfairly," answered Giancarlo.

John B. shrugged. He couldn't recall mentioning his limited experience as a percussionist to their host, but assumed he must have in the course of casual small talk. "I just hit things," he said dismissively, but took his seat behind the kit and started to compare the feel of a few different sticks and brushes.

The five began cautiously, a couple of blues standards, then slipping into a streamlined version of Ellington's *Take The A Train* that gave Stewart the chance to switch from drumsticks to the simple sound of brushes on a snare.

LaGrigio smiled benignly, like a pleased tutor. "Your rhythm and timing are good, John B. You see, you're a natural." His voice lowered, as though he was talking to himself. "It's a long time since I've heard that, my friend. A very long time."

Just for a second, John B. felt a spark – a connection, an echo from an untouchable past. Giancarlo had lowered his head over the piano again to recreate an old Fats Waller opening, leaving the wizard wondering. Something from a fragment of a dream? He shook his head briefly and turned his attention to his task of maintaining the beat, although in truth he was realising it took little effort now that he'd found the flow, and had Robi's impeccable timing in support.

Other people, like Marina and Dorothy, had indicated that they already knew John B. - Giancarlo had overtly said nothing of the sort, but the wizard had the sudden clear thought that it was true. The music was a trigger. Where, when and how they'd met were still a mystery, but that would come, he knew. For now, just be in the moment.

Leaving his piano for a while, Giancarlo took up an old Fender guitar. It was already tuned. Elizabeth suspected that there wasn't an instrument in the house that was not kept ready for instant use at any time. They played a simple 12-bar blues, with Giancarlo and Christos swapping solos like they'd been working together for years. In fact, they had.

It was an easy progression into some rock tunes: Beatles, Led Zeppelin, even a rendition of *My Sharona* which allowed Robi some fun with its distinctive bass line.

Christos led them into a new tune, unfamiliar at first, but which John B. suddenly recognised as *Toccare di Luna*. There'd been a faintly classical styling to everything they'd played, whatever the genre, and the wizard confirmed in his head the true origin of Leonardo Delocchio's successful recordings.

The wizard signalled his need for a drinks break at the end of that particular tune. Wine was dispensed all round. Christos had brought a bottle of Tuscan red, and Giancarlo proved to have a good selection in a rack under the stairs leading up to the second floor. Elizabeth did make a mental note, though, to discreetly drop a few replacements in – it was clear the session would go for a while, and the two bottles they'd brought would require supplementing.

They all sat comfortably on the floor, drinking and nibbling at cheese and salami. Thoughts of that last tune were still at the front of John B.'s mind.

"*Toccare di Luna* – that's yours, isn't it? How does that Leonardo get credit for it?" he asked.

"Both Christos and I worked on a number of recording sessions with Il Duce Grosso. It's how we met – both of us 'session' players. We – embellished some of the Duke's own compositions, and he appropriated ours."

"And you let him?" asked Elizabeth in surprise.

"It is... hard to argue with Delocchio," said Christos quietly. "He can be forceful."

"We were paid for our time and efforts. Less well than we might have hoped, of course, but ultimately, it's the music that matters, not fame or notoriety. It's enough that what we created is heard and enjoyed, and maybe even inspires," said Giancarlo gently.

The brunette had to admit to herself that neither of these men, talented as they were, could be imagined in the glare of the spotlight. "Still," she said, "I don't like to think of that fat slob making money from your ability."

"Leonardo is a very capable musician, just less creative than he presents, or perhaps even believes himself to be. He has a flair for self-promotion, though. Through him, our music is heard," replied Giancarlo in a voice of quiet satisfaction.

"He is still a fat slob, as Lizbetta says. *Feh* – he and his *stronzi*, they are bullies," said Nicola, leaving no doubts that she didn't share her mentor's equanimity.

At that point there was a weirdly discordant *yowl*. Toscanini had returned from prowling the streets and alleyways. He worked his way around the group, rubbing himself against each in turn. The volume of his bizarre purr noticeably rose when greeting the orange house's two residents, and also John B. Stewart.

'Him and animals – it's a funny thing. Another one,' thought Q to herself.

Satisfied he'd been admired by everyone, the black cat padded across the room and jumped up to his preferred spot atop the television. He curled up and may or may not have gone to sleep. His facial disfigurement made it hard to tell if he still had one eye open.

Watching the almost-feral, John B. remarked, "You mentioned he'd been injured by the – Culatello brothers, wasn't it? Are they the ugly buggers we met with Delocchio yesterday?"

"You've encountered Il Duce Grosso and his cronies? My sympathies," said Christos. "They do his bidding, enforce his wishes."

Giancarlo explained what was known of the three. "They're Leonardo's thugs. Standover men, to use an old gangster phrase. From an old Burano family, which is why they look perhaps more Sicilian than the typical delicate-featured Venetian."

"In-bred," muttered Robi, who'd been on the wrong end of the brothers' casual violence when busking.

"Possibly," admitted Giancarlo. "The family has been in fishing for generations, I believe, but I don't know that they've always been on the right side of the law. Ugo, Duilio and Luigino have just 'turned up the volume', as it were."

John B. snorted contempt. "Sounds like a family tree that needs trimming with a weed whacker."

"What is a weed whacker?" asked Nicola.

"Sorry. Slang term for a brush cutter," the wizard explained.

"Oh. What is a brush cutter?"

"Ah – right. Not much call for them in Venice, I suppose..."

Giancarlo, chuckling, interrupted. "This is Giardini, my friend. The garden district. I'm afraid their terrible noise is not unknown here."

"Oh!" exclaimed Nicola, as the penny dropped. "The loud machine with the spinning blades! Benito in the park uses one. I think he likes loud machines – he has another he uses to blow leaves across the grass. I think Benito is very lazy. A rake or broom would be much quieter."

"And probably more effective," said Elizabeth with a sympathetic smile.

Nicola nodded agreement with the brunette, and turned back to the wizard. "You are right, Jonbi. The brothers are bad men, and someone should use such a machine on them to cut them down to size!"

Evidently wanting to turn considerations to more pleasant paths, Giancarlo picked up his guitar and strummed a few chords. There was something like a bluegrass tone.

Remembering the rendition of *Giving It All To The Wind* from their first evening in the orange house, Q asked her beau, "Would you sing something, please?"

"I'm not much of a singer, really, sweetheart, but... um... a story? Do any of you know *The Wreck Of The Edmund Fitzgerald*?"

Nicola looked puzzled, but Robi and Christos both nodded as they picked up their guitars. Giancarlo moved smoothly into the correct chords. They did the song justice – Stewart's voice was a good fit for the style. Both Elizabeth and Nicola applauded at its conclusion.

Christos asked wryly, "Do you remember? Il Duce Grosso wanted to do that sad song. He made a joke of it."

"Leonardo lacks empathy," understated Giancarlo, more graciously than anyone else in the room felt was warranted.

Q leaned to John B. as she handed him a drink and said softly, "As much as I enjoyed that, could you sing something for *me*, please?"

After a thoughtful pause, the wizard had a quiet word with their silver-haired host. Giancarlo took his seat at the piano, then he and John B. proceeded to do a gentle version of Elton John's *Your Song*. Just the two of them, the other musicians maintaining a respectful silence as they nodded or hummed inaudibly along.

"About the most romantic song I know," the wizard quietly told his beloved as she hugged her thanks afterward. Her eyes shone as the jam session seemed about to continue.

It was, however, a good moment to stop for a bit and take a break. They'd all had a few drinks, and food was a very sensible idea.

As promised, *canederli* were the dish of the day. The dumplings themselves – a mix of stale bread, egg, cheese and flour, had been prepared much earlier. Simmering on the stove was a rich, heavily scented broth. Nicola had made it with beef, pancetta and a dozen fresh herbs. There was plenty for everyone to receive a generous deep bowl of the soup and a good supply of the dumplings to bob therein. It was traditionally 'peasant food', but it was delicious. Of course, a serve was laid out for Toscanini, who'd followed the procession into the kitchen.

Suitably replete, the music again became their focus. Led by Robi and Christos, they launched into a bouncy jazzy piece. Recognising the style of Louis Jordan, if not the actual tune (it was a Christos original), John B. added some scat vocals of his own, directed at their chef, saying "Thank you" in half a dozen different languages.

Nicola smiled delightedly. She was used to her mentor writing music just for her, but it was nice to have a song just for her, coming from someone else – someone she really liked.

After a few more tunes in a similar jump-jive vein, mostly instrumentals (although John B. made a point of covering Jordan's *The Chicks I Pick Are Slender, Tender and Tall* – a reassurance not lost on his beloved), Giancarlo held up a hand.

"Let's try something," he said, and went fossicking in a large cupboard.

He produced a steel tank, and handed it to Stewart. It had once been a gas bottle, the Australian realised. A series of slits had been cut in the metal, producing 'tongues' of various lengths and widths.

"I've seen something like this carved out of wood," John B. said.

""Consider this an innovation, using available material. Try it," said the instrument maker, holding out a small wooden hammer made for a xylophone.

"Your invention?"

"This particular one is my creation, but the idea is very old, and others have also experimented with its modernisation."

John B. gave the drum a few experimental taps, and grinned broadly at the tones that rang forth.

"Oh, nice sound!" he said.

Christos nodded. "Indeed. Let's see what we can do with it."

They started with some Lionel Hampton tunes, the tongue drum doing service in place of Hampton's vibraphone. They glided smoothly into rhythm and blues, and various genres of rock. Giancarlo and Nicola swapped and changed instruments intermittently, tutor and pupil both adept on a range of strings and keyboards. The others stuck to their preferred instruments, although John B. moved back to the more conventional drum kit for some tunes.

At Robi's prompting, they even played the Goon Show classic *Ying Tong Iddle I Po*, much to Nicola's delight. Her 'education' certainly was broad, Q noted.

It was late by the time they played an extended, imaginative version of *Chattanooga Choo-Choo*, each taking the opportunity to craft their own extended solo. Delighted Elizabeth applauded enthusiastically at its close, but couldn't stifle a tired yawn.

The contagious gesture went around the room in moments, with only Christos seemingly immune. He was, however, the one to say, "I'd better go. I've work to do tomorrow and I am feeling tired."

Giancarlo nodded. "We've all played long and energetically…"

"And very well," interceded Elizabeth.

"Thank you, signorina," said Christos gallantly, a sentiment echoed by the other musicians, Robi and John B. also following his lead and packing away their kits.

Toscanini circulated like a blood cell, dispensing his strange purrs evidently as his own farewells. As before, he seemed to make a special effort to press his head into the palm of John B.'s hand.

"You've won a heart, babe," observed Elizabeth, as the couple went to leave.

Just then, Nicola threw her arms around him, burying her face in the purple fabric of his shirt. She held the embrace for a heartbeat or three more than Elizabeth liked, even while Giancarlo was gallantly kissing the brunette's hand. It was a regular gesture of Stewart's, and ordinarily would have pleased and distracted her.

She could feel the resentment rising again, but then the girl completely disconcerted her by releasing the wizard and wrapping herself around her own waist in turn. If that hug didn't last quite as long as John B.'s, the difference wasn't enough to register with Elizabeth.

"Thank you both for coming," said the dark-haired nymph.

"Very much a pleasure – thank *you*," replied John B.

Elizabeth, relaxing a little again, smiled. "What he said. And thank you for dinner, it was lovely! You're going to make someone very happy one day, young lady."

Giancarlo laid a tender hand on his protégé's shoulder and said, "She already does."

The two guitarists walked with the Australians briefly, saying their good-byes at the entry of the Viale di Tavola. They would continue their walk back to their respective homes in companionable silence.

A moment's flickering eye contact from Christos as he said goodnight was as much as anyone could hope for, and Robi respected his friend's reserve.

As Elizabeth put her clothes on their spare bed, she could hear the soft sound of a single guitar through the shared wall. She wondered which musician was playing – teacher or student?

John B. appeared behind her, tossing his own clothes on top of hers. He placed one hand on her bare shoulder, and slipped the other around her waist as he stepped closer to her.

Suddenly it didn't really matter who was providing the soundtrack.

.ooo.

13

RETAIL THERAPY

The next morning was brilliantly sunny, and both Elizabeth and John B. woke with much clearer heads than might have been expected after a long late evening and night of music, wine, and other pleasures.

Rather than settle for something from their own kitchen, they decided to revisit Mac's coffee bar. As they exited the Viale di Tavola they were greeted by a loud gargling noise.

"Good morning to you, too, Tosca. You're up and about early," said the wizard, kneeling to give an affectionate, and enthusiastically-received, scratch to the cat's head.

Soon after, they were enjoying cappuccinos and pastries (ironically, sourced from the pasticerria across the way from their apartment). Tosca had made himself comfortable on the wizard's lap, to Mac's amusement when she brought out refills of the coffees.

Relaxing with his head tilted back and eyes closed, John B. was suddenly startled by an embrace around his neck at the same moment as he heard Q's surprised voice saying, "Oh! Hello! I didn't see you!"

Opening his eyes, he wasn't surprised to find Nicola at his side.

She planted a firm kiss on his cheek – it may have made his lips if he hadn't turned his head slightly at the last moment.

"Buongiorno Lizbetta! Buongiorno Jonbi!" the girl exclaimed as she gently but emphatically shoved Tosca from his resting place.

She squirmed past the edge of the table to perch herself on Stewart's lap, still warm from the cat's body. He had a moment of feeling like a department store Santa Claus, although there was still only a remote prospect of his stubble becoming an appropriate beard. As the girl wriggled he realised a slim hand was slipping into the pocket of his jeans, not removing anything, but depositing.

"What do you do today, *mi amici*?" the youngster asked, as casually as if she'd sat on a park bench beside them.

"Nothing planned," replied Elizabeth, some tension in her jaw betraying her displeasure at Nicola's behaviour.

"It is a beautiful morning for shopping, I think," said the girl, radiating innocence.

Something in John B.'s head clicked. Yesterday evening's conversation about the silversmith. Suddenly he had a very good idea of what had been put in his pocket. A name and address, he was sure. He removed Nicola from his lap, as gently but firmly as she'd dislodged Toscanini.

"I think you're right, Nicola," he said. "Once we've finished a leisurely breakfast we may well do that very thing."

For a moment, it appeared that the girl intended to invite herself along on the expedition. She seemed oblivious to Elizabeth's disapproving look. She did, however, catch John B.'s little eye movement, which her own body masked from the view of his brunette beloved.

"Ah – I would love to come with you, but my Giancarlo, he insists I should study today. I do not like the mathematic, but it sometimes is useful, I know. I like to add up prices and money in my head. It surprises some shopkeepers."

"I just bet it does," admitted Elizabeth, amused in spite of herself at the response she was sure awaited anyone who tried to shortchange this little minx.

Nicola gave an incongruous curtsey, blew a kiss to each of the

Australians in turn, then sashayed away down the Via Garibaldi, conspicuously wiggling her slim hips as best she could. The cat ambled unconcernedly beside her.

"That girl is flirting with you!" exclaimed Elizabeth crossly a few discreet moments later.

The wizard's voice was mild in reply. "Really? I thought it was a bit stronger than that."

"You behave yourself! What is she – twelve years old? Fourteen at most! That's disgraceful!"

"Darling, you did point out, *she's* the one flirting with *me*."

"But at that age..."

"Old enough to know her own mind, I think," said John B. levelly.

Elizabeth's brow knitted in annoyance even as she felt obliged to concede, "Well yes, she does seem a lot more together than a number of much older women I've met."

"Women *and* men, pretty lady. And you know, it's not that long since twelve was the legal age for marriage in some parts of Australia."

"You're kidding! Oh. No, you're not, are you? Boy, that's slipped from the collective memory!"

"Age is a number, sweetheart. 'Acting your age' is a comfort to the unimaginative, I reckon. How many petulant, immature supposed-adults have you ever met? Playful old folks? Remember April Brom-leigh on Islay? Chronologically, Nicola may be a child, but there's a whole lot of worldliness going on in that head."

"Don't you think that's a shame?"

"Yes. I do, as a matter of fact. Not least because of the circum-stances she's already had to go through to get to that point, as I under-stand things. But I reckon she's landed on her feet, with someone who genuinely cares about her and looks after her. She's much healthier – physically and emotionally, than she might well have been. Unconventional? Sure, but convention is a default when you can't think of anything better for yourself."

For some time, Elizabeth looked in silence at the man she loved. What he said made sense, in its way, but it was wildly different to what she'd been raised to believe. Life with John B. Stewart had a way of making her question some of her own fundamentals. It was a pleasant surprise to learn she'd had some of those questions herself, but had never brought them out into the light to examine them. Eventually she reached out and squeezed his hand.

"Let's go for a walk, hey babe?" she suggested.

"Sounds good to me. Can we stop at the unit? I'd be glad of a bathroom break, and I'm not all that enamoured of some of Venice's public facilities."

"I hear you, babe. Trust me, some of the Ladies' are probably worse!"

And so, a short time later they were back in Manovalo 219. Stewart seized the opportunity, while his sweetheart was Otherwise Engaged, to remove the two stones he'd kept from Henry's hoard out of the safe. While there, he quickly and quietly opened Q's jewellery case. There, as he remembered, tucked in a corner was a little black felt bag. From that he removed a plain gold band before replacing everything just as it had been.

It was the wedding ring from Elizabeth's marriage to Sonny Dance. She had absolutely no regrets about her divorce, but had brought the ring overseas with her months ago in case she needed to pawn it. The acquisition of her ancestor's treasure had eliminated that possibility, and the ring had languished in the case ever since. Now John B. had need of it, discreetly. It joined the amethyst and turquoise in a secure part of his wallet.

The safe had been resecured and the wizard was sunk in an armchair by the time Elizabeth emerged. She looked at him, the picture of indolence, legs stretched out and crossed at the ankles, hands clasped on belly, chin on chest.

"Are you sure you're up for going out?" she asked, with a chuckle.

He almost sprang from the chair, landing on one knee right in front of her, and grabbing her hand.

"Why ma'am, Ah would gladly walk tuh the ends o' the Earth if'n I was walkin' at yoah side!"

The long-running gag of the cartoon Deep South accent they

shared always made her laugh, but sometimes, too, he said just the right thing inside that silly voice. So much so that she didn't even reply in her own 'Memphis belle' tones.

"Thank you, darling."

He stood, and they embraced for some time before finally making their way back down the stairs onto Viale di Tavola, and back out towards the centre of Venice.

This time, Toscanini wasn't there to accompany them, but along the Via Garibaldi they got some cheery waves from shopkeepers who'd already come to recognise the pair. Being seen with the strange black cat and his young mistress seemed to act like a badge of acceptance into the little community. Already they felt more like locals than tourists, an unusual sensation in famously-insular Venice, but one they appreciated.

The improved weather had the tourists out in droves. Days into Carnivale, there were plenty of entertainments happening to engage everyone's attention, plenty of extravagances to lighten their wallets. That same sense of 'local belonging' for Elizabeth and John B. now extended to some shared resentment of the invading throng.

Although they walked deep into the commercial heart of Venice, they avoided main thoroughfares as much as possible. There was no shortage of lanes and alleyways, a network that connected the big shop-lined *rughe* in the same way that so many little *rielli* linked the broader *rii* and the great canals. And these little walkways often had their own shopping delights to be found.

It seemed another adventure in 'walking lost', although John B. actually had a destination in mind. He'd checked the piece of paper which had been slipped into his pocket, grateful that something more than a district and number had been written down. He'd found the *Fondamenta Margherita* on one of their tourist maps and committed the location to memory as best as he could.

Privately he doubted, though, that he would find the jewellers' names prominently displayed as 'Teasy and the Blob'. The note of introduction was written in a more childlike hand than seemed likely from Giancarlo, although what appeared to be the musician's autograph was scribbled across the bottom.

Sustained on their travels by white wine and *pierini* – tiny toasted cheese and ham sandwiches from a welcome and welcoming little bar, neither of the Australians was hungry by lunchtime, which was when they were approaching the riello that marked John B.'s discreet destination.

He'd hoped to settle in a convenient restaurant or bar, then quickly slip out while Q was occupied with eating.

"I wish we could find something that you really fancied, sweetheart," he said casually as they crossed yet another little bridge.

She laughed and hugged him as they walked. "I already have, babe. You!"

"*Grazie*, pretty lady. But I actually meant clothes or something of that sort. I feel like treating you to something nice."

"That's sweet, babe, but really, I... oh!"

John B. saw what had caught her eye. It was a small shoe shop, but if the window display was anything to go by, the leatherwork in stock was top quality. Hand in hand, they admired the goods on show.

"There's one thing about women's shoes I've never understood," Stewart said. "It often seems like the less material is in the shoe, the dearer it is. Skinny little straps like string, or uppers that are more perforation than actual leather. It's as though you pay extra for the stuff that's been removed."

"Well, my dear, the theory is that you're paying for the work involved in taking out all of those bits. And the artistry of the design. And the name on the label, of course. But there's no lack of leather in some of those, look!"

While there were a number of strappy confections displayed, Elizabeth was enthusiastically indicating several pairs of elegant boots.

"Shall we go in and have a look, my love?" asked the wizard.

"Oh, yes please!"

The range in the store was truly impressive, and the only two other customers left shortly after the Australians' arrival, so the shop-keeper could give them her full attention. She was the designer of everything on display, she explained, with a small team of talented craftspeople to assist in the art of creation.

Elizabeth swiftly decided she'd arrived in footwear heaven. She wasn't averse to fancy evening shoes, although she preferred designs which showed off their material to the 'assemblages of ribbons' that her beau decried. But really good dressy boots were to be admired, and this place had a wonderful array, from ankle- to thigh-length and all points in between. And the designs and decorations were simply exquisite, sometimes exquisitely simple.

Quickly establishing that there were real prospects of a good sale, probably sales, the shoe designer was more than happy to indulge her Australian customer's desire to "try those on, too, per favore".

Smiling broadly at his beloved's obvious delight, John B. was (after a suitable period of admiring comments and exclamations) able to excuse himself to "go and have a leg-stretch for a bit".

"Take your time, babe. There's still quite a lot here I want to try on."

"You know I'm going to think you look great in any of them, pretty lady, but you have fun! See you soon," he promised, receiving an understanding nod from the shopkeeper. She much preferred part-ners like him to those who hung around making ill-considered judg-ments about design or 'suitability', or fretting about cost. He'd already indicated he'd be footing the bill, so to speak, although the brunette had given a suggestion that, with so much to choose from, she might be dipping into her own purse as well. Both with money, and both enthusiastic – the ideal customers!

From the shoe shop it was a conveniently short walk to the jewellers who were John B.'s real objective. He introduced himself to the pudgy American behind the counter. At the mention of Gian-carlo, and more particularly his protege, Morton Overbeek's demeanour changed from 'polite formal' to 'genial bonhomie'. The switch wasn't lost on the wizard. Clearly Nicola worked her own sort of magic here.

Morton called his partner out from the workshop. After introductions and handshakes, John B. explained the purpose of his visit. In the course of his explanation he drew his viking-inspired pendant out from inside his t-shirt. Tadeusz Zybysko's eyes widened.

"Aleks! That's an Aleksander Kallaste piece, I would swear in court!" he exclaimed.

"Could be," replied John B. "I don't know the name, only that he works in Tallinn. He's, er, a friend of a friend of a friend, in Norway."

The man known as TZ laughed. "Yes, that is where Aleks trained me, after I left Krakow."

There followed a quick conference between the three men, as Stewart explained his broad idea of two matching rings, and Morton and Tadeusz made suggestions, and their first rough sketches. John B.'s finger was measured, as was Elizabeth's temporarily purloined ring. The turquoise and amethyst were handed over and admired. A price was quickly agreed.

"Leave it with us, my friend," said the Blob warmly. "We'll make these a priority!"

"Much appreciated, mate!" replied John B.

Tadeusz bowed. "Any friend of the little contessa is a friend of ours."

"The name suits her! I wouldn't be surprised if she *was* part of the nobility in her previous life!" the Australian laughed, but Morton shook his head, suddenly looking serious.

"I'm afraid there's nothing noble, or funny, about Nicola's life before she was rescued by Signore LaGrigio. There is a dark side to Venice, as there is to many cities, and her parents were deeply embedded in it."

"Were, you say?"

"As I understand it, her father and one brother are both in prison, and her mother died a victim of the very drugs they were involved in selling. The other brother is rumoured to have gone to Rome to join an uncle's business. Lamentably, the same sort of sordid businesses as were happening here," said the American sadly.

"Pushing drugs," muttered John B.

"Selling drugs, and more besides," said Zybysko. "They trade in human flesh – slavery in everything but name. Pretty Nicola would have been an ideal product for them, good looking and intelligent enough to be desirable to a certain audience. And she was being raised to be compliant, if not complicit."

All three men's faces were dark.

"I can't imagine Nicola being compliant," said John B. in a low voice.

"She was raised to know nothing else. Obey or be punished. She had spirit, which was probably part of her appeal. But standing up for herself, far less getting away from that environment – well, LaGrigio did well to encourage her, help her and care for her. It was something many of us could, or should have done..." The Pole's voice trailed off.

Overbeek put an arm around his partner's shoulders. "What's done is done. Let's be glad of how things have turned out. And be the best friends we can be to them both."

"Amen, dear heart," agreed the silversmith, returning the embrace.

"I'll drink to that, gentlemen," agreed John B. He had been found wandering the streets at the estimated age of ten, and although he had no memory at all of his life before being picked up by the police and delivered to the orphanage, he had a good imagination and an acute awareness of the possibilities.

"But now I'd better get back to my own dear heart, before she comes looking for me. I'll hear from you soon?"

"You will, sir, and thank you," said Tadeusz, his formal tone belied by a friendly smile.

It turned out that the wizard needn't have worried. Elizabeth was so engrossed in the delightful experience of trying on exclusive, hand-made footwear, that she'd lost track of time. In fact, when her beau reappeared at her side she looked up in some surprise.

"Oh! You weren't gone long! Didn't find anything you fancied?"

"Not half as much as I fancy you in those boots, pretty lady," was the more-than-diplomatic reply.

It was sincere, too, as the snug calf-length tooled leather did flatter his beloved's already shapely legs. John B.'s honest enthusiasm tipped the scales, and the pair being currently tried on got the nod for purchase.

"I think that will do me, babe," she said, smiling.

"What? Just one pair?" said John B. in mock surprise.

"Umm... no." She pointed toward the counter, where two more boxes waited by the cash register.

"Ah. Still, are you sure? It's not like you're going to find stuff like this very often in our travels."

The designer preened as she said, "*Signore*, the *signora* will not find such excellent footwear anywhere else in Venice, I promise you!"

Q laughed, replying, "Oh I believe you! We cast our net a bit wider than Venice, but I really am impressed with your work. And it's *signorina*, by the way, not that it really matters."

"Oh! *Mi dispiace!*" exclaimed the woman, genuinely surprised. The couple seemed so... well, so much a couple, in all the best ways, and she was a romantic soul.

"No apology necessary," they both said at once, bringing the smile back to her face.

"But really, JB, three pairs are plenty. I don't want to be Imelda Marcos! There's nothing with high heels, and no strappy sandals. An elegant pair of sling-backs, with beautiful carved and stitched round toes – perfect for going out to dinner somewhere special. A gorgeous pair of ankle height boots in soft black, and now these beauties."

"Sounds fabulous, pretty lady," said her beau as he walked over to the counter, pulling his wallet from his pocket.

The chain was just long enough to allow him to lay it on the glass top to extract the "magic pudding" credit card. "I'll get the two pairs of boots, okay?" he asked the store owner.

"And I'll pay for the other ones," said Q emphatically as she arrived at the counter.

"Certainly, *signorina*."

While the new acquisitions were being packaged, the Australians had the chance to pay some attention to the music playing in the background. They exchanged smiles as they recognised a quite distinctive keyboard style.

"That sounds familiar," observed Elizabeth, the wizard nodding his agreement, both of them recalling the work of Giancarlo LaGrigio.

"It's called *Giardino Della Nebbia*," explained the shoe designer. "A lovely piece, isn't it?"

"It is. By the sound of it, we know the man playing it," said the brunette with a touch of pride.

"Oh! You know Signore Delocchio? How lucky you are!"

"Umm..." For a moment, neither Australian said anything. They realised that this was another instance of Il Duce Grosso appending his name to work that was primarily performed by his session musicians.

"Have you, er, actually met him?" asked Stewart as diplomatically as he could.

"Only from a distance. He's a wonderful man," the woman gushed.

JB and Q smiled politely, made some final enthusiastic comments about the quality of the shoes, and exited as diplomatically as possible without tarnishing the image of the local hero. As they strolled along the walkway, she rested her head on his shoulder so they could converse quietly.

"Wow, talk about having a carefully crafted public image!" she exclaimed.

"Mm," her beau agreed. "Though it reminds me more of a comic book super-villain with a secret identity!"

They both laughed, but there was an undercurrent of serious caution beneath their mirth.

.ooo.

14

BENEATH A SHADY TREE

The remainder of that day had been spent on a meandering haphazard route home, investigating more shops as they went. With considerable reluctance, Stewart allowed himself to be taken into several stylish menswear shops, meeting more designers and haughty purveyors of high-fashion apparel. The haughtier they were, the less likely they were to see anything of the wizard's credit card.

In truth, he was entirely happy with living in jeans and purple t-shirts, but faced with the ensemble Q had bought for "going out somewhere special", he realised he'd have to expand his wardrobe a little. He didn't care much about his own appearance, but Elizabeth finally convinced John B. to invest in a pair of good dress shoes and smart trousers for wearing to top-class restaurants. The pants were simple, plain and black, fitted perfectly, and were really quite conservative.

The wizard's eventual choice of shoes was less so. He'd never owned anything more extravagant than deck shoes or sandshoes until their recent acquisition of walking boots. He'd resisted the idea of 'dress shoes' for as long as possible, but if he was going to go there, he was going to find something with character. What he eventually chose were long, with a pointed toe capped with silver. They were made of leather, in swirling shades of red and brown. They matched absolutely nothing he had ever worn.

Q was diplomatic enough (and loved him enough) not to make that comment. Who knows? Maybe somewhere in Venice, or somewhere else in the world, they'd find just the right pair of trousers to connect those shoes with a purple shirt. Although she struggled to imagine it. Still, he was happy, and he had actually bought something dressy for himself, which was a first.

They managed to catch a not-too-crowded water taxi to take them most of the way home. Not as romantic as a gondola, but most of those were engaged in one of the gondola races that were a feature of the Carnevale. With the crowds that were out, the queues for the few non-competitors were too discouraging. It wasn't urgent enough to 'waste' a wish, John B. thought. Perhaps some corner of his mind still privately feared that there was a finite number of them available. It wasn't like he understood the magic, after all, and every so often he had to will himself not to take it for granted.

They had a quiet night at home, sharing the cooking duties on simple steak and vegetables with creamy pepper sauce. A good bottle of Tuscan red wine with dinner, was then finished while relaxing on the couch. They tried Italian television, but nothing much appealed, so they both soon settled into reading before retiring to bed quite early.

On the following morning, their fast suitably broken by fresh pastries and home-made coffee, they agreed on a quiet day. Shopping had been fun, but contending with crowds for two consecutive days didn't appeal. Fresh air, yes. Thousands of tourists, friendly and polite or otherwise, no. A day in the local gardens – ideal.

The aged postman's satchel proved perfect for carrying Q's notebooks and reference materials. There was a temptation to add the laptop, but she reasoned that it would be too frustrating to run out of power at a critical moment, so the computer stayed in the safe. A few books for them both to relax into were added, with pens, pencils and an eraser. Finally, they squeezed in a carefully folded picnic rug they'd found in a cupboard of Manovalo 219. A whole day on a park bench may prove uncomfortable.

The wizard slung the green bag over his shoulder and saluted. "Fully equipped and ready, boss!" he said.

Q laughed and kissed him.

They ambled down the stairs and out into their little *viale*. Stopped at the pasticerria for a bag of treats to be savoured later in the day. Out onto Via Garibaldi, turned in the direction of what had become their favourite garden. Stopped at the little grocery store for some bottled water. Exchanged brief pleasantries with locals who smiled in recognition. Finally, reached the garden and spread the rug out under a large tree. Settled in for a relaxed and relaxing morning of reading and writing a good book.

Perhaps an hour later, Toscanini found them. John B. suggested he must have heard the paper bag rustling, as they'd only just extracted the first of the pastries to share. The cat had to be content with licking sweet crumbs off first Q's, then JB's fingers. But if he was disappointed he gave no show of it, purring in his peculiar way, then curling up on the wizard's lap as the latter rested his back against the tree.

Watching with quiet delight, Q smiled as within minutes both were sound asleep, warmed by the filtered sun, history book still open in her beloved man's hand.

Mere months ago, she couldn't have imagined a life like this for herself. If someone had asked what 'contentment' looked like for her, she'd have frowned in concentration, and given a vague answer about a good, well-paying job. There'd have been an unspoken desire for a supportive, non-critical home life too, but she probably wouldn't even have admitted that to herself.

"I wish you happiness," that man had said, what sometimes seemed a lifetime ago. That man sleeping under a tree in Venice, with an almost-stray cat on his lap, a trace of icing sugar on both their chins. That man who'd led her into, and out of danger across the world, in places she'd never imagined visiting. That man who encouraged her, and believed in her. Loved her.

She didn't have a home, as such. There was an apartment back in Canberra, but that was just a mailing address, and a place to store possessions not easily carried around. No, 'home' was wherever they were together, wherever on the planet this might be. And that was enough. She was content. Happy. The wish had worked.

She wrote more notes on the page in front of her. Woven into this history she was working with would have to be a love story. Not a formulaic romance, or a gratuitously steamy sex romp, but something that held some reflection of how she felt. Passion, joy, respect, gratitude, excitement and hope, all of it mutual, and all wrapped up together.

Elizabeth smiled as her story progressed.

Time passed peacefully. Engrossed in her creativity, the writer came back to the reality of a fine day in a Venetian park with a jolt when a cheery voice nearby called, "Well, hello there!"

Startled, she looked around. Strolling towards her were Giancarlo and Nicola, unselfconsciously walking hand in hand. It was the master musician who had noticed her and called out the greeting. His protégé smiled broadly and waved her free hand.

It took a moment or two for Elizabeth to recalibrate her thoughts – her mind had been on a Viking longship ploughing through a storm. Garden, birdsong and friendly faces all needed time to properly register. She managed a 'hello' in reply, instantly hoping it sounded more enthusiastic than it felt.

The two locals seemed oblivious to, or at least unfazed by, any hesitancy in her response. They stopped by her side, Giancarlo maintaining enough distance to respect her personal space, his gentle but firm hold on the girl's hand constraining her to do the same.

"A beautiful day to enjoy the garden," observed the smiling mentor. "Inspiring your novel?" he asked, with a gesture to the open notebooks.

As Elizabeth nodded, rapidly regaining her equilibrium, Nicola craned her neck to see the pages, and said, "Ooh! Can I read it? Please?"

The enthusiasm was endearing, despite the layer of reserve that

Elizabeth still retained about the relationship between this pair. The authoress smiled.

"Not yet. It's a work in progress – I'd like it to be more polished before I unleash it on anyone," she explained, a little apologetically.

"I understand," said Giancarlo, who almost certainly did.

"Me too," said Nicola, who quite likely didn't, being such a creature of impulse.

"Does that include him?" asked LaGrigio with a grin and a gesture towards the still-sleeping figures under the tree.

"Probably, for a little while yet," admitted Q, returning the grin.

The voices finally penetrated the shrouds of slumber. Almost as one, man and cat each opened an eye. Almost as one, there came a "G'day" and a *mmrrowwl*. Toscanini yawned and stretched his forelegs, but made no immediate move to leave his comfortable position. John B. likewise stretched and flexed his shoulders, but managed to suppress the yawn. All three observers didn't suppress their giggles.

"You make a lovely couple," laughed Q.

"Thank you, milady," her beau replied, both eyes now open, albeit blearily. "Good morning, sir and madam," he addressed Giancarlo and Nicola. "Assuming it is still morning?"

"Just barely," the grey man confirmed. "We were taking a stroll through the garden to whet our appetites for lunch."

His eyes flicked to the girl momentarily, as if telepathically confirming a suggestion. "Would you like to join us? There's a little trattoria we both enjoy. Good range and quality of food, not expensive, and pleasantly informal."

"It does sound good," admitted Elizabeth. "We're not really dressed for formal. JB?"

"Sounds good to me, my love. As long as they don't object to a Batman t-shirt, I'm in. Let me repack the satchel – come on Tosca, I have to move, I'm afraid, little mate."

The cat turned his head to fix his good eye on the wizard. Stared for a moment, as if considering the request, and purred in his unique way. John B. stroked the black back, but pushed gently.

"That's nice, mate, but seriously, I would like to get up and go to lunch."

"You can come too," Nicola advised the cat.

Giancarlo nodded his agreement. "The trattoria is used to us – all of us," he explained.

Still purring, Toscanini uncurled himself and deigned to climb off Stewart's lap, leaving a circle of dark fur as a souvenir of his presence.

The wizard stood, brushing some of the fur off before starting to pack away books, and the writing materials Q handed to him.

The cat padded over to Nicola and her mentor and continued purring as he wound his way around and between their legs, as if to say, "I still love you, too, of course."

By now, Elizabeth had made it to her feet. She shook the picnic rug to dislodge some leaves, dirt and grass clippings, and folded it before handing it to John B. He gave it a final light brush with his hand before packing it into the satchel, using it to secure the loose pens and eraser.

"That was a good, relaxing morning," said the wizard. "Now for a good, relaxing lunch."

Not for the first time, he'd soon learn that his dubious magical power did not include precognition.

.ooo.

15

AN INTERRUPTED LUNCH

The walk to the trattoria took them some way along the waterfront, where they started to encounter the inevitable crowds of tourists. A right hand turn soon after crossing over the Riva di San Antonin alleviated some of that. Then another turn took them into a narrow viale that reminded Elizabeth and John B. of the one in which they currently dwelt.

Only tourists who *really* grasped the idea of "walking lost" in Venice would be rewarded by finding the *Trattoria Luciano*. And that was Luciano's intention – he wanted to serve local people, and those who had made some effort to find him, not the casual passer-by who, he thought, wouldn't appreciate the difference between a mass-produced hamburger and a hand-crafted calzone.

Giancarlo, Nicola and even Toscanini were greeted like the old friends they evidently were. The addition of two extra people to what was apparently a regular, if informal, booking, created no dramas at all. The Australians were welcomed as warmly as if they'd been customers at the trattoria for years.

"Any friends of the maestro and the little contessa are welcome here," Luciano explained with an expansive gesture.

The restaurant wasn't crowded, and they were ushered to a

table near the centre of the room. Toscanini curled up quietly on the floor under Nicola's chair, as was his habit in Luciano's eatery. Menus were brought, and perused with interest. John B. and Q were a little surprised, but very pleased, to find that the trattoria offered a more cosmopolitan bill of fare than many Italian dining houses.

Nicola hugged Giancarlo's arm and asked sweetly, "Would you like a quickie?"

The musician sighed. "It's pronounced 'kweesh'. I am sorry, my friends, French is not her first language," he explained unconvincingly.

The girl tossed her head back. "I am very good at the French!" she said haughtily.

John B. resisted answering, "I bet you are," only because he was very aware of Q's foot resting on his own. She may not wear spiked heels, but he knew his canvas deck shoes would be no match for the wooden heel of her new boots.

The prospect of French cuisine did appeal to the wizard, though, and he happily ordered crepes. Perhaps in unconscious reaction to Nicola, Elizabeth went in a different direction and ordered moussaka.

Giancarlo smiled and nodded at that. "Excellent choice. I think I'll have the same, thank you Luciano."

As it turned out, only Nicola ordered a meal of local style – mussels in a rich white wine broth.

Dessert was to be crème brulee all round, glowingly described by their host as a specialty of the house, and enthusiastically endorsed by the two regular customers in the group.

The conversation was light and casual as they waited for their lunch to be served, snacking on crisp homemade breadsticks and sipping at a light Veneto red wine. The initial chat was, unsurprisingly, about music. Comparative tastes and preferences, concerts seen, albums loved.

Somehow, during a discussion of how visceral the reactions to certain music could be – good or bad – the conversation took a more philosophical turn. The question of 'nature -vs- nurture' evolved into questions about the nature of nature. Was there such a thing as racial memory, and if so, how did it work?

Elizabeth wasn't quite out of her depth, but felt very much in uncharted waters, and followed the conversation more from fascination than particular interest. She had a very definite sense that, while the master musician may have encouraged some philosophical thinking in his young protégé – certainly she could at least contribute thoughtful questions and some opinions to the discussion – it was a rare treat for him to have the depth of conversation he was sharing, particularly with her surprising beau.

Where Nicola was surprised at how much her mentor was saying (he was much more commonly a listener than a talker), Elizabeth was slightly bemused by *what* her JB was saying. She'd talked long and deeply with him, and knew he had what might be called a 'spiritual side', but he'd never revealed much interest in the detail of how human nature ticked, or how it fitted in anything like a universal context. She had the impression that much of what she was hearing was coming from somewhere deep within. A well that hadn't been plumbed for a very long time. Somehow LaGrigio was calling up something long untouched, or perhaps even forgotten. Intriguing.

The meals were delivered by Luciano himself, taking obvious and justifiable pride in their presentation. And they tasted as good as they looked. Greek, French and Italian, each of the cuisines represented at the table had been done justice to.

Discussion of humanity's place in the universe, and the place of the universe in humankind, was shelved while everyone's attention was turned to food. Even Toscanini had been discreetly served a plate of shredded chicken and fresh herbs in a white sauce. Somehow the cat was able to purr between mouthfuls.

Engrossed in their lunch, none of them noticed another foursome entering the trattoria.

It was pure chance. Pasqualina had been on a shopping excursion. She knew Luciano sometimes was prepared to sell ingredients that were difficult to obtain anywhere else in Venice, and there was a particular type of mushroom she wanted. The Culatello brothers had accompanied her simply out of having nothing more useful to do. Maybe they could get a good free lunch here, although the cook had made it clear she didn't want to jeopardize the quite useful relationship she'd started to cultivate with Luciano.

It was Luigino who first spotted who was sitting at the table in the middle of the room. In particular, he spotted the Australian girl who'd made him look stupid in front of his brothers. Galling as that was, though, he also remembered that Il Duce Grosso had made it clear that he wanted the woman for himself. The nudge to his oldest brother had triggered the same thought in Ugo's head too.

The three Culatelli stopped just inside the doorway, exchanged silent looks and slow nods. They didn't need words to understand each other's malevolent thoughts. Pasqualina understood also. She tried to lay a restraining hand on Ugo, but to him, she was only a woman. Favoured by Il Duce, sure, but not someone to give him orders. Delocchio wanted the Australian girl. What he wanted, the brothers provided. End of story. The three moved quickly.

The first intimation of trouble that John B. had was the startled shriek of another customer and the feeling of an arm crooked around his neck. As his head jerked up from his meal he saw that Giancarlo was held in a similar grip. The wizard didn't know their assailants by name, but recognized that it was the biggest, presumably eldest brother who'd grasped the musician.

It was Luigino who grabbed Elizabeth under an arm and yanked her to her feet. So, it must be the other brother who now held him. The wizard tensed, about to create some mayhem with a well-aimed elbow.

"No!" cried Elizabeth, sensing his intention. She'd seen the glitter of blades in the brothers' hands.

Ignoring, or oblivious to that threat, Nicola stood and lunged for Ugo, shouting, "Let them go, *stronzi!*"

Luigino managed to grab her long hair with the hand that held the knife and pulled her back into her chair. As tears of pain sprang to the girl's eyes the oldest brother struck her face with the back of his fist, never relinquishing his grip on LaGrigio's neck.

Giancarlo said nothing, but John B. saw the look in his eyes. The older brother was a marked man.

The grip on his own throat tightened, but as he watched his beloved being wrestled toward the exit, he glared at her assailant and gritted out, "I wish all of you, especially you, would get to blazes out of here!"

The other customers were sitting transfixed, by fear, or recognition of the brothers, or by the all-too-common desire to "not get involved". But the commotion had been quite audible, and the kitchen door flew open.

Luciano stormed out, a small but florid bundle of fury, still clutching the miniature blowtorch with which he'd been finishing off the desserts. He roared something unintelligible in Italian and strode forward.

The brothers paid him no mind, confident in their own strength, individually and in numbers. But the distraction was enough for Elizabeth to use her free hand to punch Luigino in his ample nose. Not hard enough to do real damage, but enough to get his attention. It was the second time she'd struck him, and now there was real feeling behind her actions. As he hoisted her painfully up off the ground by one arm she brought one of her wooden bootheels down forcefully onto his kneecap. An automatic send-off in hockey. And painful enough to do proper damage.

Cursing and struggling to hold his grip on the girl, Luigino staggered. He longed to use his knife, but Il Duce wanted her, presumably intact... Reeling and not concentrating, the youngest of the Culatello brothers stumbled into Luciano.

The chef hadn't consciously intended to use the blowtorch as a weapon – it just happened to be what he'd been holding when the fracas had erupted. But the little blue flame caught one of the many patches of grease on the thug's grubby sleeve and the fabric erupted into fire.

Luigino shrieked and dropped the knife. He also let go of Elizabeth, freeing up his hand to try to beat out the flames on the opposite arm.

Duilio was momentarily torn between helping his brother and maintaining his grip on the shaggy-haired Australian. His loss of concentration couldn't be seen by the wizard, but it wasn't lost on Nicola. She'd polished off all the mussels, but there was still broth in her bowl, and it was still hot. Without hesitation she grabbed the bowl and flicked its contents over the Australian's head and into Culatello's face.

The Buranese yelped, let go of his victim, and cursed as he pawed at his eyes. It was all the opportunity that John B. needed to drive his elbow into the groin that was at a convenient height behind him. Duilio collapsed in a pain-stricken heap.

The oldest of the brothers wasn't distracted. He had a grip on the grey man's throat, and he wasn't about to let it go. The other two could take care of themselves, even if it didn't look it at this moment... There was a weird sound from around his feet, like something trying to snarl while it gargled. Suddenly a sinewy bundle of black fur scampered up his body, claws extended to snag jeans and flannel shirt. The same extended claws that raked the swarthy face. Unlike his brothers, Ugo didn't shriek or scream or shout. But he did surrender his grasp of the musician's neck, and take a step back as he flailed at the feline menace on his face.

John B. was up out of his chair in almost the same moment, and stepping around the table.

"Tosca – drop!" he said sharply.

To Nicola's surprise the cat seemed to obey instantly, or perhaps he'd merely had enough of the close proximity to Ugo's breath. Either way, he jumped off the brother's face at just the right moment for the Australian to land a hard left cross that turned a couple of the scratches around the cheekbone into full-on splits in the skin. Ugo reeled and fell.

Culatello was about to get up and resume hostilities when Luciano strode forward to stand over him.

"You stay still!" the chef commanded. "I know who you are, you three. You think, you work for the fat man, no-one will argue with you, try to stop you." He jabbed the blowtorch in Ugo's direction.

"This is Luciano's house, not Delocchio's. You think the *carabinieri* will not touch you? Me, I am not so sure, but I will call them and find out, hey?"

The chef made a meaningful step towards the counter where a telephone stood. Some of the *Arma dei Carabinieri* – one branch of the Venetian police, may well have held Il Duce Grosso in respectful awe, but the three brothers had a sufficiently unsavoury reputation that a formal complaint might well cause some difficulties. Leonardo didn't like difficulties.

"No! No – we will... go. Go away quietly, eh? A misunderstanding. I... apologize." That last remark of Ugo's was directed at Luciano, not at any of the actual victims of the assault, a fact not lost on some of them.

Nonetheless, Elizabeth and John B. held their tongues, the brunette now standing by her wizard, each with an arm around the other's waist. This was Luciano's property. Whatever their own inclinations, they were willing to let it be his call. Elizabeth contented herself with 'helpfully' upending a carafe of water over Luigino to aid in quelling the small fire on his arm. A snarl broke through his whimpering, but he made no move. Not without instruction from his oldest brother, who appeared to be reluctantly giving in to the man from the trattoria.

Now that man turned to glower at Pasqualina. The red-haired woman had stood by the door, avoiding any involvement in the violence. If there was anything she might have subtly or otherwise been able to contribute to the proceedings, she'd chosen not to do so. Instead, she'd watched, with a mixture of amusement and intrigue, as the brothers' bullying had failed. She had a suspicion that something unseen was at play, and that there was more to this latest object of Leonardo's desire than met the eye. But now she realised that Luciano was advancing on her.

"If you ever bring these *stronzi* into my trattoria again, you will never see any of the specialties you look for from me, *capire*? Now, you bring them, you take them away. Now!"

There was nothing to say in response. Certainly not in front of the thwarted henchmen of her lord and master. Pasqualina nodded, doing her best to look contrite. She had no need to encourage the departure of the Culatello boys – their public humiliation was enough to have them in slinking retreat already. All three were already imagining what they'd do next time they met the Australians, preferably in a dark viale with no witnesses. Although Il Duce did want the woman... Still, on past experience, that wouldn't last long, and then she'd pay.

Those dark thoughts were stamped on their already unattractive faces as they exited, closely followed by Pasqualina, who did make some attempt to apologize to Luciano before leaving. He waved her away with a curt, "Not now!"

Luciano turned to address his customers, the audience of the unexpected floor show. He apologized for the unpleasant scene, and offered a complimentary carafe of the house sangria to every table.

"Actually, it's very good and we should take him up on it!" Giancarlo said quietly to Elizabeth as they all resumed their seats, rubbing gently at spots that had been hurt.

John B., in particular, was flexing his left hand gingerly. It was the hand he'd broken on the jaw of an American colonel, what seemed like a lifetime ago, when his magic was first roused. Ugo's skull was uncommonly hard – a trait which Stewart shared, ironically – and he worried that he may have reopened an old fracture when he hit the Buranese cheekbone.

When the sangria was delivered, the wizard quietly asked for a small bag of ice which he promptly laid across his knuckles. Toscanini had resumed his place under the table, rewarded for his efforts by hugs, pats, and another plate of chicken. The nerves and tempers of the four humans at the table gradually settled, helped by the excellent crème brulee which their host finally had the opportunity to serve. His apologies to them had been especially profuse, even though all five of them knew the event had been in no way his fault.

"It's encouraging to know, at least, that there are some parts of Venice where Il Duce Delocchio isn't held in reverential awe," said Giancarlo. "His thugs are regarded as just what they are."

"I don't want to talk about them, please," said Elizabeth. "I don't want that creep's hands on me ever again!"

"The fat pig, you mean? Or Luigino?" asked Nicola, sympathetic, still upset, and angry all at once.

"Is that the greasy sleazebag's name? Him. Either of them, actually!"

With his good hand, John B. caressed his beloved's arm. "I wish that'll be so, sweetheart."

The wish comforted Elizabeth, and elicited no comment from their companions who took it as no more than an affectionate expression of support.

The sangria cooled anger and distress, and the ice soothed the throb in John B.'s left hand. Conversation turned back to gentler matters. By mutual, unspoken agreement, Il Duce Grosso and his repellent henchmen weren't mentioned.

Elizabeth talked about some of the shops they'd visited, amusing Nicola in particular with accounts of successful haggling. They talked of some of the street performances they'd seen as part of the Carnivale activities – jugglers, a fire-eater, and musicians of varied types, styles and quality. It was no surprise that the naturally reticent Giancarlo didn't join their number, but it was thought that the more gregarious Nicola might have taken the opportunity to display her talent publicly, perhaps earning a few euros from the effort. But a mob of jostling tourists, crowding the Piazza San Marco, chattering amongst themselves with most of them having no real appreciation of what they were hearing, was adamantly not the audience she wanted.

"It is good for Robi," she said. "He can play with no effort, and people will give him money because he'll play whatever they want to hear. I will play only what I want to play."

Giancarlo quietly observed that this sounded a little more harsh on Robi than was warranted, but conceded that their friend had a very casual approach to his music. To most things in life, actually.

John B. mused to himself that that was probably why he'd felt such a quick rapport with the guitarist. It was an attitude he'd held for almost as far back as he could remember. Even the awakening of his magic hadn't changed it much. His love affair with Q was the first thing he'd taken truly seriously, he thought. Which went a long way towards explaining earlier failed relationships, but there was no point in mulling over them – he had a new opportunity, and was determined to get it right this time. All of that flashed through his mind in seconds, the only evidence being a smile and a gentle squeeze of his beloved's hand.

It was noted that tomorrow there was to be a parade of gondolas and other boats in the Grand Canal. It would deservedly attract a large crowd, but Giancarlo was able to recommend some good viewing spots that were likely to be less populated. Upstairs in any of a couple of waterfront buildings, he suggested.

Not least from some sense of loyalty to Mario and his older friend, the idea appealed to John B. and Elizabeth.

"And, ah, in the evening, I should confess that Nicola and I will be participating in the Carnivale revels, in our own small way," admitted the silver-haired musician.

He explained to his intrigued friends that he had been engaged to provide the music for a masked ball in one of Venice's more up-market hotels. A three-piece ensemble of himself, Nicola, and Robi (who would be obliged to 'dress up' – fortunately there were appropriate outfits in Giancarlo's home, one of which could be made to fit).

There were a number of such events in different venues across the time of the celebration. Ordinarily LaGrigio ignored them, but he'd accepted this particular invitation because 1) he knew and respected the hotel manager, and 2) he reasoned it was time for his protégé to make her public professional debut, and this would be a good, small environment in which he'd have some degree of control, if it was needed.

"This ball is an expensive proposition," he said. "All of these high-end events are, I'm afraid. But I believe I can arrange two tickets to be at the door for you, if you'd like to attend?"

The Australians looked at each other in surprise.

"I've never been to a masked ball," said Elizabeth. "It sounds like fun! Shall we?"

Her beau shrugged. "Darling, you know I dance like a bookshelf, but if you're keen, then sure. Yes, it does sound like fun, and it's certainly not something I've ever experienced. Okay, my friend. We accept your kind invitation. You've done well keeping it quiet, though. Both of you."

For the first time since they'd met him, Giancarlo looked a little embarrassed.

"I didn't want to seem... boastful, I suppose. I had sworn this little widget to secrecy..."

"I know when to keep my mouth shut," said Nicola primly, causing Elizabeth to raise an eyebrow but say nothing.

"But perhaps it would be good for Nicola to know there are some friendly faces in the audience, even if they are hidden behind masks," Giancarlo concluded.

"Oh! Masks! We've looked at lots, but not actually bought any to wear," said Elizabeth. "And clothes – what should we wear to a masked ball?"

The musician shrugged. "Unlike some, this one is not fully formal."

"That's a relief! I reckon I'd be about as comfortable in a suit and tie as a gorilla would," admitted the wizard.

"Even a purple suit?" teased Nicola.

"Even that!" John B. laughed, along with the others at the table.

Giancarlo continued. "No, not formal. But something good."

"Elegant, classy? We can do that, can't we, JB?"

"Um... we? I'll try, sweetheart."

The gathering broke up with shared laughter. Luciano waved away requests for the bill. His 'good friends had put up with enough', he explained, and he would not add to their inconvenience. The four stilled their protests and accepted the courtesy, confident that they'd be back in the near future.

They walked homewards together, chatting amiably, with the cat trotting just ahead of them. The food at Luciano's had been excellent, but the interruption of the Culatello brothers had obviously soured the occasion.

Finally letting the matter intrude on their conversation, they wondered what had motivated the attack. It seemed to be a matter of chance, as indeed it had been. The brothers happened to have walked into the wrong place at the wrong time, as far as they were concerned. And the assault itself, well, it was presumed it was Luigino's impulsive response to having lost face to the Australians, particularly Elizabeth. There was no reason to think otherwise.

At the entry to Viale di Tavola they took their leave of each other, exchanging affectionate hugs, with a characteristic set of distinctive yowls from Toscanini before he trotted on ahead. Ostensibly, Nicola was going to spend the afternoon studying, although it seemed far more likely she'd be making music with her mentor. Well, that was study of a sort. Elizabeth was looking forward to reviewing her morning's work. And John B. planned nothing more demanding than a good book, a small bag of ice for his hand, and perhaps an anaesthetising drink. The Scotch they'd bought at the local store was a blend, not his regular preference, but frankly, just at the moment it would do.

"Mask shopping tomorrow, babe, and maybe some fancy clothes, hey?" said Elizabeth lightly as they climbed the stairs to their apartment.

The wizard chuckled. "Okay, pretty lady. We'll see what we can find. Tell you what, though – I wish I don't lay eyes on those damned Culatello brothers tomorrow!"

Q squeezed his undamaged hand as she slipped the R2D2 keychain from her purse. "That sounds fair, babe," she agreed.

.ooo.

16

VANISHING ACT

After their satisfying lunch – well, food-wise at least, Elizabeth and John B. had enjoyed a light evening repast. Little more than a grazing plate of meats, cheeses and other deli items they'd already stocked up on.

It was an early, gently affectionate night for them both. The brunette had been more disturbed by the assault than she'd let on, even to herself. She loved that her beau leapt to her defence, and hated that it was necessary. Hated more that he was in pain because of it, however much he downplayed the injury, now firmly bandaged to limit the movement of his fingers. John B. had remembered clearly how the earlier, similar damage had been treated by an excellent doctor in Central Australia.

Indeed, by morning he claimed that the hand felt fine, although he acquiesced to his beloved's insistence that the strapping stay on for a day, at least. Longer, she hoped. Elizabeth loved what he could do with those hands, and didn't want any long-term impairment, thank you very much.

They took their time setting off for their shopping expedition. It was mid-morning by the time they were strolling over the now-familiar bridges that took them into Venice's shopping precincts.

Indeed, the way was now familiar enough that they knew a few of the back ways that allowed them to dodge the worst of the tourist crush. Still plenty of time to acquire the finery needed for the night's formal event!

They made their way to the Mercerie district. There was a good concentration of mask sellers there, and John B. remembered one particular shop where the wares had caught his eye.

Locating it, they were even able to talk with the craftsman who made the masks in a workshop above the store. 'Talk' overstates things a bit. Vito the mask-maker spoke very little English, and the Australians' command of the local dialect was limited. Elizabeth understood slightly more Italian than she spoke, which was minimal. John B. was an adept linguist, but his vocabulary was still rudimentary. Although he could understand, and be (mostly) understood in casual conversation, complex or rapid dialogue was beyond him.

Nonetheless Vito gleaned and appreciated his visitors' enthusiasm for his work, and was able to guide them to selections that seemed most appropriate.

Both of the chosen masks were full-face. Elizabeth's was mostly in a rich shade of ivory, subtly deeper and more distinctive than the usual white, and which somehow lit up the emerald green of her eyes. That brilliant colour was prominent in the three-leaved curling crown that topped the mask, scattered with tiny faux gems and fringed with glittering gold. The only other ornamentation was a deep red heart on the left cheek.

Hardly surprisingly, John B.'s chosen mask had a strong purple element. A diagonal line ran from above the right eye, across the bridge of the nose and down across the left cheek, just brushing the corner of the mouth before curving into the corner of the jaw. Above the line was glossy royal purple, shot with tiny gold stars. Below the line was mostly simply white, but around the right eye was a gold starburst, the north and south 'compass points' of which extended in fine glittering lines to the edges of the mask, while the 'lateral' lines reached to the right edge, and the corner of the left eye.

There were no others like them, Vito managed to make clear.

Indeed, that was much of the appeal of these artisan products. Uniqueness was a rare commodity amongst Venetian masks. Even these had design features that were common in the mass-produced facewear that was on show in so many shops, but little touches in execution and embellishment would identify Vito's hand to a serious collector. The price reflected that, but John B. was determined on nothing but the best for his beloved – she wanted something special for a special occasion, and that's what she would have. These, he insisted, were his treat, from his account. Quietly pleased, Q didn't argue.

Considering mask options had taken surprisingly longer than they'd expected, so before braving clothing stores for fine evening-wear, they decided to break for lunch. It wasn't a long walk to the banks of the Grand Canal, even skirting the crowded Piazza San Marco, to hopefully find an upstairs restaurant offering a view of the boat parade.

The first ideally situated location they found was already packed. Undeterred, they continued their way along the Riva degli Schiavoni. Some of Venice's most opulent (and expensive) hotels were to be found in this locale. And of course, these were well-populated by the well-heeled, as keen as any cut-price tourist to see one of the spectacles of Carnevale. Fortunately, nestling amongst these were some more modest buildings. They may have lacked a certain grandeur flaunted by their neighbours, but a few also lacked the crowds.

Prestige and glitz weren't factors in the Australians' choice. They wanted a good view, and at least reasonable food. The *Casa di Cozze* seemed to offer just that combination. Seafood was the specialty – the name meant 'The House of Mussels' – and Elizabeth was happy with a bowl of those molluscs served in a white wine and garlic broth. John B. contented himself with a couple of *pizzette*, miniature pizzas with a simple cheese and smoked meat topping. A bottle of Veneto white was an acceptable accompaniment to both.

What the *Casa di Cozze* mostly had in its favour was a good vantage point looking out over the water of the Grand Canal. This meant the diners could easily enjoy the spectacle of the brightly decorated small boats that bobbed in the parade.

"I presume Mario must be among them. I wonder which is his gondola?" mused Q.

"No way to tell from here, pretty lady, more's the pity. Still, I'm sure you're right and he's out there in the thick of it somewhere. Ha – just as likely he'll be out front leading the way, or at the very back, shepherding the rest like a mother hen."

They both laughed at the mental picture that conjured up.

"I suppose Marina will be watching from somewhere, boats being her specialty," said Elizabeth.

John B. nodded. "I'm sure she's seen it plenty of times before, mind you. I wonder if she's involved with any of the decorations for the participants?"

"That seems a bit – frivolous for her. She's a very serious woman, I think. Maybe when her Mario was still alive."

"Mm. That's a loss keenly felt, hey? Understandable." He just stopped short of saying, 'I know how I'd feel without you'. That had been far too close to the truth in Norway.

Engrossed in the sight of the floating parade, neither had noticed the head waiter watching them intently. They were unaware that he'd taken note of their accents, or that he'd been more than usually interested in studying Elizabeth's face, particularly her distinctive green eyes. His surreptitious phone call had likewise gone unseen.

The parade had reached a point where the participants seemed mostly to be small fishing boats, kitted out with pennants and streamers. The gondolas the couple so admired had passed, or perhaps more were still to come.

"This is a good moment for me to duck out to the Gents. Sorry sweetheart – I won't be long."

"Take your time, babe. A man's gotta do what a man's gotta do, hey? I'll be fine sitting here enjoying the show."

John B.'s destination was actually outside the restaurant itself, tucked in a far corner of the upper storey of the building, past a number of dingy small offices. As soon as the wizard had gone out the door of the restaurant, the head waiter pressed the intercom button that connected his station to the kitchen.

The kitchen doors swung open, and there rapidly emerged three figures that Elizabeth would have recognised immediately, if she'd seen them coming. Alas, she was facing in exactly the wrong direction. Before she knew what was happening, Ugo had hoisted her from her chair, pinning her arms behind her. Duilio had clamped a sweaty hand over her mouth, and Luigino held a knife against her face, its blade lying across one eye so its glittering edge loomed large in her vision.

"Not a word!" he hissed.

In moments she was hauled across the room and out through the kitchen doors. The head waiter appeared at the table, and swiftly removed her plate, glass, napkin – any and all evidence that she'd been there. Even her purse was gone, conveniently still slung over her shoulder.

He deposited the items in the kitchen just in time to see the Culatello brothers exiting through the back door with their prey, who had enough sense of self-preservation to not struggle. He very nearly patted himself on the back. The *Casa di Cozze* was one of several businesses in which Leonardo Delocchio had an interest, financial or otherwise.

Il Duce Grosso had contacted all of them, providing a description of a young Australian woman, good figure, brunette with distinctive green eyes. If she was seen, he was to be told immediately. This head waiter happened to be the one who recognized Delocchio's 'target' first, and had called the number that had been provided.

Duilio Culatello was never without his mobile phone. He and his brothers had been loitering around the square adjoining the church of San Zaccaria. They had no interest in the Renaissance beauty of the church, or the famous Giovanni Bellini artwork it contained. It was simply a coincidence. They'd been part of the waterfront crowd watching the parade on the Grand Canal, but their interest had quickly waned. They'd had enough of boats in their younger days.

The Campo San Zaccaria was a convenient place to sit, drink coffee, and eat slabs of takeaway pizza.

As it happened, it was also conveniently close to the restaurant where the Australian girl was reported to be. Luigino was all for an immediate dash – he wanted to get his hands on her as soon as possible. His oldest brother, however, restrained him. The woman had just arrived at a restaurant. She would be some time there. No need to abandon, or even rush, their own food and drink.

Inwardly the youngest brother seethed. Ugo was right, and he could no more stand up to him than he could fly to the moon. But that damned green-eyed cow had twice gotten the better of him, publicly. The skin on his arm still smarted from the burn, even under the dressing and ointment that Pasqualina had provided. As soon as Il Duce was bored with her, he'd get revenge. And the sooner Il Duce got his hands on her, the sooner he'd get bored. But no, Ugo wanted to finish his pizza, so they waited.

Not for long, though, and the way to the restaurant wasn't long. And the 'snatch' had gone smoothly, thanks to the waiter's collusion. They walked briskly back to the Palazzo Grossi, Elizabeth's wrist held unobtrusively but tightly by Ugo on one side, her ribs on the other side equally inconspicuously poked by the sharp point of Luigino's blade. Although the youngest Culatello never quite touched the girl, the two brothers kept as close to her as a pair of lovelorn swains, with the third barely a pace behind. He was thought to be the fastest of them, and in the unlikely event of their captive managing to somehow get free, he would ensure she didn't get far.

They swiftly got through the jostling Carnevale crowds, taking back ways and alleys until they reached the Ghetto, where the numbers were typically less, even at this busy time of year. As they neared their destination, Duilio called to announce their impending arrival. Delocchio's was the first number on his mobile phone's speed dial, of course.

Reaching the Palazzo, Ugo propelled Elizabeth through the portal, the door held open by a quietly grumbling Septimus Smith, who considered 'acting as doorman' to be well outside his duties.

The heavy door was slammed emphatically shut behind the arrivals just as soon as they were inside. Duilio's heels were almost grazed by the action. Smith drew three heavy bolts into place. Barely bothering to glance at the newcomers, he started to stalk back to his studio.

He was called to a grudging halt by the owner of the Palazzo, who reclined on a sturdy couch in the front room, surveying all that went on. Leonardo's face was wreathed in a broad, satisfied smile. He looked like a particularly happy whale (albeit a whale wrapped in a heavy silk brocade smoking jacket and baggy pants).

"Now then, Sceptred, dear boy, no need to be surly. I realize you're irked at the loss of your room, but I assure you it's only temporary. Please join me in welcoming the lovely young lady to her new home," the big man said smoothly.

Elizabeth had reached a point of being speechless with frustration and rage, but Delocchio's artificial charm was the trigger for that to detonate. Still gripped by Ugo, she launched a stream of invective that would have been worthy of a bullocky who'd just had his foot trodden on by the largest of his beasts. It's doubtful that John B. would have been shocked, but he'd probably be surprised by the range of his beloved's colourful vocabulary.

AT THAT MOMENT THOUGH, John B. Stewart had much greater concerns than how well his lover could curse. He'd re-entered the restaurant after a relatively short 'comfort stop'. The trip to and from the toilet took only slightly less time than he'd spent there. As he'd gone back into the restaurant he'd been planning a witty remark about "inconvenient conveniences". He stopped in his tracks a little way short of his table. His unattended table. It was conceivable that Q had followed his lead and gone to visit the Ladies' room, but while his own glass and napkin were where he'd left them, all evidence of his partner's presence was gone. The seat opposite his own was neatly tucked under the table. The cloth was pristine, a set of clean cutlery, folded napkin and an unused wine glass sitting, apparently waiting for a diner who hadn't come.

Under the table he could see the brown bag that held the masks they'd bought, apparently untouched. Baffled, he went to the table and stood, tapping the fingertips of his good hand unconsciously on its edge. Abruptly he turned and strode to the head waiter's station. Barely controlling his emotions, he asked the man what had happened to the young lady.

"*Scusi, signore*? Young lady?" the waiter asked with bovine density.

"My dining companion. Brunette. Extremely pretty. Was sitting with me when you brought us our lunch, remember? You brought her a bowl of the house specialty. The mussels in broth."

The waiter spread his arms helplessly. "*Signore*, I brought only the *pizzetta* you ordered. And a bottle of wine. I thought it odd that you would want a whole bottle to yourself, but the customer is always right, *si*?"

Stewart blinked, uncomprehendingly. "You're kidding, right?"

He got a blank look in response.

"This is crazy! She was right there! She's been right by my side for... for... bloody ages. She sure as blazes was here with me having lunch. *You* led us to that table, told us about how good the view of the boat parade would be..."

"*Si, signore* – I told you that. But only you, no one else."

Bewildered, his sheer bafflement overwhelming even his anger and fear, Stewart turned and shouted to the other customers in the restaurant, then walking amongst them agitatedly calling, "Hey! Anybody! You saw her! Someone must have. Good looking woman, I'm used to her getting second looks – she's worth it. You – you were watching her as we came in!"

The middle-aged businessman being addressed looked anywhere but at the Australian's eyes. He managed a helpless shrug before concentrating very intently on the last traces of his meal. Every one of the patrons had been speedily approached with a three-pronged attack – a free lunch, a handful of cash, and the words "Signore

Delocchio". The combination seemed to have worked. No-one met John B.'s gaze.

The waiter made a great show of producing a docket that showed only the pizzetta and wine as being ordered. He'd managed to deftly prepare it while Stewart was watching the other customers. If John B. had actually touched the docket (it was held well out of his reach) the ink would have smudged, so fresh was it.

Clearly his beloved wasn't in the restaurant. Growling, Stewart strode into the kitchen, ignoring the shouted protests of the head waiter. He also ignored the shouts of the kitchen staff, and even the brandished cleaver of the apprentice chef who advanced on him. The young man, keen to earn the approval of Il Duce, closed on the Australian. He was more enthusiastic than effective, though. Interested only in looking for Elizabeth, John B. barely glanced at the approaching figure.

When the white-jacketed fellow loomed too near, the wizard simply planted the palm of his undamaged hand in the sweaty face and pushed. Expecting a rather different reaction to the weapon he held, the young man was caught off balance literally as well as figuratively. Staggering backward, he flung out an arm and upset the large pot of the simmering broth served with the signature mussels.

Chaos erupted as the other kitchen staff rushed to limit the damage, as the soup pot acted like the first in a series of dominos across the crowded stovetop. It toppled a pot of pasta, which in turn knocked over a saucepan of meat sauce, the handle of which caught the edge of a pan of frying pancetta. The frypan flipped up, and the fat really hit the fire.

The wizard remained mostly oblivious to all this, quickly making his way around the kitchen checking for any clues or trace of his beloved. Without success.

Without a backward glance either, John B. went back into the restaurant. The head waiter had seen everything that had happened in the kitchen, and frankly wasn't sure what to do. He decided to brazen it out.

"Signore - il conto?"

"The bill? You expect me to pay you, after you make the love of my life disappear? Magic is supposed to be my department..."

"Eh? *Non capisco.*" He may not have understood the reference to magic, but there was no mistaking the look on the face staring at him.

Il Duce Grosso may pay well, but neither he nor his musclemen were here right now to protect him. And it seemed very likely he'd need protection if this shaggy man was provoked any further.

"Ah – *signore*, you are... upset. No charge. No charge, eh?"

He snatched back the docket and tore it in two, scrunching the pieces into a ball and tossing it away. He ventured what he hoped was a reassuring smile, that in fact did nothing to disguise his nervousness.

John B. continued to glare at him for a few more moments, then suddenly turned away. He snatched up the shopping bag from under what had, very definitely, been *their* table, and stormed out. There was clearly nothing to be achieved here.

Down the stairs and back on the broad walkway that fringed the canal, he looked in exasperation at the throng still crowding the area.

"I just wish I had some clue of where you are, darling," he said.

He couldn't just stand there and wait for the wish to work. It didn't happen that way – well, not usually. But what to do? Retrace their steps of the morning? Head back to Manovalo and wait there? Pound the streets of Venice with his fingers crossed?

He took a few steps in the direction of the Piazza San Marco. It would be crowded, but it was in some ways the hub of Venice. From there, perhaps he could... think of something.

Then, amidst the tourists he spotted two men in uniform. They walked in the measured, rather world-weary manner of constabulary on foot patrol all over the world.

John B. had a sketchy idea that policing in Italy was a multi-tiered system, with different organizations having different areas of responsibility. But surely a copper was a copper, and even if his experience with policemen hadn't always been positive, these two might at least be able to point him in a helpful direction.

The pair might have been father and son by their appearance, although there was no such relationship between them. One in his forties, the other twenty years younger, both had dark hair, long faces, and rather sad eyes. The older man's face was more creased, and there were streaks of grey hair visible at his temples.

They were members of the *Polizia di Stato*, what might be considered a 'middle tier' of policing. Less militarized than the *Carabinieri* or the finance-crime specialists, the *Guardia di Finanza*, they tended to be more professional than the *Polizia locale*.

The *Polizia di Stato* operated a number of boats in Venice. Indeed, a couple of their sleek, light-blue-and-white craft had been part of the parade on the Canal, and these two had made sure their patrol had given them a satisfactory view. It was near the end of their shift, and they were making an unhurried way back to the stationhouse, ironically not far from where John B. had just left.

Taking a deep breath to calm himself as best he could, the Australian approached the uniformed men. In broken but hopefully comprehensible Italian he tried to explain that his girlfriend had gone missing.

The expressions he got in response were barely a step up from bored.

"*Inglese?*" asked the older officer, after John B. had stopped for breath.

"No. Australian. Does that matter?"

The older man shrugged. "*Non parlo inglese,*" he said casually.

"And you?" Stewart asked the other.

"*Parlo un po'. A che ora... scusi...* what time did this happen?"

Determinedly patient, John B. repeated himself, mostly in English, using such simple language and phrases as he could think of to make himself understood. The faces in uniform didn't seem to register any change in interest.

The younger man did, at least, take a notebook and pencil from his pocket, and appeared to be about to write down a few details.

"Where did this happen?" he asked.

John B. tried not to grind his teeth. He'd just explained all the detail. But he realised that this was questioning by rote. The procedure of habit, and probably defaulted to when the 'investigation' wasn't being taken very seriously. He pointed back along the Riva degli Schiavoni.

"Upstairs, in the *Casa di Cozze*. There's something seriously not right about that place. Something crooked, I think."

Suddenly the older policeman discovered his English language skills.

"No, *signore*! That place is owned by the esteemed Signore Delocchio! It, like the man himself, is beyond reproach!"

"Delocchio? The douche grosso owns it? That's – interesting."

If either police officer caught the deliberate insulting pronunciation of the 'esteemed' man's name, they didn't pursue it. The younger man did, however, close his little pad.

He looked at the Australian, perhaps with a trace of sympathy, but no sign of helpfulness.

"Signore Delocchio is a respected and generous man." There was a very slight emphasis on the word 'generous'. "I do not think that there would be anything to be gained from pursuing enquiries at the *Casa di Cozze*. We know it well."

They should. It was a popular dining venue for many at the nearby police station.

A light had come on inside the wizard's head, though. He'd wished for a clue, and this was it. Of course he should have suspected Delocchio's involvement somehow, but not knowing the direct connection he hadn't seen the link. His mind racing, he barely acknowledged the younger policeman handing him a slip of paper with the telephone number of the *polizia locale*.

It was a hollow gesture in any case. That particular force wasn't noted for their helpfulness, especially in response to phone calls from folk who didn't speak Italian. And the presence of Il Duce Grosso in the matter seemed to guarantee that any enquiries would quickly hit a brick wall.

Thanking the officers with more courtesy than they'd expected, Stewart turned and headed for Manovalo 219. He didn't quite run, but his pace was rapid. From time to time he glanced into the shopping bag he still clutched. A sliver of ivory mask could be glimpsed through its tissue wrapping.

"Keep your defences up, darling," he muttered. "Be safe. I'll find you."

It wasn't a wish. It was a vow.

.ooo.

17

IN THE HALL OF THE SILVER DUKE

Delocchio had shown only amusement at Elizabeth's fiery tirade. She *was* a spirited wench, wasn't she? Sufficiently so that he deemed it prudent for Ugo to maintain a firm grip on her. She seemed the type to lunge at him with claws out.

The scratch of a woman's fingernails could be quite entertaining under the right circumstances, of course, but it was necessary that he control those circumstances.

Eventually the brunette stopped swearing, and drew her breath in a ragged gasp.

"All finished? No matter if you're not. I'm speaking now, and you'll hold your tongue please. Or it will be held for you."

"Let anyone try! I'll bite their bloody fingers off!"

Il Duce laughed. "Yes, I believe you'd try! Duilio, please apply a gag to my new toy. And I think, yes, tie her wrists and ankles. A little security, until such time as she comes to fully appreciate her new situation."

As Elizabeth was being bound, the big man continued to speak with an infuriating casual geniality.

"Your new situation: welcome to the Palazzo Grossi. This is my home, and you will share it with me. In time, I'm confident you'll come to accept that. It's not like I'm offering you an alternative. You're an attractive woman, Elizabeth – I believe that is your name? Yes, and I want you. Simple as that. I am a man who gets what he wants. When I want your affection I will have it, by whatever means necessary."

Outrage shone in the flashing green eyes, but already she was too well tied to do more than strain uselessly against the ropes, squirming against the chair she'd been deposited on.

"Obviously you've encountered some of my associates. The Culatello brothers are inclined to be crude, but they're very useful, and commendably loyal. You'll meet my cook later..."

If Pasqualina had heard herself being described so dismissively she might have been irked. Not surprised, but irked.

"But she's busily engaged in the kitchen. The gentleman who so gallantly opened the door for you is my other houseguest, Mr. Sceptred Smith. A more than capable artist, as you'll soon see. I expect you'll soon be in a position to have your own room, at such times as you're not sharing mine. But until your mood settles and you become more tractable, I'm afraid you'll be confined to the only securely lockable bedroom in my palazzo. Unfortunately for Mr. Smith, that happens to be his room, hence his irritation. I am sorry, Sceptred. I'm sure this will be only a temporary arrangement. I don't believe Elizabeth is a stupid woman. She'll soon see what is best for her."

Smith scowled and said, "But it's my *studio*. I *work* there, not just sleep. And I have projects that you want finished..."

"Yes, yes, I understand. A little inconvenience. We can take the time tomorrow to move whatever you require into one of the upstairs rooms. For now, go and remove whatever effects you'll want for this evening. Take the small guest bedroom three doors along from mine. It's cosy, but I gather the bed is comfortable."

"I'm not worried about 'comfortable'! I have work to do..."

"And it's work on my behalf, dear friend. And I say it can wait until tomorrow. Relocate yourself. If it will help your peace of mind, go for a walk along the canals afterwards. Muse on the unfairness of life, if you wish – I know that's often how you feel. But right now, I want that room tenanted by Elizabeth, and secured, with all haste."

Spurred by Delocchio's imperious gesture, Smith went to obey. He wasn't happy about it, but he was seldom happy anyway. As he stalked away, he pondered the state of his bank balance. How soon would he be able to walk away from here? The fat man paid well, admittedly. Better than any other employment or commission he'd be likely to find. He realized that unfortunately he did still need considerably more money to finance his dreams. Morose as he habitually was, he still never allowed himself to see the reality that his self-sustaining daydream would almost certainly never be anything more than that.

Il Duce didn't even acknowledge the artist's departure, turning instead to Ugo. "Give Mr. Smith five minutes. Then take Elizabeth to the room, and lock the door."

The eldest brother nodded and replied, "Duilio can help me. Better not let Luigino get too near her, boss."

Again, Leonardo laughed. "Oh dear, you're still bearing a grudge are you, young fellow? Well, I suppose she has damaged your pride. And other bits too, eh?"

Luigino glowered, but wasn't foolish enough to react further to his employer's amusement. Or his brothers'. He could be patient. For a little while.

Once more, the host turned to his reluctant guest. "Don't worry about young Lui. His temper will cool. As will yours. My dear girl, I think a period of contemplation in a quiet room will be good for you. As I said, you have no other option. Take this time to come to terms with that. Accepting your fate can make it so much easier to bear. Enjoy even. I mean, how many Australian girls get to live in a palace?"

If Elizabeth could have spat through her gag, she would have. As it was, the emotion on her face was clear. Her captor, though, was utterly unmoved.

"Shall you join us for dinner? Or will I have it sent up to your room? I insist on a high standard of food here, and our cook does deliver that. I trust you enjoyed lunch. The *Casa di Cozze* isn't the best dining establishment I have an interest in, but it's reliable."

Suddenly the Australian grasped what had happened. For a moment, she cursed their carelessness in choosing to eat in one of Delocchio's businesses. But almost immediately she thought better of any recriminations. They could hardly have known. His name wasn't displayed anywhere. Leonardo's reputation in Venice was as expansive as his appetites, but he kept the details of his multifarious interests well hidden.

"Farewell for now, my dear. Rest. Try to calm yourself. 'Resistance is futile', as I recall being said in an old TV series. Though of course, I'm no doctor."

He laughed at his own little joke, even as he waved a hand to order Ugo to his task.

The older brother grabbed Elizabeth under her arms and lifted. He tilted his chin at Duilio, who promptly seized her bound ankles. They hoisted her like a sack of produce. She didn't struggle. There was clearly no point. Better to wait, and think. She saw Luigino standing back. Could his temper be somehow exploited? As she was carried, she tried to take stock of her surroundings.

The main room was substantial. And judging by the doors she passed, open or otherwise, there were plenty of other rooms, although not all of the same size. She was carried up tiled stairs, multiple flights of them. They'd gone up two floors, and it seemed that there was at least one more above. Artwork hung on the walls, but there was no theme or consistency to it. Abstracts, landscapes and portraits, oils, watercolours and charcoal, not arranged in any evident order. A gallery without a curator. A collection without rhyme or reason.

Then she was dumped on a bed. Little more than an elevated palette. Septimus Smith didn't require luxury, barely even comfort. He slept only because his body sometimes insisted on it. He'd have preferred to work 24/7, but did at least recognize the necessity for sustenance and rest, distracting as they were.

The Culatellos said nothing. Ugo wiped his hands theatrically.

Duilio pulled his phone from a pocket and took a quick photograph of the captive, lying awkwardly and embarrassingly dishevelled across the thin mattress like a good-sized, recently-landed fish. He grinned and showed the image to his brother, who didn't react.

It was only after they'd left the room and locked the door that Ugo quietly said to his brother, "Better not let Il Duce see that on your phone, hey."

The photographer waved a casual hand, but heeded the older man's advice. Their employer could be mercurial in mood. What amused him one minute could provoke him into a towering rage soon after. While the boss was still fixated on this woman, better to keep the picture to himself.

Ugo considered rifling the bag that had still been over her shoulder, and which now lay on the bed. But no, that could wait. While she held Il Duce's favour it would be better not to provoke her. The situation would soon change, he was sure. He led his brother out, securing the door behind them, and stomped back downstairs.

Lying still, Elizabeth listened to the brothers' heavy footsteps fade. Slowly she wriggled around and began to look around the room. It was a good size. Currently illuminated by daylight from a window on the wall opposite her. Curtained and, yes, of course, barred.

The bed and accompanying table occupied a small proportion of the floorspace. Near them, a small wardrobe and an umbrella stand which held an assortment of canes and walking sticks. Funny, she hadn't noticed the man Smith limping.

Not much in the way of personal effects, she noticed. Most of the room was given over to painting. There were several easels. Two bare, one holding a canvas that had a pencil draft scratched across it, and another holding a partially-completed 'still life' in oils that looked vaguely familiar. At the far side of the room, another easel holding what was evidently a large picture, completely hidden by a heavy canvas draped over it. And amongst the easels and against the walls, an assortment of small tables, laden with canvas, paints, brushes and similar paraphernalia of the artist's work.

Curiously, this one room had no artwork on its walls.

By now, Elizabeth had her breathing back under control. She certainly wasn't resigned to her fate, as Leonardo had blithely suggested she aspire to be, but she could think clearly. The ropes holding her hands and feet weren't going to co-operatively unravel or snap. She could move enough to reach the annoying gag, and with some difficulty remove it.

Reaching the rope around her ankles was at least possible, if somewhat uncomfortable. Doing anything about that rope was, however, beyond her. The knots tied by the fisherman were complex and tight, and positioned so as to resist a decent grip anyway.

Still, being rid of the gag (which now circled her neck like a grubby cravat) meant easier breathing. John B. had passed on some of the things he'd learned from his Hawaiian friend Harlan: shamanic techniques for calmness and clarity. She was going to need that sort of self-discipline to survive, she realized.

Her mind went back to the little island of Tepatamwa, off the coast of Maine. There she'd been held captive by a group of pirates, modern-day rogues who'd modelled their activities on buccaneer legends. Their leader had turned out to be a delusional man with an underlying sense of honour. His brother was a greedy psychopath. What to make of her current captor? He was a different individual again.

An egotist, obviously. Egomaniac, possibly. Acquisitive, which was not quite the same as greedy. Not to be trusted, that was for sure. His 'charm' was transparently false, although it seemed there were plenty of people in Venice who had fallen for it. She thought that, as discussed earlier with John B., it was only when you were in close proximity to Il Duce that you spotted his insincerity. And the Silver Duke was loath to let people get that close.

That prompted a new train of thought. What about the other residents of this 'palace'? How close were they to Delocchio? As close as the big man assumed? There was no chance of her forging any sort of alliance with any of the Culatello brothers. She'd probably feel safer cosying up to Il Duce.

The usual resident of this room might be a possibility. There was little indication of Smith's personality evident in her surroundings. As though he didn't have one. But although he hadn't actually stood up to the fat man's orders, there were at least signs of discontent. Could she insert any sort of wedge between them, and somehow turn it to her advantage?

And then there was the cook who'd been mentioned. There'd been a sense of that individual being taken for granted. Perhaps there was some simmering resentment there that could be exploited, if she could get to meet her.

What about that red-haired woman who'd been present at the Musee Barche? Where did she fit in the scheme of things? Elizabeth had no way of knowing that the redhead was the cook she'd just been contemplating. Why would a cook be at the museum? She lay there wondering if perhaps the woman was a secretary, or maybe even a lover. Thrown over for the fat man's new object of desire? If she was still around, Elizabeth would try to convince her of the truth – that there was absolutely no reciprocal desire. A possible ally, some support for whatever effort to escape she might devise.

The brunette had no doubt that even as she lay there, somewhere in Venice her beau would be doing his damnedest to find her and free her. She had faith in him. The man, even more so than the magic she'd come to believe in (even if she didn't understand it). But she wasn't going to lie there just waiting and hoping. That wasn't in her nature.

Two approaches to be taken. One was to plan. Use her imagination, work out a course of action, then look for the opportunity to make it happen. Which led neatly to the second option: stay alert, and seize any moment that presented itself, whether it suited her plan or not.

Nothing useful in her bag, dammit, even if she could get into it effectively. Just her purse and a couple of tissues. For a moment she recalled a small hairspray she'd once repurposed as a flamethrower. But now, there wasn't even a comb she might find a way to use as a weapon. When she got out of this mess, she'd have to think about that.

Imagination, intuition, initiative. They'd be what she needed. A wave of tiredness washed over her. The adrenalin that had been pumping relentlessly since the moment she'd felt herself being seized, finally abated as she lay on the thin mattress. Imagination, intuition, initiative. And a shaggy-haired white knight in a purple t-shirt who would brave any obstacle for her.

John B. Stewart's face swam behind her eyelids as she slipped into an exhausted sleep.

.ooo.

18

SIR GALAHAD

John B. Stewart had a long history of disenchantment with police officers across the globe. He wasn't really surprised at the lack of help from the two uniformed men he'd encountered. That was consistent with his experiences, and those of Q and other friends, in the USA, Europe, and back in Australia. Indeed, some of his experiences with police in Australia had been considerably worse than unhelpful.

'Expect nothing, and never be disappointed', he'd heard. At best, that was his feeling about officers of the law. Oh, he'd met a few decent individuals, but he felt that they were the exceptions who proved the rule. Policemen were like politicians, he thought cynically: anyone who wanted to be one should be automatically disqualified from the job.

Elizabeth hadn't agreed, even after some less than positive experiences of her own. She still respected the job, just not some of the individuals in it.

Perhaps it had become self-fulfilling prophecy, he mused. Working in some way like his magic, getting what he expected rather than wished for? An unhappy thought.

To be fair, the *polizia* had been helpful, even if it was inadvertent.

Oh sure, it *might* be a coincidence that the restaurant where Q had disappeared was owned by a man they'd already come to deeply distrust, who'd already made a lecherous interest in Elizabeth clear, and whose thuggish henchmen had already attacked them. But coincidence had become so much the touchstone of Stewart's existence that he didn't believe that for a moment.

He turned the Wookie-decorated key in the door of the apartment. Upon entering, he carefully laid the masks on the spare bed, then prepared a coffee for himself. He forced himself to be still and to concentrate.

Leonardo Delocchio was a prominent man in Venice. He surely couldn't be hard to find. But even assuming that was true, what then? He could hardly burst in, shouting demands for the return of the woman he loved. Or could he? Maybe not quite so dramatic, but there was no reason not to confront the big man.

Okay, he'd get no support from the authorities, that seemed clear. And yes, Delocchio would almost certainly be protected by his three swarthy thugs, plus who knew who or what else. But on the other side of that ledger, it seemed safe to assume that it was rarely, if ever, that anyone stood up to Il Duce, and the sheer audacity of such a move might work in his favour. He may just have the upper hand from the outset in a confrontation with someone not used to defiance.

Ha! The fat man would already be learning about defiance if he really had made a prisoner of Q! The wizard frowned. Just so long as his beloved's wilfulness didn't anger him too much too soon. He couldn't be sure of what Delocchio was truly capable of, but the little he knew didn't auger well.

The coffee soon finished, John B. had already determined his next move. Finding Leonardo Delocchio. And the first person to ask was right next door. He knew Giancarlo had worked closely with Il Duce, and knew that despite the thin veneer of professional courtesy, the grey maestro disliked his erstwhile employer. Yesterday's dramatic interaction with the brutal brothers had added a lot of heat to that feeling. He'd seen it in the older man's eyes.

As he approached the violin-maker's shopfront, the wizard could hear Toscanini's distinctive voice already raised in greeting. No need for a doorbell! And yes, in response to the cat's noise, Nicola had the door open before Stewart could raise a hand to knock.

"Jonbi!" she said delightedly, and threw her arms around him in her usual enthusiastic embrace.

Almost immediately, though, she released him. There was a tension in his body that she neither recognized nor liked. "What is wrong?"

"Elizabeth's missing," was the short reply.

"Lizbetta...? Oh! What...?"

"Is Giancarlo home, contessa? I could do with his help."

"Si, of course. You will have my help too. But I will fetch him."

The girl turned and scampered upstairs. Her mentor was rummaging for something in a storeroom and had made it plain that there was only space for one to work in amongst the jumble. John B. sat cross-legged on one of the big floor cushions, and stroked the head of the black cat who'd climbed onto his lap.

Nicola returned at a run, and dropped to her knees beside the cushion. Her small hands gripped one sleeve of the purple t-shirt, fear written on her face. She'd read her visitor's mood all too well. Giancarlo appeared soon after, not quite at a run, but moving faster than the Australians had ever seen.

The musician stood before the wizard, wearing a look of great concern.

"Tell me," he said.

John B.'s voice was calm, but the tension was unmistakable as he narrated the events surrounding Elizabeth's disappearance.

"It feels crazy. Straight out of Hollywood. But they're the facts. And based on them, I can only come up with one conclusion. Unless there's someone or something else at play here, that I don't know about," he concluded.

This last comment was an admission that, in the last little while, a number of bizarre and dangerous circumstances had impinged on his life, and on Elizabeth's. It was possible that there was some explanation for the mystery that had nothing to do with Il Duce Grosso, he conceded.

"I don't think so," said Giancarlo, slowly. "I think that, as you say, the coincidence of his owning that restaurant is too big to ignore."

"Just like the fat pig himself," added Nicola.

"It may not be the smartest strategy in the world, but I want to confront him," said Stewart. "Watch his face as I ask questions. Listen to his answers."

"And then?" asked the maestro.

"I have no idea. Making plans isn't my long suit. I tend to make things up as I go along. I've a way of making things work out."

"Yes. Yes, you do." Giancarlo's tone was conspiratorial, hinting at shared knowledge and experience which Nicola didn't catch, and John B. was too distracted to properly notice.

"But first and foremost, I need to know where to look."

"Do you want company? Moral support, or back-up? Such help as we can offer..."

"Would be welcome, but I think, not yet. You have a show to put on tonight, anyway – I'm sorry, mate, but it looks like I'll have to miss that. Let me scope things out first. See how Delocchio reacts. What I need now is an address, and directions, please."

The offer was made to delay their preparations for the recital, and lead John B. to his destination, but he declined. He wasn't sure that his friends, especially Nicola, could contain themselves enough to not go in with him. He wanted to face Leonardo on his own. He was worried enough about Elizabeth, and didn't want the added stress of anyone else putting themselves potentially in harm's way.

Giancarlo knew the Palazzo Grossi well, and explained the best ways to get there by land or water. The canals would be quicker, but today of all days, the chances of finding a convenient boat were much slimmer than usual.

"I'll go on foot," John B. declared. "Gives me more time to... not plan, exactly, but at least run through a few scenarios in my head. Consider some options."

The grey man looked worried, and laid a hand on Stewart's shoulder. Reflecting that concern, Nicola hugged 'Jonbi' tightly.

"You call us if you need us," the girl said. It wasn't a request.

"Better give me a number, then, hey? And yes, as soon as I know something, I'll be in touch. It may take a couple of hours, mind you. If you haven't heard from me in, say, three hours, then you can start to worry."

"Too late, my friend, we're worried already. But three hours, yes. After that, we'll... ah... well, we'll think of something."

There was no doubting Giancarlo's sincerity, but the wizard wondered fleetingly what this odd couple *could* do if he was unable to contact them. Well, the trick was to not let that situation arise, wasn't it? He grasped the maestro's hand as reassuringly as possible. The cat got one final encouraging scratch of the head.

The wizard turned and held Nicola's shoulders firmly and looked into her eyes. "Thank you for your care and your concern, darling girl, but I want you to concentrate on your performance tonight. I will be fine, so will Elizabeth. This is an important event for you, and I want you to focus. Lose yourself in the music. We'll be with you in spirit, and we *will* see you in person as soon as we can afterwards – I promise, contessa. Be brilliant!"

There was a slow nod. "Si, Jonbi. I will be brilliant. For you, for Lizbetta, and for my Giancarlo. I will trust you, and we will see you – both – tomorrow. And I will tell you how brilliant I have been, si?"

"Damned right you will!"

The embrace they shared was passionate, but powerful, not romantic in any way. They were sharing energy with each other, consciously or otherwise, and LaGrigio's eyes twinkled approvingly as he watched.

After storing the appropriate number in his phone, John B. went back out to the Via Garibaldi. He walked in long, purposeful strides. As he'd said, while he walked he imagined different scenarios. Some involved negotiation, some involved violent confrontation with Delocchio and/or his henchmen, some involved Il Duce calling the local *polizia* for support.

Not one included the possibility that he was wrong, and that Leonardo had nothing to do with his beloved's disappearance. And he refused to allow himself any that envisaged already being too late. There would be a rescue. Only the detail was to be worked out, and that would happen as required.

.ooo.

19

IN THE HALL OF THE SILVER DUKE II

The Carnevale crowds impeded John B.'s progress like the Red Sea impeded Moses. Maybe it was an aura of steely determination or barely controlled anger, but no-one amongst the still milling throng of sight-seers got in the wizard's way. Instinctively, people stepped aside, not even aware that they were doing so.

All of which meant that Stewart made it to the Ghetto district in good time, considering it lay at the opposite side of Venice to the Giardini area.

Had he been in a 'tourist' frame of mind himself, John B. might have admired some of the architecture and history on display around him. There was evidence of the Moorish influence in Venice's past, and of the Arab merchants who'd been based in the area, alongside the otherwise insular Jewish community. He'd already passed the Ca' d'Oro, arguably the city's most splendid museum, which he and Q had visited on one of their first days there. It was adorned with gold. Had its proximity influenced Delocchio's passion for silver? The question flitted across Stewart's mind like a finch in a field.

As he went, he removed the strapping from his hand, and stuffed the bandage in a bin. No sense in showing any evidence of a weak point, and besides, it really did feel better already. Having made his way through a phalanx of tenements of varying degrees of preservation, John B. stood before the large building that was his target. Rising four storeys up from the street, it was surprisingly unspectacular. The façade was clean and tidy, painted in a neutral shade of pale blue. The windows on each floor were barred, a sensible precaution on the lower levels, but hinting at a certain paranoia in the upper reaches. Stewart didn't think Venice was noted for its cat burglars. Then again, he was aware that Delocchio hoarded things of value, so perhaps the security was understandable.

With a shrug, he walked up to the heavy wooden door. There was no bell, or knocker. A subtle indication that the owner didn't encourage visitors. Too bad. The timber was thick enough that a rap with the knuckles was unlikely to be heard inside, so the wizard picked up a substantial loose cobblestone and used that to pound on the portal.

There was no response to his first knocking, so he started a steady regular rhythm. In his head, he was beating out the underpinning of an old blues standard, a metronomic timing he could sustain indefinitely. He was confident that anyone indoors would get sick of it before he did.

Correct. It was Sceptred Smith who was once again despatched to see to the door. The 'confounded knocking' happened to be right at mealtime, and Smith was the only one there who wasn't engrossed in food. Well, neither was Elizabeth, by choice, but she was still tied and locked in an upstairs room at the back of the Palazzo, and couldn't hear the stone-on-wood anyway.

Having drawn back the bolts, the Englishman opened the door just enough to peer out. He raised unimpressed eyebrows at the scruffy figure confronting him.

"Yes? What?"

"G'day. I'm looking for Leonardo Delocchio."

"He's busy. Go away."

The artist went to close the door, but Stewart had already dropped the cobblestone into the gap, and was holding it there with his foot. The rock was large enough to prevent the heavy door from crushing his toes.

"We met when the Signore was examining a collection of silver that I've got an interest in."

"Oh." The magic word, silver. "Wait here."

"I'll wait in there. I don't do business out in the street." John B.'s reply was the sort of terse, professional thing that Smith expected from some of the people his employer did business with, so he accepted it.

"Very well. Come in. Wait in the foyer."

With a curt nod, Stewart did as he was instructed. It was a start. The Englishman walked away with an exaggerated hobble. The wizard waited, gleaning what little he could from the small anteroom.

One narrow window, barred horizontally as well as vertically. Tiled floor – old and good quality, if he was any judge. Two pieces of art, on opposite walls. Beautifully framed, but they were rough pencil sketches of female nudes that looked like they were the work of a hormonally inflamed teenaged boy who had been copying and embellishing his fantasy figures from a comic book.

Meanwhile, Smith had gone to the dining room. The new arrival was an Australian, judging by the voice, he explained. Something about some silver that Il Duce had been looking at?

"I know who that will be. Not an unexpected visitor, I suppose, although I am surprised he found his way to me quite so quickly," mused Delocchio.

Ugo rolled his shoulders. "You want us to get rid of him?"

"Oh, I don't think that'll be necessary. It's not like he can do anything anyway. He knows nothing, I'm sure, and I'm happy to contribute to his helpless ignorance. You and your brothers, keep your tempers in check until I tell you otherwise. Bring our guest to me, Sceptred. I'll have a little fun."

Grumbling under his breath, the artist limped back to the foyer. The intended object of Delocchio's amusement was leaning casually against a wall, taking in his surroundings with a discreetly analytical eye.

That eye appraised the man who'd reluctantly admitted him. Stovepipe jeans and a long-sleeved shirt, black and white stripes, all emphasising his tall spare frame. Dark hair and dark eyes, and an expression of habitual gloom.

"You're not the butler?" Stewart asked mischievously.

"No." Smith had plenty of practice at not rising to Leonardo's baits, but he allowed himself the mutter, "Just treated like one."

That won him a sympathetic grunt just before they entered the dining room.

"Ah! Mr... Stewart, isn't it? Welcome to my humble little abode! You find us in the midst of a light meal, I'm afraid, but do please pull up a chair."

"Thanks."

John B. parked himself on a spare seat against a wall. Far enough away from the table to easily watch every diner. He'd see anyone coming if they made a hostile move, although admittedly that didn't look immediately likely. Everyone was giving full attention to eating.

Il Duce Grosso was, of course, at the head of the table. None of his chair was visible as he lolled back, having his food served directly to his mouth by the red-haired woman sitting beside him. Under orders from their boss, the Culatello brothers concentrated on their meal, although three pairs of eyes did occasionally flash venomous glances toward the new arrival.

Septimus Smith had resumed his place at the table, and picked at his pasta. It was good, and he'd have said so if asked, but the little appetite he'd had was diminished by feeling treated like a servant. He was an employee, yes, but an artist, not a blasted doorman.

Speaking in the brief moment between mouthfuls of *farfalle all'a-matriciana*, Leonardo addressed his visitor. "I understand you're here about some silver?"

"No. I simply explained how we'd met. I'm interested in something of much greater value," replied Stewart evenly.

Ugo belched loudly. The oldest brother was messily stuffing his face from a mound of ricotta that John B. couldn't have held in two hands.

Barely suppressing a giggle, Leonardo managed to say, "Please excuse Ugo. He's not very sophisticated."

As if to emphasise the difference in class, Il Duce turned towards his server, mouth open like a baby bird greeting its parent. The redhead neatly spoon fed the art dealer from the saucy pasta in his bowl. Each spoonful was only modest, but the process was steady and constant, and the dish was rapidly being emptied. Watching the farfalle being rhythmically deposited in his mouth, Stewart was reminded of a stoker feeding coal into a hungry furnace.

"Value is such a subjective thing, isn't it?" asked Delocchio between spoons. "I greatly value my Squila here. An excellent cook and reliable server. She's a good companion. Not everyone regards her as such, however I do."

"*Grazie, ciccino mio,*" the woman said pleasantly.

John B. blinked momentarily at the description of her 'little fleshy thing'. Only in his late 30s, Leonardo Delocchio had a physique that, if he continued his current gustatory form, would eventually require its own area code.

Recovering himself, the wizard continued, "Speaking of food, I was at a restaurant today that I understand you have something to do with."

The big man waved a hand airily and replied through a mouthful of farfalle, "There are many restaurants in Venice that I routinely visit. And my investments are many and varied. I no longer pay a lot of attention to them. I have more important matters on my mind."

"Really? Such as?"

Delocchio smiled as Pasqualina carefully wiped a dribble of sauce from his chins. "You must have noticed that it's Carnevale time, Mr. Stewart. My favourite time of the year, when Venice devotes itself to amusements and the joys of the palate. A tradition, like the old Saturnalia, of breaking rules. Or at least, of ignoring the rules that supposedly 'order' society. I am to be the featured performer at the climax of this year's Carnivale, Mr. Stewart. This requires some preparation, and I will be memorable."

"If you do say so yourself."

"I most assuredly do, Mr. Stewart. I expect others will also say it of me, but it will be deserved praise. My new work will pay homage to the dark parts of Venetian history which lurk behind the beautiful masks, costumes, and facades. Where distinctions between social classes break down, and the disguise is more important than the identity. All in my own little way, of course, but it will be my joyous anarchy."

Nobody noticed the look on Pasqualina's face as Il Duce spoke. As far as she knew, her expression hadn't altered, but a shrewd observer would have seen a flash of wild excitement in her eyes. Not festive jollity, but something much darker. Malevolent. Alas, no such shrewd observer was watching her.

John B. was watching the Silver Duke instead, probing for a reaction as he asked, "So do rules not apply to anyone, or is it only to you? You're above them, or is it below?"

The big man's smile slid off his face like bacon fat off Teflon. "I have been diagnosed with Asperger's Syndrome, Mr. Stewart. I can't be expected to conform with the pettiness that dictates other people's lives. I am simply not able to function under the rules of polite society – it's the price of my artistic genius – it's not my fault, and I'll accept no criticism for it. My masterpiece for the Carnevale is a way of giving something to the society that I'm not able to engage with."

Stewart didn't know a lot about Asperger's, but he was pretty confident that many, if not most people with it, didn't use it as an excuse for anti-social bastardry. This one did though, his ego excusing his lack of conscience, arrogantly putting himself above 'right' and 'wrong'.

The wizard had learned enough. He may not understand this man, but he had a good idea of what he was capable of.

"What have you done with Elizabeth?"

"I've no idea what you're talking about." Delocchio lied easily. It was more than a habit, it was the foundation of his world.

"Bull."

The two younger brothers started to rise (Ugo was still eating) but Leonardo stilled them with a gesture. John B. expected Delocchio to lean forward threateningly - that seemed to be the appropriate body language. Then he realised that Il Duce couldn't. The big man's stomach had swollen so large that the haughty, backwards leaning posture was pretty much his only option when sitting. The anger and threat were in his voice, though.

"You no longer amuse me. Get out of my house."

"Not without the woman I love."

"I've told you – I have no idea what you're talking about. If you want to walk out with a woman, here. Walk with this one. Squila, escort this man out of my Palazzo. Ugo – take your face out of the food for a moment – you and your brothers, make sure he leaves."

"And after?" asked Luigino with sadistic anticipation.

"I just want him out. Then come back here."

None of Leonardo's coterie seemed happy at his peremptory behaviour. Smith was still smarting at being treated as the doorman. Ugo just wanted to finish eating, and his brothers rankled at the implication that they weren't to pursue their violent vendetta. And while Pasqualina had said nothing in response to Il Duce's dismissive comment, the look in her eyes showed that a raw nerve had been poked.

Nonetheless, the redhead got up from her chair, laying down the spoon she'd been using with exaggerated good grace. She moved to stand beside Stewart, her hands behind her back.

"It would be best for everyone if you leave," she said. "For *everyone*."

John B. nodded slowly. "Alright," he replied to her, then turning to his less-than-genial host, continued, "Whatever chicanery it is you've got going, I wish that it'll be a washout."

The fat art dealer snorted derision. "If wishes were horses, every poor man would own a stable. Get out."

Accepting the light touch of Pasqualina on his arm, John B. walked back to the door. The three brothers stayed a pace or two behind, barely restrained aggression quivering in the air around them. At the portal, the redhead turned to face the Culatello family.

"I'll make sure he doesn't loiter. Go back inside. There's food left," she said.

Ugo, at least, shrugged. He nudged both of his siblings. They'd done as they'd been told. There would probably be other opportunities later, when their quarry didn't see them coming, further from home, and when there wasn't still part of a meal on the table. Reluctantly, the younger pair followed his lead and went back into the Palazzo.

Fingertips still lightly resting on the Australian's arm, the cook guided a path between old tenements.

"He lies, of course," she said casually.

"I thought as much."

"He does so out of habit, I sometimes think. It is his little way. Another of them."

"He has a number of these foibles, does he?"

"Foibles?" Although her English was good, this word was strange to her.

"Quirks. Bad habits."

"Oh. Yes. It is his medical condition, he says."

"I know a number of people who live somewhere along the autism spectrum, but manage to find ways to cope with the world. They function without routinely treating people like a child playing with toys." He pictured Christos, a study in concentration over his guitar, and probably much the same over the ledgers in his office.

Pasqualina shrugged. "His attention span is not great. Or perhaps I should say, even though he is an avid collector, he tires of things quickly and soon is seeking new things."

"What sort of things? What does he collect?"

"Silver, as you know. Art. Women, if the mood strikes him."

"And what happens when he loses enthusiasm for his new toys?"

"Once he has something he wants, he will not give up possession to anyone else, even when his own interest has waned. I have seen it before. Such things are simply put away."

"Even the women he collects?" Stewart's voice was flat, a dangerous sign, if one knew him. "Put away, how?"

"There is a lot of water around Venice. It is not just the secrets of antiquity that lie at the bottom of the canals."

"You've survived."

"I know how to be submissive, but also how to be interesting enough when I have to be. I have skills in many areas."

John B. suspected that Pasqualina had not arrived at the Palazzo di Grossi as cook.

"And you know where the bodies are," observed the wizard.

She shrugged. "That would not prevent me from joining them." Her voice took on a note of warning as they approached one of the narrow waterways that crisscrossed the Ghetto. "The authorities will hear no evil of Il Duce. He is a pillar of the community."

"No bloody wonder the city's sinking into the mud, then."

As Pasqualina tossed her had back haughtily, a small pendant popped out from the neckline of her red shirt. The movement caught John B.'s eye, and instinct made him peer at it, trying not to do so obviously.

Evidently hand-made, it was cut in the shape of a hexagon. A concentric hexagon was etched inside that, and within that shape were engraved seven weird symbols that might almost have been a child's attempts at Arabic text. It wasn't pleasing to the eye, but what was worse was that he recognized it.

The last time that Stewart had seen this symbol it had been on a computer screen in a secret underground base in South Australia. It had been a key element in a plan to unleash an ancient demon-lord and his army. Overcoming that insane scheme had been the first real test of John B. Stewart's new magical power.

The memory seared through his mind in an instant, but he determinedly didn't let it show in his reactions. Or if he did, Pasqualina didn't notice.

She looked across the narrow strip of water they'd come to, and said, seemingly as much to herself as to Stewart, "Leonardo is like a child in many ways. Spoilt, yes. But he is a child with influence. Power. And he knows it, which makes him dangerous. Whatever you decide to do, Signore Stewart, I suggest you do it carefully."

"And you?"

"I will be of no help to you."

"You'll stay loyal to him?" the wizard asked in some surprise.

She snapped a sudden angry response at him. "My loyalty is to... is to myself." Just as suddenly her voice softened. "For all his – what was the word – foibles – I am best served by remaining near to Leonardo. For now, at least."

"Tell me this, at least. Is Elizabeth still alive? And in that house somewhere?"

A half smile played on the redhead's face. "When last I saw her, yes, in an upstairs room at the back of the Palazzo. I will not pass on your greetings if I see her, signore. I would not like to raise false hopes. Goodbye, Signore Stewart."

With a final inclination of her head toward the canal, as if emphasising 'where the bodies were', Pasqualina walked away, brisk strides taking her back toward the Palazzo.

Before losing himself in deep thought, John B. made a quick phone call to Giancarlo. It wasn't quite a reassuring call, but at least the wizard was alive. Alive, and planning.

Meanwhile, Leonardo had made his way to the room where Elizabeth was being kept. He'd had no objection to her managing to remove her gag. Indeed, he'd come for "a little chat". His ample girth filled the doorframe but he didn't enter. He made casual small talk about his collection of silver, particularly the *grossi*.

It seemed as though he presumed these were a point of common interest, from which they might build a conversation. Certainly, he'd intended to impress her. It didn't work. Neither did his offer to have a serving of the "excellent meal" brought to her.

"Ah well, your loss," he said casually. "You can have tonight to yourself, my dear. I'm a little full, anyway," he announced, unconsciously rubbing his belly.

"A little?!"

He ignored the sarcasm. "But tomorrow, my dinner will be digested and I'll be hungry again. And I think I'll be hungry for you."

He lumbered away, closing and locking the door behind him.

Elizabeth was left alone to fume, and try to push from her imagination the forced affections of Il Duce Grosso.

Back out in the Ghetto, John B. was walking slowly and thoughtfully along the fondamenta beside the little riello where Pasqualina had left him. Suddenly his reverie was interrupted by a stentorian voice calling a greeting.

Mario Vespucci's gondola glided alongside him, and pulled in against the path. John B. clambered into the craft. After sharing an embrace, they talked. Mario discreetly moved them out into open water, ensuring that they couldn't be overheard, accidentally or otherwise.

The gondolier was appropriately outraged. His sympathetic advice was action, but considered action. Nothing rash, or unplanned. Perhaps a raid, under cover of darkness. The windows may be barred, but that didn't make the old building impregnable. Walls could be scaled, bars removed with some effort.

"One problem, I don't travel with a lot of tools and ropes," John B. pointed out.

"Leave such concerns to me, my friend!"

They agreed to meet at the Giardini pier at three in the morning. They'd arrive and leave the Palazzo di Grossi silently travelling by water. Mario could navigate to a spot even closer than where he'd found the Australian.

As the gondola pulled up to Giardini, Mario rubbed a powerful fist into the palm of the other hand as he said, "I prefer not to fight, but if that is what's required I won't be found wanting. Side by side, again, *si*?"

"Absolutely. I just wish it won't come to that. All I want is for Elizabeth to be out of there, safely."

They shook hands, and the wizard clambered onto the pier.

"It will be like old times again," said Mario as he pushed the boat off.

"Yeah," agreed John B., thinking of the fracas outside the Museo dell' Accademia.

"Venice, too, has its old ghosts. But we should not need their aid for this!"

The voice was faint. The gondola was speeding out along the Grand Canal before Stewart could assemble a coherent question. A vivid image of a cliff in Hawaii leapt into the wizard's memory. It lingered as the wizard made his way down the Via Garibaldi, but was soon displaced by thoughts of the task ahead. And of Q.

Home, he forced himself to eat. A cold Danish and a dark beer. Then tried to rest for a few hours. Part sleep, part meditation. Part planning. A wall to scale. Windows to be surreptitiously looked through. Bars to get past. Doubtless there'd be some sort of security to be overcome.

Could the redhaired woman's word be trusted? Was it a trap? Even if she'd been being honest, anything might have happened subsequently. Elizabeth may have been moved. Or worse.

Fleetingly he thought of Giancarlo and his protégé, performing in splendour that neither seemed an appropriate fit for, and wished out loud for them to be as successful as they wanted. He suspected that the grey man had very carefully moderated ambitions for his young student just as yet, and saw dangers in too much profile, too much success, too soon. As though he'd seen such a scenario play out before.

Intriguing as such musings were, his own and Q's situation crowded those thoughts out. Mulling over possibilities and contingencies occupied his mind during the times he wasn't able to sleep. Other questions about Mario Vespucci and the man he'd once known as Courtesy could also wait. His only priority right now was the woman he loved.

.ooo.

20

WAY OUT

In the room recently occupied by Septimus Smith, sleep eluded Elizabeth. She was tired, physically and emotionally, but too fired by the determination to get away from her repellent captor. She did her best to be calm and to meditate, but by the early hours of the morning restlessness overwhelmed her.

Tied wrist and ankle, Ugo's fisherman's knots defied her. She needed to move, though. Wriggling off the flimsy mattress, she managed to struggle to her feet. Balance was initially a problem for her, especially as the blood flow returned to her lower legs.

She wobbled for a bit, but stubbornly stayed upright. As soon as she felt a little more stable, she began to hop awkwardly about the room. 'I'm glad I used to pogo dance when I was younger,' she mused wryly as she explored her surroundings in hope of inspiration. Enough moonlight came through the window for her to navigate, if not clearly. And she'd had plenty of time for her eyes to adjust to the conditions.

Almost toppling at one point, her knee clipped one of Smith's several small tables, knocking it over. A long wooden box lost its lid as it hit the floor, and a selection of brushes fell out. But not just brushes – there was also a small palette knife, its metal glinting briefly in the lunar glow as it fell.

Squatting, she managed to pick it up, then bounced back to the bed, a little more optimism in her heart. The angle was tricky, but she went to work on the binding on her ankles. The blade was duller than a butter knife, but Elizabeth was persistent. What better use of her time did she have? Even with her wrists tied she gradually managed to make progress on cutting through the rope.

What she didn't notice was that also on the upset table had been a jar of brushes soaking in spirit. They'd been there for quite a while, though. Smith was fussy about whatever piece he was working on at any particular time, but once that was done and he was ready to move on to the next, his clean-up process was regularly forgotten until brushes and leftover paint were unsalvageable. Such as in this instance. The combination of spirit, dust, varnish, and whatever had bound the bristles of some of the cheaper brushes together, had resolved into a thick gel.

It would be inaccurate to say it 'splashed' when the table fell. It looked more like a large animal had sneezed about half-a-cupful of unpleasant snot onto the cold wall. Elizabeth was oblivious to the small mess, being far more focussed on her efforts with the palette knife. But as she sat on the bed, patiently sawing at the thick rope, the goop slid down the wall, albeit at the speed of a lethargic snail.

But as glacial as it was, gravity was still doing its inexorable job. The sickly green-tinted gel slowly descended, straight into a power point.

There was a sudden flash, accompanying a brief sound like *fzzt*, and a plume of smoke wound out of the socket. At least a third of the electrical equipment around the Palazzo di Grossi suddenly ceased to function. Even more critically, the smoke activated the sprinkler system that Il Duce had insisted on having installed. Many of the buildings of the old Ghetto had a deserved reputation as firetraps, and Delocchio had investments he wanted to protect.

Now, though, he woke with terrible clarity to the realisation that some of those investments were threatened by his own security precaution! Rolling off his bed and getting to his feet with surprising agility, he threw on a heavy silver brocade gown, found a torch, and left his bedroom with all the speed he could muster. The Performance Room! He had to get to the Performance Room!

As he charged along the corridor like an angry elephant, he bellowed for Ugo. "Get to the basement! Turn the damned waterworks off!"

"But if there's a fire..." the oldest of the Culatelli started to ask, having just emerged into the corridor himself.

"Idiot! Do you see any flames? Or smell any smoke? Get to the basement I say! Pasqualina!" he roared, seeing her emerge from her own room. "Is this your doing? Something in the kitchen?"

"It shouldn't be! I've left nothing on the stove." She saw the likelihood of being blamed though, and knew enough to make herself scarce. "I'll go and make sure," she called over her shoulder as she ran in the direction of her domain.

Now Septimus Smith appeared in the hallway, wet hair plastered to his forehead and a look of blinking agitation on his face, suddenly illuminated by Leonardo's torch.

"Leonardo, I must get into my room! It's urgent!" he cried.

"Never mind that! I've got to get to my studio!"

Smith grabbed at his patron's sleeve. "That Pollock is in *my* studio! I've got a canvas over it, but if this water soaks through that, it'll be ruined. I'll never be able to reconstruct it in time for next Monday, as you demanded!"

Delocchio stopped his lumbering progress, the import of Smith's word's sinking in. He had a collector lined up who was going to pay a very high price for what he thought was a rare Jackson Pollock original. Just then, the youngest of the three brothers stumbled into the corridor, fumbling with the fly on his trousers.

"Wha...?" was all he had time to say before Leonardo spotted him.

"Luigino! Go with Smith to his room. Make sure my painting is secure, and make sure my woman doesn't go anywhere!"

It fleetingly crossed the big man's mind to wonder if the green-eyed wench had anything to do with this sudden pandemonium. But, how could she? She was tied up, in a locked room. And she was only a woman, anyway. Inconceivable!

Obediently, Luigino ran for the stairs up to the next level. Sceptred Smith loped close behind, giving no thought to his 'damaged' knee.

Duilio was the last to emerge, and was summarily despatched to the top storey to confirm that there was no fire up there. That seemed unlikely – those rooms were mostly used only for storage, except for what Leonardo called a "playroom". That was fitted out with a king-sized four-poster bed, a bedside cupboard containing "toys" of unusual and intimate nature, a grid of stout wooden bars securely fixed to one wall, and an incongruous small selection of gym equipment. Nothing to spontaneously combust there, certainly not when Il Duce wasn't indulging himself in the use (or abuse) of any of it.

The Silver Duke himself made it to his Performance Room, and headed straight to the mixing and recording desk. Damnit, yes! There was water seeping under the loose dust-cover. But it wasn't the equipment itself that mattered so much as the digital files. Equipment could be replaced quickly and easily. Not so all of the multiple backing tracks that he'd been preparing for the Carnevale closing event, the launch of his new masterpiece. Were they intact? Why were these damned sprinklers still going? What was that fool Ugo doing?

To be fair, Ugo was doing his best, hitting switches with agitated force. Even though he'd managed to hit a light switch, with the power out he was still fumbling in the dark. There were no sprinklers in the basement, so he couldn't even be sure if he *did* manage to turn off the waterworks. It was only when he barked his knee against a metal wheel the size of a dinner plate that he realised that there was a stop valve to cut the water supply.

He spun the wheel, then stopped with alarm. Was that the right direction? He could feel the vibration of water through the pipe under the valve. He was making it worse! He reversed his efforts, and was pleased to feel the vibration cease. He tugged at the wheel, making it as tight as possible. It would probably take a lever to loosen it again, such was the force of his agitation.

Now to restore some light. He felt around for the switches he'd so frantically dealt with. Forced himself to approach the task more calmly, and methodically started flicking them. One of them would eventually give him some light to see what he was doing.

While all of this was going on, Elizabeth had continued patiently sawing at the rope on her ankles. Added a soundtrack of curses at the unexpected shower, but didn't let the water distract her from the task at hand. Or foot. There! One rope cut! With difficulty, hampered by her wrists still being bound, she unwound the several loops around her ankles.

With a sigh of relief, she stood up beside the bed, bending and flexing her legs, together and each in turn, wincing as the blood flowed in stiff muscles and joints.

Then, over the hissing of the sprinklers, she heard a rattling sound. The door was being unlocked!

The rangy figure of Septimus Smith dashed into the room. He was making straight for the shrouded easel in the far corner, and showed no interest in the prisoner. She couldn't take the chance of that remaining the case for long, though.

An image from one of the football matches she'd watched with John B. leapt into her mind. Without hesitation she kicked the back of the forger's leg. She wore dress boots, not football boots, but the impact was quite enough. She'd chanced to connect with just where Smith's leg had been damaged in the accident, long ago. He'd been overstating it for years, but now a very genuine burst of pain shot up from his knee. With a cry, the artist collapsed.

As he fell, a flailing arm upset the umbrella stand in which he kept several of his walking sticks. The canes spilled out across the bedroom floor.

"Hey! You're not supposed to be loose! I fix that! Fix *you*!" came a snarl from the doorway behind her.

Realising the danger, Elizabeth instinctively ducked low to evade a swinging arm, and managed to grab one of the scattered canes. It was dark wood, old and satisfyingly heavy. Just for a moment, she was wielding a hockey stick again. She turned, light on her feet to dodge her clumsy, moonlit assailant.

That was the moment when, down in the basement, Ugo finally managed to stem the water flow. The sudden cessation of the sprinkler distracted Luigino far more than Elizabeth – he was focused on following orders and inflicting pain for his own satisfaction, whereas she was concentrating on her own freedom. A far more powerful motivation.

While the thug glanced upward at the ceiling, she swung the cane in an old familiar arc. Here was a 'deserving case' if ever she'd met one! There was a loud *crack* as she hit. Two, in fact, as the walking stick broke, and so did the shin.

Luigino screeched as he fell, landing heavily on the prone figure of Smith. Instinctively, the forger lashed out, his bony foot catching Culatello's already fractured leg.

Tempting as it was to land another blow, Elizabeth realized her time was better spent getting out of there. She grabbed her bag from the bed, and another walking stick to use as a weapon if required, and wished her wrists were free. That only seemed to work for John B., unfortunately.

What was in her favour, though, was an unimpeded route to the front door. Pasqualina had remained in the kitchen, checking her precious old books for water damage. Ugo was still in the basement, now trying to replace the fuse which had been blown to start all the pandemonium. Duilio was making his way down from the top floor, but with no sense of urgency now that the sprinklers had stopped. And Leonardo was totally absorbed in his music. Most of it was intact, but typically he was concerned only for the one track that wasn't.

When he discovered that one file was compromised, the air around him was blue with curses and obscenities. Some very un-Venetian curses and obscenities, if anyone had been near enough to be paying attention.

Seizing her opportunity, Elizabeth ran for the front door, stick at the ready to clatter anyone who got in her way. But nobody did. She propped the cane against the portal, then while again cursing the ropes that bound her wrists, she dragged three bolts open. No-one was going to have an easy time breaking in to Palazzo di Grossi! Getting out was bad enough, she thought as she emerged out into the street.

Now what? Now where? She had no idea where she was. Obviously still in Venice – she'd come to recognize the distinctive marine aroma. But it wasn't a small city. It was dark, and nothing looked familiar in the moonlight that made it down between the buildings.

Splashing! She heard splashing. There must be a canal nearby. Well, of course. There were canals everywhere in Venice. Still, a canal was less likely to be a dead end than many of these narrow streets and lanes, so she ran in the direction of the sound she'd so briefly heard.

Two figures stepped out from beside a battered old tenement block. Instinctively she swung her faux hockey stick at the nearer figure.

The man jumped over its dangerous arc, and threw his arms around her, preventing another swipe.

"Hey! I'm on your side, pretty lady!"

"J.B.!? Wh...?" The question, whatever it was to be, died on her lips as she buried her face in the dark purple cotton covering his shoulder.

Not crying. Definitely not crying. But great racking deep breaths of relief, and the release of pent-up tension.

"*Buongiorno, signorina*. It might be best if we weren't here, *si*?"

After almost colliding with her beloved, it was scarcely a surprise to find him in company with Mario Vespucci.

"Si," she gasped, and allowed herself to be led to the *rio* where Mario's gondola was moored.

The ropes and tools that the two men had carried were clearly not required, but the small collection included a sharp knife. John B. wasted no time in slicing away the bonds around her wrists. Tough as the rope was, it was still a far quicker operation than had been possible with a palette knife.

"Well, my love, I was on my way to attempt a rescue. But here you are – free, if inexplicably wet on a fine night. I'm clearly superfluous."

She threw her newly-released arms around him, softly saying, "Oh babe, you are never, ever, in any way, superfluous to me. Thank you for coming for me."

Mario smiled broadly as the two lovers kissed before and after getting into his boat. Whatever her story was, it could wait. The waterways were almost deserted at this hour. A gondola ride by moonlight was meant to be romantic, and – ah, yes. They'd worked that out. He whistled softly as he glided them right across Venice, towards what, for now, was home.

.ooo.

21

COUPLES

Venice, mid-morning. On opposite sides of the city: two men, two women. Each pair deep in conversation. Both planning, both conversations with a strong element of anger at their core.

In a bar in the Ghetto, Leonardo Delocchio fumed. He was affronted on multiple levels. The damage to some of the furniture and artworks in the Palazzo was annoying. Most things were replaceable, one way or another, but he disliked the prospective expenditure of money and effort.

Although there'd been a moment of some satisfaction when Sceptred Smith had limped up to tell him that the pseudo-Pollock painting was safe and would be ready for sale, that had evaporated when Luigino had hobbled in behind Smith. The damage to his underling was of no consequence, but the news that his most recent acquisition had made her escape was infuriating. He'd wanted her, and he hadn't had her yet. He'd been too nice, that was the problem. Not insistent enough.

Most aggravating of all, though, had been the realization of damage to one fragment of his masterpiece. It was three minutes of fairly basic acoustic guitar – little more than extended riff, played several times with different small variations. The intention was that it be 'looped' repeatedly as part of a background 'wash' of sound, over which he'd be performing his magnificent soaring keyboard solos.

Leonardo was obsessive about several things, and vain about many more, but his music was at the top of both lists. 'His' music encompassed anything he'd had any involvement in, however small. His presence overshadowed the contributions of any other writer, musician or producer, in his own mind and in any publicity that he promoted. But the Carnevale closing piece – there would *be* no others to deflect from his glory. Every note was his and his alone. But having to take the time to re-record something he'd already done, that was intolerable. He couldn't see it as an opportunity to refine or polish that particular fragment. One could not improve on perfection! It would have to be reproduced, that was all, and that was an imposition on his time that he begrudged.

As ever, Pasqualina was a patient ear, nodding when required, and making suitably sympathetic comments when the big man occasionally stopped for breath. The chaos of the night before had brought her no harm – her precious books were safe – only a measure of amusement which she carefully concealed.

Her 'den mother' role had seen her ensure that Luigino did actually go to a doctor early in the morning. Septimus Smith had accompanied the youngest brother, gloomily convinced that his own leg was irreparably damaged again. The Englishman's response to being told he had nothing more than a bruise, was to confirm in his mind the conviction that Italian medical practitioners were incompetent. But as far as the redhead was concerned, her responsibilities there were finished with.

She'd cleaned up the kitchen almost immediately. Ugo and Duilio had been set to the task of getting the rest of the Palazzo back in order, and she'd correct their clumsy efforts later. For now, her task was to indulgently minister to Il Duce Grosso. She was used to that.

She assured him that, by now, the brothers should have removed any remaining water from his Performance Room, and he could commence work on recreating the assuredly excellent guitar piece.

Pasqualina had her own plans for the closing of the Carnevale, and Il Duce's performance was integral to them, not that he knew nor would have cared.

Mollified by his companion's encouragement, and the half-dozen flaky pastries that had accompanied his coffee, Delocchio allowed himself to be assisted to his scooter. A few other customers were discreetly struck by the apparent ease with which the red-haired woman seemed to lift the outsized man from seat to feet. She didn't look powerfully built, but was obviously much stronger than she appeared.

There was a lot about Pasqualina which she didn't make obvious.

ACROSS TOWN, at another bar, this time on the Via Garibaldi, Q and JB were also enjoying coffee and pastries (although a lot less of them than Il Duce Grosso). Toscanini was curled contentedly on John B.'s lap, seemingly purring at the sound of Elizabeth's voice.

"I know it sounds crazy when I've just gotten out of the place, but there's a part of me that's really itching to get back into that damned house and do some sort of damage."

"You mean, beyond whatever the sprinklers did, and beyond bruising his ego by getting away?"

"Well, yes. I just have a really strong sense that something needs to be done about that man."

"Is that our job, sweetheart? I thought we agreed a while ago that we're not some odd Agatha Christie-type couple of crime busters."

"I know, babe, but this has become personal. Even if I'm safe for the moment, I don't like the idea of laying low, then skipping town with my tail between my legs, knowing he's so confident that he can get away with anything. Believing he's so special that consequences don't apply to him."

"Okay. I can wish that he learns about consequences, and that he cops some serious ones. We don't have to see the results."

"But I'd like to. I owe that fat grub."

"Well, yeah. I can see that. And I share the sentiment. As do a few other folks we know, I think. Maybe we should get together and toss some ideas around."

Elizabeth looked thoughtful. "Giancarlo and his musician friends, you mean?"

"And Mario the gondolier. There may be some others, too. I have a feeling that Delocchio and his bully boys have upset a few people around Venice. Maybe it just needs someone to harness all that enmity together and do something practical with it."

"They say you can only fool some of the people some of the time. Okay, babe, let's start by talking to Giancarlo. I want to hear all about how last night's grand ball went, too! I really wanted to go to that – just one more aggravation I owe that fat ball of slime. Tosca – would you care to take us to your lord and master?"

The cat opened his good eye, curious at the mention of his name. John B. laughed.

"Darling Q, I don't think Tosca regards anyone as lord and master! And conversely, I don't reckon Giancarlo sees himself as lord and master of anybody."

"Not even Nicola?"

"Least of all Nicola! Sweetheart, even if, and I say 'if' with some emphasis here, what you're still wondering is true, have you seen any evidence – even the slightest hint – that Nicola is anything but very happy with her life?"

"Well, no..."

"Exactly. I think, my love, that that young lady knows what she wants and is making her own choices."

"Oh, I'm sure you're right. It's probably my mother's influence at the back of my mind. I still have a tiny worry that he's got some sort of hold on her."

"Beyond affection and loyalty? Are you watching them? I think she's more likely to have a hold on him."

"Mm. And I bet I know what she's holding."

"Be nice. Let me finish this macchiato and we can go visiting."

John B. drained the last of his coffee, and was trying to gently dislodge the cat from his lap when his phone rang. Greatly surprised, he managed to wrestle the mobile from his jeans pocket despite Toscanini's inconvenience. He was even more surprised to see the identity of the caller.

"Scarlet! Wow – this is an unexpected pleasure! How are you?"

"Excellent, John, thank you. Better than excellent! I've got news to tell you."

"Cool! Oh, hey, listen – before you do, let me ask this while I remember. It's been bugging me and I'm sure you're the right person to ask..."

He described the pendant he'd briefly seen on Pasqualina, and where he believed he'd seen the design before. Elizabeth looked puzzled as he spoke. She knew something of what had happened in Central Australia, but not a lot of detail. And she certainly didn't know that her former workmate Charlotte ('Scarlet') Burke was an assiduous student of the occult.

"That's the Talisman of Yhe alright," came Scarlet's voice over the phone. "Nobody wears that just as an ornament. There must be something behind it. What do you know about this woman?"

"Next to nothing, sorry."

"Assume she's dangerous."

"I get that, just by the company she keeps."

Q smiled wryly at her beau's response. She knew nothing more about Pasqualina, and now regretted not having had the chance to engage the cook in even a casual conversation that might have helped.

Scarlet made a worried clicking sound with her tongue. "I could teach you some spells perhaps – identify some detail of what she truly is."

"For one thing, she's the girlfriend, or something like it, of an unpleasant local egomaniac. She's a cook of some ability, I'm told. And Scarlet, I don't know that spells, as such, are quite my thing."

"You were very adept when we fought the Ancient Dark One in that cavern."

"I just read out what you wrote for me." Unpleasant thoughts entered John B.'s mind, and sat there like dog droppings in a punch-bowl. "Maybe you'd better send me that incantation."

"John, I do not like the sound of this."

"I'm not fussed about it either, mate. But call it a precaution. Can you text it to me?"

"I don't have the detail with me. I'm at Murph's, and my books are in my apartment. Can I message you later? I won't be back there for a few hours – I've just arrived for dinner."

"Yes please. I don't know that it's urgent, yet, but I'd appreciate having it handy. So, my friend, what's prompted the call? You're dining with Murph and the Mob – I assume things are going okay there?"

The laugh audible through the phone surprised Elizabeth. In the office, Charlotte had been notorious for her serious nature and extreme focus on her work. Plumbing her memory, Q couldn't recall ever hearing a genuine light laugh from the woman.

"Oh, John, yes. Better than alright. I'm telling you before we tell the Mob around the table tonight – Murph and I have decided to get married!"

John B. grinned broadly, and took a moment to let the announcement sink in. The look of bafflement on Q's face was exquisite but he refused to let himself laugh.

After a deep breath he said, "Scarlet, that's wonderful! So, the two of you really have worked out, hey?"

"Oh, I know some people think we're an odd couple..."

A bookish librarian with a feisty red-headed temper, and the rough-edged aboriginal leader of a bike gang, who's larrikin exterior concealed a canny business brain. Odd? Yep.

"... but we've realized that we're good with, and for each other."

"I can relate to that, mate. Congratulations, to both of you. And good luck breaking the news to the Mob."

"Thank you. They'll be fine, though. Nothing much will change. They'll just see even more of me than they already do. Marrying is largely symbolic, although, if we do decide to have a family – I was brought up very conservatively, and though I've put most of that behind me..."

"Some things run very deep. I get it. A family, eh?"

"I did say 'if'. But we'd at least have a good stock of baby-sitters to rely on."

Both Scarlet and John B. laughed, envisaging the beefy Berg, or Pretty Boy, or Curls or Geezer changing nappies. It was beyond incongruous, although they'd probably turn out to be good at it.

"Seriously Scarlet, I'm very, very happy for you both. Elizabeth is waving and sending her best wishes, too. Thank you for telling me. Let me know your where and when."

"As soon as we get things arranged, I will. How much notice would you need to get to Alice Springs from... wherever you are?"

"Venice at the moment, but that will doubtless change. I shouldn't think it'll take us too long. If there's anyone who can organize travel, it's my darling."

Q smiled at the compliment, which she also knew was quite correct.

"You go break the good news to the Mob, mate, and just keep us in the loop. Oh, and please remember to send that – *other* text."

"I will. And you please be careful about that. These are dark forces."

"I remember. I may not have ever fully understood, but I do, definitely, remember. Take care, mate, and be happy."

"I am, thank you, John. You also. Bye for now."

As the connection ended, Elizabeth looked at her beau with eyebrows raised.

"Well, that was a few kinds of interesting," she finally said. "I know you said Charlotte had 'changed a bit' out in Alice Springs, but she sounds like a whole different woman."

"Maybe the change of environment brought her out of a cocoon she'd spun for herself. I dunno – it surprised me, too."

"And what was all that about a talisman?"

"Ah. That, my love, is a long story. Not an entirely pleasant one, and I admit, there'll be a few gaps in what I tell you. Things I don't understand, and, well… let's just say I had a fair quantity of single malt on board. Helped me to cope, when I didn't have much else to rely on, but it's made some things a bit blurry. Shall we have another coffee? I'll try to explain, as best as I can, and we can go see Giancarlo a bit later. I reckon they're going to be needing a late morning after the ball last night!" Q nodded, and JB waved to attract their waitress's attention. "Mac? Two more macchiatos, per favore."

.ooo.

22

A MEETING OF LIKE MINDS

Not surprisingly, Giancarlo supported the idea of a gathering to consider the subverting of Leonardo Delocchio. He might never have been the one to initiate such a project, but he smiled broadly at the suggestion, and immediately offered his *casa* as the venue. Nicola was equally enthusiastic. There was a shrewd twinkle in her eye as she told John B. and Elizabeth that she knew "a couple of others" who would help.

Elizabeth did notice that the girl didn't mention *asking* for their help. She suspected it wouldn't be necessary - equal parts of resentment of Delocchio, and the girl's own charisma.

Delight at Elizabeth's liberation was at the forefront of conversation, but there was also due discussion of the masked ball, and especially the performance of the small ensemble. Giancarlo's pride was not in his own performance, but that of his student who, he said, showed all the signs of nervousness he expected – none.

"I promised Jonbi I would be brilliant for the two of you, so he would not worry about us and concentrate on you, Lizbetta. And so I was," the girl explained without a hint of arrogance.

"Control was excellent. Technique, especially so. Your timing was not always flawless. You are sometimes inclined to rush things, widget. Patience is as much an asset as enthusiasm, and you will learn it in time," the mentor explained with a smile.

"I would like to learn patience more quickly!" Nicola replied. Possibly guilelessly.

"And how did Robi cope with dressing up 'posh', I wonder?" asked Elizabeth.

"Like a duck to a waterfall?" ventured John B.

Giancarlo guffawed more loudly than they'd ever heard.

"A remarkably accurate description, my friend. My suit being at least two sizes too big, despite my widget's artful adjustments, didn't help, but in truth he wriggled and squirmed every moment that he wasn't actually playing. Those times, however, were as reliably excellent as I knew they would be. Robi is a masterful musician, who could be greatly renowned if he had such inclination."

"He wants to be a hermit," explained Nicola.

"And yet, he's good company," observed Stewart.

"He's good with people, individually. Humans are just not his favourite species," said Giancarlo, perhaps with a hint of regret.

There was some interested discussion about the music that had been chosen, and how well it was received. None of the pieces which had become associated with The Silver Duke had been performed (not unexpectedly), and none had been requested (perhaps more surprising). Maestro LaGrigio had carefully chosen a range of music that was more than adequate to entertain their audience without any hint of reference to the self-styled 'local hero'.

The mention of that individual did, however, swiftly bring their conversation back to the task at hand: the curtailment of the big man's influence. Stewart, especially, felt a peculiar sense of urgency about this, although as yet he couldn't, or wouldn't say precisely why. But he was glad of the prospect of support.

Nicola also undertook to feed everyone that turned up to that night's hastily-planned gathering. As good as her word, she spent the afternoon preparing a small mountain of *polpete* – nicely herbed pork and veal meatballs, to be served with a tomato and basil sauce and lashings of rice boiled with whole cardamom pods.

That evening, there were no complaints about the catering! And as good guests do, everyone brought wine of at least decent quality. Everyone, in this case, being John B. and Elizabeth, the taciturn Christos (it seemed that Robi had slipped out of Venice straight after the strain of unaccustomed formality at the ball, preferring rural peace and quiet to the crowds of Carnevale), and the couple who Nicola introduced as "Teasy and the Blob". Tadeusz and Morton introduced themselves more formally to Elizabeth and John B., all three men carefully not mentioning their previous meeting, or the rings currently being crafted.

Good food and good wine were allowed to be the first order of business (well, second, after the guests' obligatory fussing over Toscanini) – sustenance to 'grease the wheels' of creative thought.

Raising a glass of excellent Tuscan red, Giancarlo recited, "Ah, wine! The subtle alchemist that in a trice, Life's leaden metal into gold transmutes!"

Smiling at his young protégé he explained, "The 43rd Rubai credited to Omar, the son of the tent-maker."

"I've heard of the Rubaiyat of Omar Khayyam," said Elizabeth.

"The very one. A rubai is a quatrain, and Rubaiyat is the plural. It's an old Persian word, 11th or 12th century. As is Khayyam, which means maker of tents," explained LaGrigio. "What English speakers are most familiar with is a translation prepared in 1859 by Edward FitzGerald. A creative chap in his own right, was Edward. Certainly, he did Omar's work justice."

Something under the surface of the grey man's voice suggested just a hint of first-hand knowledge, or even proprietorial pride. But no-one commented on it, if they noticed.

With a little sigh, Christos gazed into his own glass, swirling the fine red as he said, "Personally, I've always liked number 46. 'For in and out, above, about, below, Tis nothing but a magic shadow-show, Play'd in a box whose candle is the sun, Round which we phantom figures come and go.' I wonder if Shakespeare knew the rubai when he wrote about there being more things in heaven and earth? Certainly has the same sense of futility."

"Futility? Never thought of it that way," remarked Morton with some surprise.

John B. was quiet. His thoughts had turned 'outside the box', recalling the experience in an underground cavern with a thing that purportedly dwelled in something called The Outer Dark. The conversation with Scarlet had thrown up unpleasant memories of the demonic Shub-Niggurath. A chill went up his spine. That had been an experience he did not want to repeat. He hid behind a polite smile as the conversation turned to favourite poetry.

Eventually, the meal finished, and with Toscanini curled up asleep atop the old television, discussion moved to what had brought them together – the toxic activities of Leonardo Delocchio, and how to end them.

"He's like a puppet master, but the strings are invisible. He's never directly seen to be doing anything illegal himself," observed TZ.

"*Feh*! He kidnapped Lizbetta! Surely that's illegal, even here in Venice," said Nicola sharply, betraying some of the cynicism forged by her own past.

"Indeed, widget, but as Elizabeth has told us the events, it was the brothers Culatello who actually abducted her. And they're never going to admit to acting under his orders. They're too well looked after," said Giancarlo.

"But his was his house that she was taken to! Surely that would mean something?"

Christos shook his head sadly. "At best it would come down to Elizabeth's and John B.'s word against his, and whoever else he'd call in. The fool in that restaurant, for example. And while everyone in this room has a strong opinion about Il Duce, his reputation among many of the local population, especially those in authority, remains good."

"You can fool some of the people some of the time," said Elizabeth bitterly.

Morton "Blob" Overbeek snorted in response. "Delocchio is a

high-profile benefactor to the city. You, alas, fair lady, are a visitor. There's little doubt about who'd be believed!"

His partner Tadeusz was looking thoughtful, though. "You're right to suggest that he's built a high profile, both by his carefully publicized donations, and his music. Not necessarily *his* music," he corrected himself, spotting the expressions on the faces of Christos and Nicola.

Giancarlo maintained a studied neutrality as the silversmith continued, "I think, though, that it is not the man who is well known, but rather, certain *things*. He himself, his true character, is not so high in profile."

At this point LaGrigio nodded and said, "His public spiritedness is a useful mask."

TZ nodded agreement. "In the same way that he hides behind the activities of his henchmen, yes? The Culatello brothers are a shield, and they will be blamed for any and all misdeeds that correctly should be laid at the fat man's feet."

"Not quite all," said Elizabeth, thoughtfully.

She explained what she knew of the activities of Septimus 'Sceptred' Smith. "I don't know that all of the art that Delocchio sells is fake. That's probably *too* risky. Maybe he even started out as a legitimate dealer or trader. But some of what he's selling now certainly is forged. If that ever comes out, though, I'll bet it's Smith who carries the guilt while his boss wriggles out like a fat flounder. A poor innocent dupe, cruelly misled, or some such rubbish. Yes, I reckon Smith would be well looked after to be another one for him to hide behind."

John B. had been silent, and deep in thought, for quite some time. Now, his eyes staring into the distance, he spoke. "I've been thinking about how Delocchio talked about Carnevale. He's got plans, I know, but there's something – unpleasant, about his attitude."

"The end of Carnevale is to be the launch of his new musical masterpiece. That's been well publicized," said Christos.

"I think there's something more. I think Delocchio's music is another mask. His talk of 'joyous anarchy', and 'the dark parts of Venetian history'. I'm thinking of something I read recently.

Wonderful author named Terry Pratchett. He said 'there's a kind of magic in masks – they conceal one face, but they reveal another'. Masks are intrinsically a deception, but they are a 'public face', and they do convey something themselves."

"You think that the end of this Carnevale may be an opportunity to damage Il Duce Grosso's image, and so take away some of his power?" suggested Tadeusz approvingly.

"I think… more than that. I've an instinct that whatever he's got planned is something that *needs* stopping, and I can only wish that doing so will mean an end to his malign influence."

Elizabeth caught the concern in John B.'s voice, and thought of the recent conversations with and about Scarlet Burke. She shivered involuntarily as she said, "I'd love you to be wrong, babe, but I trust your instincts. What do we do?"

"You've got me there, pretty lady. I mean, in a general sense, we want to stop whatever he's up to, but without knowing exactly what he's got planned, we're in the dark. All we can do is try to be in the right place at the right time to react, and hope that it's the right reaction."

"We can do better than that." The brunette's innate talent for organisation was beginning to assert itself. "We can disrupt, distract, disarm – to some extent at least, even before he starts whatever it is he intends to start. Make things difficult for him, however and wher-ever we can."

"But discreetly. His performance is being seen as something of an artistic coup by some of Venice's elite, and our… disruption, as you put it, will be resisted officially," warned Christos.

"So, we'll be as low key as possible," agreed Elizabeth. "But look for opportunities. Anything that looks like an option for the fat slug's bastardry, try to cut it off or at least complicate it, in advance. I know we don't have much detail to go on besides this show he's putting on…"

"One trouble is, so many of his tendrils and influences are unseen. I hadn't realised he had any link with the *Casa di Cozze*. I won't be eating there again!" said Morton emphatically.

"All we can be is as alert as possible. Look out for those we know to be his catspaws. Although, on the final day of Carnevale, I fear most of Venice will be masked and costumed. Delocchio's cohorts included," observed Morton's partner.

"And so should we be," said Elizabeth. "The fat bugger might still be having eyes out for me, and while I don't know that he'd associate any of you with me, other than JB obviously, I'd rather we didn't take chances."

Nicola grinned impishly. "I've got just the outfit."

Perhaps John B. elected not to let his imagination pursue that, or perhaps he genuinely was distracted by other thoughts as he said, "I'd like to get our gondolier friend Mario involved. Marina, too, if she'd willing."

"Old alliances, eh?" Giancarlo mused, seemingly to himself. "Perhaps it is time." He brought his attention back to the group. "My apologies. There is some... history, which may be problematical, but yes. Any and all help will be valuable."

For the next hour or so, they made such plans as they could about who would be where on the final day of Carnivale.

Teasy and the Blob would be spending most of what should be a good trading day in the store, but would ask careful questions of such neighbours as they felt could be trusted, and would meet the others as soon as possible after closing.

Christos would not be required in the office, and so would be available for whatever 'foot patrol' could be co-ordinated.

Giancarlo and Nicola undertook to do likewise. Together or independently would be for them to decide. Probably both at different times of day – Giancarlo balancing his impulse to protect the girl with recognition that she could, in some ways at least, operate more effectively on her own.

They'd all have one day to organise their own costumes and contact any other allies who they thought could be trusted. Elizabeth made sure everyone had her mobile phone number so she could act as a central communication hub.

Eventually, with much exchanging of hugs and handshakes, the little coterie broke up and went their separate ways. There was a strong positive sense of an alliance formed against a deserving adversary. But no-one truly knew how important the fight would be, or how high the stakes.

.ooo.

23

RECONNAISSANCE AND RESEARCH

John B. had made no specific plan of contacting Mario Vespucci. He assumed from experience that the gondolier would turn up at an appropriate time and place. And that's how it turned out. As the Australian couple walked over one of the smaller *ponti* on their way towards the Musee Barche, a booming voice from below hailed them.

After a quick exchange of greetings, the gondola was moored nearby and the three adjourned to a convenient quiet bar. Mario knew the proprietor and was confident that this was not one of Delocchio's 'little interests'. Nonetheless, they kept their voices down as they conversed – there was no way of knowing who might pass information to Il Duce Grosso, either for reward or from misguided loyalty.

The gondolier expressed his admiration for Elizabeth's determination and courage. It would have been easy, and forgivable, to keep a low profile after the abduction. It was reasonable to assume that, whatever else his distractions, the art dealer would still be smarting over the escape of his latest 'prize', and may have his 'network' primed to watch for her.

"I don't want him to have the satisfaction of thinking I'm scared of him," she said.

Mario, of course, was willing to offer whatever help he could to "Operation: Get Fatty", as Elizabeth wryly described it. He undertook to quickly put the word about amongst the other gondoliers who he trusted (most of them, he averred) to watch for Delocchio and his henchmen. Any overtly dangerous, or even suspicious, activity would be reported via the 'boatman's grapevine'. That channel of communication had existed for generations, even maintaining its own unique dialect.

John B. gazed into the pattern of coffee grounds at the bottom of his cup. Without looking up he said, "I should have asked this last night, but tell me, Mario, how *does* Carnevale traditionally end? I've heard things about 'joyous anarchy' and ceremonial breaking of rules, but what does that actually mean? What exactly is Delocchio going to be doing, or attaching himself to? I've got a feeling that's far more important than we're giving credit to. If I'm wrong, and everything is fine and jolly, then I promise no-one will be happier about it than I am!"

"But you're not convinced, are you babe?"

"No," he replied gloomily.

Mario, meanwhile, assembled his thoughts, then launched himself into a 'tourist advisory' speech.

"One of the key points about Carnevale's history is the recognition of the change of seasons. Not just a change in the weather, but a change in the jobs that were required to be done. Different tasks, different skills required. In many parts of Italy, as in other communities across Europe, indeed, the world, that transition is signified by a ritual sacrifice. Many of these old rituals live on as bonfires. Such is the case in Venice, but perhaps not surprisingly, the city has evolved its own history and traditions interwoven into the oldest ways.

"According to the records of the City Executioner, back in 1721 a young man was executed – beheaded then quartered, actually – for murdering a prostitute then robbing her corpse. He may or may not have actually been guilty. The boy worked in the pharmacy at the

Campo San Luca, outside of which there was a large sign depicting an old woman wearing a white cap.

"Somehow that image came to become the sacrifice. An effigy of an old hag would be hung up and then cut in two, releasing confetti and flowers for the children. In time, that ceremony morphed and merged with that of the bonfire, and the effigy of the old woman was burned instead of butchered."

"The Campo San Luca – according to the advertising I've seen around town, that's where Il Duce Grosso will be performing tomorrow evening," said John B. thoughtfully.

"There is a tradition that the square of Campo San Luca is the heart of Venice," explained the gondolier.

Elizabeth grimaced. "It would fit with his ego to choose the 'heart of Venice' to debut his masterpiece," she said bitterly.

"As you say, *signorina*. The square will be grandly decorated, and perhaps he intends that the burning of the Old Lady is to provide a suitably spectacular backdrop to his music. The marble pedestal in the square is, I suppose, a focal point for the celebrations marking the end of Carnevale before Lent begins."

Something about the words 'focal point' resonated in the wizard's head. He thought back to his earlier encounter with the demonic Shub-Niggurath, recalling that the mad sorceress who'd called forth the ancient evil had used that term, or something like it, for the place she'd prepared in a cavern under the South Australian desert. Again, his mind's eye saw the symbol that the red-haired Pasqualina wore about her neck, and as he thought about where he'd seen it before, he shuddered.

"Babe, are you okay? You look like you've just seen a ghost."

"Sorry sweetheart. Just a really disconcerting memory. I think we're onto something with this burning thing."

"But John B., *mi amico*, whatever its gruesome origin, the burning of the Old Lady has become an occasion of joy and abandonment. Music and much good wine abound!"

"Music provided by Il Duce Grosso himself," mused John B. "I think we need to keep an eye on this Campo San Luca."

"It's not a long walk from here. Why don't you go and look at it?" suggested the boatman.

He gave clear directions to the couple, then, admitting that he should try to make a few euros while the opportunity was there, headed back to his gondola.

The Australians made their way to the Campo San Luca, noticing as they walked more posters for Il Duce's 'Special Performance'. Perhaps they simply hadn't paid attention before, or perhaps there was a greater concentration of them closer to the actual venue itself. Or perhaps there was a last-minute promotional 'blitz' happening, to maximise attendance.

The square proved to be brightly decorated with bunting and swathes of coloured cloth. There was the marble pedestal that Mario had mentioned, already roped off, which was clearly going to be where Delocchio's equipment would be set up. As yet, there was little of note to see on the pedestal.

But standing some way behind it was a platform perched on a scaffolding tower about five metres tall. This too was bedecked with pennants and garish cloth, and rising from the middle of it was a steep cone of dry wood. It resembled a tepee of sticks and kindling, secured at its top by a red ribbon. Clearly, this was where the effigy of the Old Lady was to meet its fiery end.

There were quite a few people milling about the square. Like pretty much any other *campo* in Venice, this was a convenient and popular place to relax throughout the day. John B. and Elizabeth looked like any other pair of tourists, out for a stroll. They were alert though, checking potential entry and exit points while also keeping discreet, wary watch for anyone seeming to take more than a passing interest in them.

"Gut feeling tells me we should be here for the galah performance, tomorrow, pretty lady."

"I'm not sure I want to spend the whole day camping out here, though. Sorry, no pun intended."

"That's a shame – it was a good one."

"Sometimes, sir, your sense of humour is quite... what's the word...?"

"Lucid? As in San Luca-d?"

"No. Definitely not. Stop that at once," she said, trying to sound stern while suppressing a giggle.

"I'll Luca elsewhere for inspiration, shall I?"

"Stop it, I said! You'll make me San-guine about your jokes!"

"Touché, darling!"

Their laughing embrace turned into a kiss. And they really didn't care if anyone was watching.

Carnevale crowds did slow their progress as they resumed their walk to the Musee Barche. And the museum itself was hosting a good crowd when they arrived. That meant conversation with Marina DeNucci was, by necessity, carried out in short quiet bursts, snatched between the questions, comments, and spendings of the other visitors.

The curator was supportive in principle. She held Signore Delocchio in low regard, more by instinct and observation than first-hand experience of his crookedness. She was sympathetic, and only a little surprised, at the story of Elizabeth's abduction. (The green-eyed Australian did ponder to herself if the mild surprise expressed was along the lines of 'what would he see in you?', but kept her own counsel.)

But no, she would not be able to take an active role in their 'operation'. She expected an even busier day than this one was proving to be – one of the year's best for income. And there was, she said, a good prospect of speaking to a potential buyer of coins who might offer both a good price, and a respectful home, for the St. Clair collection.

"That will be another reason for me to be in contact with you later in the day, as well as passing on any observations I may happen to make that are relevant to your... efforts. I do, sometimes, see things. And hear them. I will reach you when required, be assured."

John B. silently reflected on the reserve that Giancarlo had expressed about the prospect of Marina's assistance. What was this 'history' the grey man had alluded to with the curator? Was it the musician's, or his own? Again, this frustration – people who apparently knew him but who held no place in his own memory. A long and serious talk would have to be had with someone. But it wouldn't be with Marina DeNucci, he thought.

Instead, he thanked her for such support as she was able to offer, thanks echoed by his beloved who likewise diplomatically did her best to mask her own reserve. They left the curator trying to explain to a determinedly inquisitive Carolina girl why gondolas had different geometric shapes "at the pointy end of the boat".

They'd not long left the museum when John B.'s mobile phone blared out the fragment of a Beatles' track he'd managed to set up to announce the arrival of a text message. ("Gonna write a little letter, mail it to my local DJ...") It was from Scarlet, as promised. The wizard grimaced. It was too long to be casually read while strolling the *fondamenta*.

"When we get home," he said, trying not to sound as grim as he'd immediately felt, and shoved the phone back into the pocket of his jeans.

Elizabeth only nodded, catching the edge of his change of demeanour. She made chatty small talk as they walked back to Manovalo 219, succeeding in lightening her beau's mood with observations of curious characters they passed as they strolled.

A shrewdly-considered stop at a good little taverna helped too. John B. may not drink as heavily as he had previously, but the restorative properties of a decent Scotch or three were never to be underestimated. It wasn't one of his preferred single malts, but it was at least a very good blend of a small number of those, and did put a smile back on his face. Her own choice of Tuscan white wine also went down well, it had to be admitted, accompanying as it did a small platter of lightly crumbed squid pieces.

Even as they ate and drank, the pair stayed warily vigilant, but this was not one of the venues in Leonardo's network of "little interests".

They were both more relaxed by the time they made their way up their narrow stairwell to the apartment. Looking forward to the contents of the little bag of fresh light pastries they bought at the entrance of Viale di Tavola added to the positive vibe.

As they went to deposit themselves on the couch, John B. pulled the phone from his pocket. But Q reached over and laid a hand across the screen.

"Not yet, hey?" she said softly, and placed a tender kiss on the side of his neck.

The pastries, too, could wait, as she set about lightening their hearts by indulging their bodies. Nothing urgent or intense, but gentle delight. The sort of intimacy that was the best gift that two people could share. If John B. was going to confront something that he so clearly found deeply disturbing, he was going to do it from the best frame of mind that could be managed, his beloved reasoned.

It was a good strategy.

By the time the wizard did open his phone, he could hardly have been feeling more positive. And that was well.

Scarlet had begun by reminding him of the gesture and incantation that had worked previously to combat Shug-Niggurath. Contorting his fingers into the Sign of Koth would certainly be easier without the hand having just been broken on someone's jaw, he was pleased to realise. The words of the spell still looked to him like gibberish, just as they had the first time. *Imas weghaymnko quavers yewet...* they began, and got no closer to resembling any of the languages that he had even a passing familiarity with.

What Scarlet had added was context. For a number of reasons, there had been little conversation after the incident under the South Australian desert about the detail of what had happened. The experience had been just too raw, and frankly, too weird. John B. had heard the term "the Ancient Black One" used to describe Shub-Niggurath, and had picked up that he/she/it was a demon, or maybe the boss of demons. 'Black' was a serious understatement. He recalled something like an animated mass of, not just darkness, but the extreme opposite of light. He'd met evil, and didn't like it.

Now Scarlet had attempted to explain, in simple terms, the

mythology of Shub-Niggurath. Except that they knew, from experience, that this wasn't just a story.

'*Ages before the rise of man, there were things on Earth that had come from somewhere else. Perhaps the stars, perhaps another dimension,*' he read. '*They'd long gone by the time of humanity, but there were traces and echoes in dark places, and a cult arose dedicated to reviving those Ancient Ones, who in some way spoke to those believers. That cult would not die until those old 'gods' returned to rule the planet as they once had. It would be their time when mankind itself behaved in the old ways – wild, free, beyond good and evil. When laws and morality are thrown aside, Shub-Niggurath, the Greatest of the Old Ones can be summoned to teach men new ways to shout and revel and kill in joy, and all the world will burn in a holocaust of destructive freedom and ecstasy.*'

"And Charlotte believes all this?" asked Elizabeth, perplexed.

"Fears, I think, rather than 'believes'. Or more to the point, fears the people who *do* believe in it."

"And you reckon there are such people?"

John B. took his beloved's hand and looked her squarely in the eye as he replied, "Darling, I've met one. And that one was more than enough. The... thing she was able to conjure up was, well, it radiated malevolence."

"Sounds awful. All fur and fangs and claws?"

"No. No, nothing like that. Did you ever see the old Steve McQueen movie, *The Blob*? Yeah? It was like that. Black, shapeless, it kept getting bigger and was, well... blobby."

"Blobby, but dangerous?"

"Oh yeah. Trust me. The woman involved definitely had nothing to do with laws and morality, as Scarlet puts it."

"I do trust you, babe. And Mario's explained that the whole point of this party is to 'break all the rules', so that fits, too. And you think that Delocchio is a part of this cult? I wouldn't have picked him as the type to worship anyone but himself."

"Yeah, that's certainly true, sweetheart. It was the red-haired woman who was wearing the talisman. Oh, look, maybe I'm over-reacting. Maybe it's nothing. One of those instances where someone sees a design and likes it, without having any idea of its meaning. Like some kid drawing swastikas 'cos they like the shape, and have no knowledge or memory of Nazis or Hitler or the War. And this is a much older symbol…"

They hadn't released each other's hands, nor shifted their gaze from each other's eyes.

"You don't believe that, though, do you, babe?" Q asked.

"As much as I'd like to, no. It's an instinct warning me."

"We'd better listen to it then, and be careful. Try to memorize this spell that Charlotte's sent you. I still can't get over that she knows this stuff."

"Turns out there was, is, more to Scarlet than anyone realized. Just like you and me, pretty lady."

That won a small laugh which broke the tension.

"Cain't argue with that, sir!" Elizabeth replied in her Southern Belle voice.

.ooo.

24

THE COVERT WAR: PRELUDE

Some of the 'Allies', as they styled themselves, met over an early breakfast at Casa LaGrigio, to go over such plans as they'd made and acquaint themselves with what each other would be wearing. In a city full of disguises, they wanted to be able to recognise each other in an emergency!

TZ and the Blob weren't in attendance, being busy setting up their shop for a hopefully busy day's trading. They'd sent a message explaining that they'd be doing no manufacturing work, so as often as possible, one or other would be available to wander around their part of the city. Of course, they'd be in costume. Morton described his outfit as "an appropriately stylish long gown in gold and black, white wig and a simple domino mask, black with gold trim on the left, white with gold trim on the right". TZ would be dressed in a dapper suitcoat of patchwork shades of aquamarine and sapphire blue with a contrasting black collar, black trousers with bright blue piping, and a mask that was the exact mirror image of his partner's.

"Well, the suitcoat sounds distinctive," admitted Elizabeth.

"It may not be quite as unique as Signore Zybysko hopes," warned Christos. "I think your idea of each of us wearing a sprig of lavender pinned over the heart was a very good one, John B."

Christos' own attire for the day was characteristically low-key: over a conventional dark suit he wore a long grey coat, collar and cuffs trimmed in the deep dark red of a good shiraz. His mask was a simple black band, his headwear a slightly oversized beret in the same red that trimmed his coat. He carried an elegantly painted Spanish guitar, which would allow him to wander freely as he played, watching for any of their quarry.

Mario had visited briefly, wearing his usual striped shirt, but with a floppy broad-brimmed black hat covering his distinctive hairstyle. Like Christos, his 'mask' was no more than a band of fabric tied around his head, with eyeholes cut into the blue material. His lavender adornment may prove useful in distinguishing him among the other gondoliers, some of whom were of similar build.

There'd been no more word from Marina, but it was early and no contact had really been expected.

Giancarlo was dressed in a variation of a harlequin costume, mostly in black and white. The top was diamond-patterned, with loose black sleeves, the same matte black that was on his calf-length trousers and stockings. A conical white felt cap was decorated not with the usual fluffy pompoms, but black enamel musical notes. They were the right accompaniment for the lute slung over his shoulder on a length of stout gold rope. His full-face white mask bore a stripe on the left side, patterned after a piano keyboard.

His musical protégé was dressed beyond her years. Not surprisingly. Nicola wore a tight-waisted jacket (that gave an illusion of a bustline that would surely come with time) with a short, flared skirt in a matching crimson fabric, over fire engine red tights and long red boots. Elizabeth could almost hear her own mother's voice making a sour comment about, "You know what they say about girls who wear red", and hoped she gave no hint of that herself. The girl's red motif continued into her headwear – a long wig of ginger tresses was topped with a three-pointed jester's cap in red and yellow. In a plain hessian shopping bag, she carried a tambourine, flageolet, and a rather incongruous bright pink ukulele. She was equipped to play accompaniment to Giancarlo, or to busk happily on her own when her mentor so required.

Scouring some high-end costume rental shops had secured for Elizabeth a long extravagant ball gown – these would be a common sight out in Venice today. But it had been carefully chosen for more than just opulence. The emerald satin and damask overlaying pale green tulle were typically full at the back, but the hemline swept up dramatically from the sides, scalloping well above the knees. "If I'm going to have to break into a run, or give someone a bloody good kicking, this'll give me legroom!" she'd declared. The bare shoulders and plunging neckline in fact gave the dress a look that wouldn't have been entirely out of place in a Wild West saloon, although Q had made an effort to soften that by adding an almost-demure white faux fur stole and long white satin fingerless gloves. The ensemble ideally suited the ivory-hued, emerald-embellished mask they'd bought earlier.

And of course, John B. had been unable to resist the colour purple. His shirt was uncharacteristically white, but all that was visible of it was the massive ruffle that seemingly burst from a long velvet frock coat. The coat, knee length britches, and stockings were all purple, with gold sequins, stitching and small features that picked up the little details of his mask. Like Q, he'd also had a mind for the practical. His shiny black shoes with their large silver buckles looked innocently formal, but concealed serious steel toe caps that would hurt, a lot, if applied forcefully to anyone's shin or elsewhere. And the black tricorn hat (with attached fringe of white curls) he'd hired had been 'adapted' in a way Stewart had learned while visiting Scotland. A broken piece of razor blade had been inserted in such a way that two of the hat's three edges could make it an effective slashing weapon at close quarters.

Fighting 'fair' didn't come naturally to him, and hadn't since he was young. It was a matter of survival, he figured, even though he remembered nothing of his apparent life 'on the streets'. When John B. got into a fight, he fought hard, dirty, and effectively. Discreetly, though, he hadn't mentioned his hat's modification to anyone, hoping he wouldn't have to use it.

As they finished their light breakfast, Giancarlo looked around the assemblage and spoke.

"My friends, I know we have a serious purpose ahead of us today. John B. especially has a powerful sense of danger, and we would all do well to take that to heart. But that said, please remember that this is meant to be a day of joy and fun for the people of Venice. Don't lose sight of that either – look for the fun and the happiness. Enjoy yourselves as much as possible, wherever and whenever possible."

"Be aware of trouble, but don't go looking to make it? That sounds fair," admitted Elizabeth, for all her own determination to resolve matters with Il Duce Grosso.

Handshakes and hugs exchanged, they made their separate ways out into Venice, into the maelstrom that would be the last day of Carnevale.

If the little group could somehow have been observed from above across the day, the watcher might have seen a resemblance to something under a biochemist's microscope. Cells getting separated, splitting up and recombining in different combinations, disconnecting and reconnecting again.

The musicians played, together and independently, at spots across the city. Giancarlo rarely lost sight of his young apprentice for long, even when she was apparently 'soloing' on a busy corner. Behind his mask, Christos was, at times, almost genial in interacting with people who stopped to admire the flamenco stylings he'd chosen for the day. Mario ferried passengers hither and yon almost continually, but always with one eye watching activities ashore, even as he kept up his normal stream of patter.

Morton and Tadeusz, as they'd hoped, enjoyed a busy day of trade. But with neither choosing to occupy the workshop, they were able to socialise a little with some of their neighbours at different times. There was a moment of tension in the morning when TZ spotted the recognisable figure of Ugo Culatello further along the *fondamenta*, but the Buranese was alone and apparently not looking to cause trouble at that particular moment. He evidently didn't recognize the silversmith, who made a mental note that the other's 'costume' apparently consisted of a long silver-and-black robe thrown over his usual street wear, and a black-and-silver banded mask on the top part of his face.

A uniform of sorts, pandering to the vanity of Il Duce? Were all three brothers similarly attired? It seemed plausible, and the information was swiftly relayed to the other Allies.

Elizabeth and John B. were doing their best to take Giancarlo's advice and enjoy the event, notwithstanding their nervous anticipation, and the sometimes manic jostling of the crowds. The latter, at least, was for the most part, good-natured. Pickpockets were out in force, naturally, and the wandering *poliziotti* were kept busy, albeit unaware that on a few occasions their efforts were abetted by an alert pair of Australians.

Q's ankle-high boots and John B.'s reinforced toecaps were judiciously applied to deserving shins and tailbones, creating enough consternation for pilfered wallets and phones to be reunited with their startled owners. The little beaded white purse on Elizabeth's arm was tempting bait (her real purse and phone more carefully secreted in a hidden pocket of the white stole), as were the apparently gaping side pockets of her beau's frock coat. His wallet and phone were secure inside inner breast pockets. The phone, especially, was not going to be risked. Stewart did not want to rely on his memory alone if it became necessary to use The Spell.

There was another 'ally' whose presence was even more circumspect than the masked figures. Toscanini prowled far afield from his usual territory around the gardens. In the morning and early afternoon, he stayed in the vicinity of Giancarlo and particularly Nicola, watching without being seen. Ignored or unnoticed by tourists or residents, outside his own neighbourhood he was just another one of the multitude of feral cats populating Venice – cats sufficiently absorbed in their own business to ignore him as thoroughly as he ignored them. Tosca prowled along walls and balustrades, sometimes sauntered and weaved around the ankles of crowds, and sometimes sat quietly in dark corners and alleyways. He watched the maestro and his apprentice as they performed, and kept his good eye on the people around them. His good eye, and his keen sense of smell.

It was mid-afternoon when the black cat, evidently satisfied, redirected his attention. He picked up the scent of the two Australians. He tracked them along *fondamente* and over bridges, eventually reaching the Campo San Luca. The gradually growing crowd wasn't a comfortable environment for a cat, especially one who'd suffered as he had in younger days. But somewhere in that damaged little black head was an imperative that kept Toscanini crouching on ledges and in doorways, watching the pair who'd suddenly come into his life – especially the shaggy one he'd felt a powerful instinctive bond with.

Around midday that pair had made their way over to the Musee Barche, but were surprised to find it wasn't open. There was no sign of trouble, though, just a locked door and a Closed sign. Nothing to legitimately raise suspicion, cautious as they were.

"She did say she was hoping to meet up with some silver collector, didn't she?" said Elizabeth. "Maybe she's had to go to them, instead of them coming to her. Perhaps had to make some compromise herself – that'd be a challenge!"

The wizard had to laugh. It had sounded harsh, but he suspected that his beloved's assessment of Marina DeNucci's character wasn't far wrong. "We can check back later, maybe. I'm sure she'll call us if she has any news, or in the unlikely event that she needs us."

It wouldn't turn out to be that simple.

Most of the residents of the Palazzo di Grossi were similarly scattered about Venice for much of the day. Like the Allies, they came together and drifted apart at various times, each with their own tasks or agenda. For the most part, they were keeping clear of the Silver Duke himself. Pre-performance anxiety manifested itself in the big man as worse-than-usual temper, and his entourage were glad to stay well away. Only Pasqualina seemed unperturbed. Her polite request to 'borrow' the services of the three brothers got a perfunctory "Yes, I don't need them".

Delocchio would be spending the afternoon setting up his array of keyboards and equipment in the Campo San Luca. He'd hired a road crew to assist, led by a veteran road manager named Dino who aspired in vain to be a jazz pianist like Thelonious Monk. His crew were men with vastly more appropriate skills and experience with musical gear than the sons of a fisherman.

Dino was capable enough to serve as the sound producer for the show itself, manning the vital mixing desk. The muscle of the Culatello brothers would be useful for haulage and little more today, and that task was better handled by people with some affinity for the instruments. Frankly, Leonardo had neither use nor patience for their dull-witted company in the morning.

Sceptred Smith was, as ever, content to labour at a quiet easel, while the cook had her own plans for the three bruising siblings.

They didn't ask questions. Il Duce had told them to put themselves at Pasqualina's service as if it were his own, and so they did. It was late morning when they met, as she'd instructed, near the Musee Barche.

Duilio had a storeman's trolley, to which was strapped a large wooden box seemingly filled with long loose coloured rags. He didn't know why, and didn't care to ask. It wasn't especially heavy, and if he'd cracked a few ankles among the crowd as he'd walked, so what?

Conscious as she was of the history of the day, Marina herself had given considerable regard to her outfit. Moorish splendour would be a fair description. A blue tunic with wide sleeves, swathed in a long wrap of darker blue and gold. The same material had been used for a turban which topped a jet black mask trimmed with crimson beads. Only her gold 'Curator' badge distinguished her from the museum's costumed visitors when she left her counter to mingle and answer questions.

The deed was done swiftly. The redhead's own silver-and-black attire included a hood, so even if the curator might have remembered the distinctive hair, it wasn't visible anyway. She simply walked up to Marina, apparently just another visitor. From the pocket of the plain blouse worn under the robe she pulled a small bottle of a potion of her own devising, and with a thumbnail flicked open the hinged lid.

A sudden discreet punch to the solar plexus was just hard enough to cause Marina to inhale sharply, at the very moment the little bottle was held in front of her face. Behind the black mask, the colour drained from DeNucci's face and her eyes began to glaze.

Marina's legs buckled. The cook caught her as she sagged, exclaiming, "Oh! She's fainting! It must be this hot outfit – please, give us some room!" as she steered her prey to collapse onto a chair.

Unseen, she transferred the museum badge onto her own robe, then turned to address the visitors, only a few of whom had even noticed anything.

"I'm sorry – Signora is not well! I must ask you all to leave, while I attend to her!"

She shooed out the tourists like a farmer herding chickens. A few tried to protest, but were mollified by the promise of 'free admission later if they presented their tickets for today'. No need to reveal that there wouldn't actually *be* a 'later'.

Within minutes the brothers had been ushered in through the rear door that was used for deliveries. Burly Ugo lifted the unconscious woman and deposited her in the box. She was hardly a neat fit, but once Luigino had replaced and rearranged the brightly-coloured scrap fabric to blend with the blue and gold stripes, it would take more than a second glance to be aware there was a human form among the material.

Neither Ugo nor his brothers questioned the task. That was Rule 1 in working for Il Duce Grosso. The reason for doing something didn't matter, only the obedient doing. They'd been told to do as Pasqualina bid them, so that was it. Ugo vaguely wondered if it had something to do with the Australians' silver that he knew was here somewhere, but there was no mention of it.

Leonardo Delocchio was in fact oblivious to his cook and sometime lover's actions. Her plans were her own. Pasqualina's intuitions were raw, trained only by what she'd read, but she'd sensed a type of power in her new captive when she'd come to the Musee. There'd been something similar about the Australian woman, but when the green-eyed brunette had inconveniently managed to get away from the Palazzo it had been no great imposition to do things differently. The outcome would still be the same, of that she was sure.

The foursome made their way to Campo San Luca, as quickly as Luigino's moon-booted limp would allow. He walked in front, his job to prevent anyone coming inconveniently close to the trolley. Duilio and Pasqualina did similar duty on either side as Ugo did the heavy work of pushing.

At the edge of the square was a small canvas pavilion that had been set up to house the fireworks and other paraphernalia which would be used in the evening's pyrotechnic display. The silver-and-black outfits were as good as a backstage pass for the two security guards. The staff of the esteemed Signore Delocchio could go anywhere and do anything, it seemed. The guards waited politely outside while the 'stage crew' set up whatever interesting props Il Duce would be entertaining them with.

Among the things inside the pavilion was a garishly painted wooden box. It was shaped to fit securely amongst the pyramid of kindling on the high platform behind the pedestal where the music was to be performed. There was no chance of it sliding off into the crowd – as the fire burned it would just fall back into the blaze.

It was the Old Lady. The painting was a caricature of a hag, with wild staring eyes and a cartoon witch's leer.

At the command of the cook who was more than a cook, Duilio prised one side off the mannequin box. With his brothers' help, he pulled out the kindling – sticks, rags and paper, which had filled it. And replaced it with Marina, repacking enough around her limp form to hold her securely as Ugo drove the nails back into the wooden frame.

No effort was made to bind their victim. Pasqualina gave no such order, entirely confident that her potion would keep the older woman unconscious for many hours yet. Long enough to be oblivious to the winching of the mannequin into position. More than enough time for her to meet her fate when the Old Lady was burned.

Even the Culatello brothers must have grasped what was intended for Marina. But they'd dealt before with people who'd crossed their boss, and accepted without demur that this must be one more such instance. They knew better than to ask anything. The notion of a ritual sacrifice would never occur to any of them. They would never understand what they'd helped achieve, thought Pasqualina with sinister delight – the morons weren't likely to live that long.

The brothers were dismissed, to again wander Venice as they wished. She would remain at the Campo San Luca, quietly sitting at the fringe of the gathering crowd and watching the preparations. A show of support for Nina Carina, the harried young woman who was acting as a stage manager for the evening's big show. A word here and there, if required, to ensure the Old Lady was hoisted and swung into place correctly – yes, that box was heavy, wasn't it? Must be the wood it had been packed with, hey?

Some reassurances for Delocchio when he arrived, soothing his nerves as he ordered Dino and his crew around, setting up and testing equipment. His performance would not be the Carnevale high point that he expected, but she expected the music to do much to set exactly the right mood.

Perhaps he'd understand, a little, as he surely died. It would satisfy his ego, she thought, to realize that he was playing a central role in the holocaust that would be the return to power of the Great Old Ones. Nothing else mattered.

.ooo.

25

THE COVERT WAR: OPENING MOVEMENTS

A day of peace and quiet at the Palazzo was a rare treat for Septimus Smith. No capricious orders or sudden changes of direction from his employer. No obligation for meaningless small talk in the kitchen if he wanted to make a cup of tea for himself. No risk of encountering any of the buffoon brothers – sometimes he swore he could feel his own I.Q. dropping when he was forced to spend any time in their presence. And no requirement to go and mingle with the mob out on the streets of Venice. He'd really rather stab himself in the leg with a fork than do that, thank you very much.

He had his own room back. He'd just about completed the "Pollock", only a few final fake 'aging' touches were required, and he had a new Constable he was looking forward to producing. He stood at his easel, glancing back and forth between his blank canvas and the broad description of the piece that had been 'sold' to a rich collector – *A Suffolk Hayrick*, supposedly one of John Constable's early works before he started producing large landscapes. Excellent! An English countryside scene, he could do that from memory.

Then, of course, just as he was about to apply the first stroke, there came a loud knocking at the front door. The first and strongest impulse was to ignore it. The sound repeated.

Il Duce Grosso did not get many visitors. He desired an audience, but at a distance. Anyone coming to the Palazzo could be expected to be here on business, and Smith knew that his employer would be irked if any opportunity for profit was missed. An irked Duce was even less pleasant to be around than usual. So, with a sigh, Smith turned from his canvas and made his way to the door. The painful limp, which had mysteriously vanished in the absence of anyone else in the house, slowed his travel, so there was a third knocking at the portal before he reached it.

'Persistent sod,' the painter thought to himself as he undid the latch. The door was swung inwards just as the visitor was raising a hand to rap on it yet again. The mere fact that the knocking on the heavy door had been so audible was testimony to how hard the man's bare knuckles must be. Septimus was silently impressed.

"Ah, thank you. I'd like to speak to Signore Delocchio, please."

Smith blinked. The man's English was impeccable, but there was something slightly odd about the pronunciation of his employer's name, as if the letters of the word didn't quite fit. At first glance, the artist took the man to be in a traditional 'plague doctor' costume – a black hat, long black coat, and mask with dark crystal eye covering. Then he realised it wasn't a mask. The man's nose was prominent, but not grotesquely elongated, and he was wearing conventional, if very dark, sunglasses. The black attire was evidently his normal streetwear. He carried a black leather briefcase.

"I'm sorry… Il Duce is not home at present. He's preparing for a performance this evening. Was he, er, expecting you?"

"Oh, I would think not. Pardon me, do you work with Signore Delocchio? A musician, perhaps? You have the air of a creative man."

His ego stroked, Smith invited the stranger into the front room and directed him to a chair. The man introduced himself as Signore Medici, and explained that he wished to discuss a number of business matters with Signore Delocchio. Perhaps Signore Smith could offer some advice? The benefit of his knowledge and experience?

Septimus, of course, dissembled about the precise nature of his own 'consultancy', and gave what he hoped were suitably vague answers to some interesting questions about his employer's range of business interests. The vanity of having as his patron "one of the wealthiest men in Venice" did slip into some of his responses, though.

It dawned on Smith that what he considered to be some of his most innocuous remarks prompted the most energetic flurries of note-taking in Medici's little pocket-book, bound in the same sombre black leather as his briefcase.

After a few minutes of this conversation the dark man drew a finger down the bridge of his nose and considered his notes.

"The Campo San Luca, you say."

"Well, yes, but he'll be very busy with preparations for this evening's show. And of course, I expect there'll be a very large crowd. Il Duce is very popular. His music sells well, you know."

"So I understand. Well, there are perhaps a number of other addresses for me to call on before I speak directly with Signore Delocchio." He looked over the top of his dark glasses with a gaze that made Sceptred Smith feel uncomfortably like a specimen being pinned to a display board. "You have been very helpful, Signore. I shall speak further with you soon."

With a formal handshake, Medici departed. As he closed the heavy door behind the figure in the long coat, Septimus Smith abruptly decided that wasn't a conversation that he wished to be involved in. Nor, he realized, did he want to be around if – no, make that when, Il Duce Grosso found out about the conversation that he'd just had. It dawned on him that he didn't know exactly who or what this Medici fellow was, and as circumspect as he thought he'd been, there was a distinct feeling he'd revealed something he shouldn't have.

His pay was up to date, or close enough to it. It would be a shame to go when there was work still incomplete, and he hadn't yet accumulated enough funds for the much-anticipated boat. However, that particular escape was still to be aspired to, and there would be other employers. He'd paid some attention to who'd been Delocchio's clients and contacts, and had an idea of who might share the fat man's disregard for honest provenance.

He could, and would, be packed up and gone very quickly, his 'bad leg' no impediment when it suited him. A water taxi over to the mainland, then a flight from Marco Polo airport to London. He could lose himself there for a short time while he pursued Other Opportunities.

ON THE *FONDAMENTA MARGHERITA* a good crowd had gathered not far from the small high-class jewellery store owned by Teasy and the Blob. It wasn't the quality of those two worthies' wares that had drawn the numbers (as exquisite as their work was), but the quality of music being performed by a succession of buskers. There had been a man in a harlequin costume who had played extraordinary baroque tunes on an old-fashioned lute, first alone, then accompanied by a young woman dressed all in red. She'd added delicate trilling high notes on a little flute-like thing (most of the watchers couldn't have named a flageolet for good money), or played surprising harmonies on a ukulele.

When the lute player had stopped, slipping away into the costumed crowd, the young woman had continued alone for a while. The crowd had grown – few, if any, had heard a ukulele played like this before. Admittedly, most had probably never heard a ukulele played at all, but the fact that the young woman was extracting from the small instrument the sort of arrangements that might otherwise be expected from a 'full-sized' guitar, was intriguing and greatly entertaining.

And then another fellow had come forward to join in. A man in a grey coat and red beret. He played a beautifully decorated guitar, and at first offered clever counterpoints to the ukulele. To the laughter of the crowd, the masked pair performed a most unlikely, but cleverly executed, version of *Duelling Banjos*.

Then it was the turn of the young woman to bow graciously before seeming to melt into the crowd. The grey-coated guitarist shifted his styles smoothly. A lot of flamenco, some classical, and even some cunningly 'tricked up' familiar pop tunes.

There was a cloth-lined wooden pail on the ground near the musician's feet, into which enthusiastic audience members had been tossing money which would later be shared equally between the three performers, each of whom was wearing a discreet but distinctive piece of lavender. The pail was getting quite full, with notes as well as coins. It was a tempting target for one skulking individual who'd forced his way towards the front of the crowd. A solidly-built individual in a silver-and-black hooded robe, who'd been surreptitiously using his mobile phone to take voyeuristic photos of women in what he regarded as interesting costumes (read: short and/or otherwise revealing).

Duilio stared greedily at the bucket of money, then flicked his eyes around his near vicinity. Leading with his shoulder, he moved around to his right, getting even nearer to the leading edge of the crowd. Measuring his angle. A short fast crouching sprint, he could grab the pail of cash and lose himself in the mob squeezed onto the small bridge before anyone had realized what happened. Take the money and run. He felt a moment of jostling, someone nearby must have bumped him – no matter. He tensed, set his shoulder to charge, and sprang forward.

The very first of his long strides went awry. His knee smacked into the ground painfully. In a tangle, he almost bounced back up to his feet, but a small lithe figure in red appeared under his tumbling body and ramped him up. The guitarist swayed back out of the way of flailing limbs. Culatello's momentum carried him over the pail of cash, and almost upside down he crashed into the guardrail. With the small of his back as the pivot point, he was up, over, and into the canal before he knew what was happening.

At first glance, you might expect a man of Duilio's build to be a bit buoyant. But no, perhaps he *was*, as he'd sometimes said, "big boned", because he sank like a big rock.

The clumsy somersault into the water attracted only the mirth of the crowd. The guitarist played a quick riff appropriate to a slapstick movie to emphasize the comedy of the moment. A quick exchange of whispers among the onlookers had identified the hooded figure – none of them moved to assist the floundering man.

As he kicked and splashed, Duilio realised his boots had been tied together – a trick he'd enjoyed tormenting others with when younger (though surely, he'd never used anything as tough as... as whatever this was). Closely bound up with that flash of memory were images of people he'd delighted in pitching into the canals and lagoon, including his sister Antonella. He'd made sure no-one ever jumped in to help her. As the water filled his nostrils and ears he realized, all too clearly, that nobody was coming to his aid, either.

He'd barely had time for a deep breath as he'd fallen. Already the blood was pounding in his head and he desperately wanted to exhale and inhale. The cloak was wrapping itself around him as he flailed, its weight helping drag him down deeper. He was about to drown, and nobody cared enough to rescue him. And with the awful clarity of impending death, he knew he couldn't blame them.

He had to gasp, and got another mouthful of water. He managed to free an arm from the black-and-silver shroud, and thrashed frantically, trying to claw his way to the surface. What was that? A rope, against his wrist, fleetingly. He twisted and turned, unable to see in the murky water. As he gagged on another mouthful of water, the urge to retch and take in a final, fatal 'breath' almost overwhelming him, his fingers caught the line, heavy and taut.

Desperately he clung to it. Stopped the mad threshing, tried to control the panic, enough to free his other arm. The shining dots swimming before his eyes weren't in the canal, he realized – they were in his brain. He was dying. No, not dead yet. Hand over hand he hauled himself up that wonderful, precious rope, his mind almost adrift from its own moorings. He barely even felt the top of his head smack into something solid. Only the now-mechanical action of scaling the rope brought him up out of the water.

A sudden, massive intake of air. An equally violent reaction –

uncontrolled coughing and projectile vomit. His eyes streaming, Duilio felt his way with trembling slowness around the hull of the moored boat. Here – the set of metal rungs enabling the climb up onto the *fondamenta*. A climb that should take seconds felt like it took ten minutes before he flopped onto the footpath, looking and feeling like something his father might have dumped onto his deck to expire.

A small, functioning part of his mind feared that someone would immediately kick him back into the canal. It was what he and his brothers would have done, he knew. But no, he was ignored. Not helped, but shunned. A couple of tourists had taken a tentative step forward, but a restraining hand and some quiet words from locals, notably a slim girl in a red costume, and a white-wigged man in a patchwork suitcoat of aquamarine and blue, swiftly changed their minds.

Duilio never knew that. He only knew that as he forced off his sodden boots, still entangled in some sort of thin wire or metal strings, he didn't want to be so close to water ever again. Instant hydrophobia. No more Venice for him, effective immediately.

He wrenched off the soaked Delocchio cloak that had so nearly killed him, and flung it to the ground. As he staggered away he pulled his mobile phone from the pocket of his shirt. A stream of water ran out of it. Ruined. No bad thing. He flung the object back out into the canal that had already claimed it once. There was nothing on it he wanted to keep.

The middle Culatello brother reeled and weaved his way back to the Ghetto, and the Palazzo Grossi. By the time he arrived, Sceptred Smith had already decamped, leaving the front door unlocked, though not actually ajar.

Duilio wasted little time packing. He didn't own much, and there was little of that he wanted to keep. A canvas bag for two changes of clothes, a towel and a razor. The 'petty cash' tin he knew was kept in the kitchen. His first impulse was to simply take the tin and all his contents, but as he reached for it he stopped.

It was a newly-fledged thing, this conscience. But he realised that if he was really going to be a better man, as he'd vowed to himself in the watery shadow of death, it had to start here. Il Duce owed him unpaid wages, but it was less than the substantial sum required to operate a kitchen to feed the big man's appetites. He pulled a few hundred Euros from the tin. That seemed about right.

He looked about the kitchen. It struck him that he'd never before seen it so quiet. There was nothing simmering on the hob, or slowly baking, or marinating. Odd. What would they be eating after the big performance? That was usually when Leonardo was most ravenous, after a show. Ah well, Pasqualina must have something planned. She always seemed to. And not his problem any more.

Gritting his teeth at the prospect, he walked away to catch one final water taxi. The mainland beckoned, and there he'd head for the hills. Literally. He was strong. A willing worker. And determined to start a new life, among people who didn't know him, who he had never hurt. And away from his brothers, especially Ugo, who he knew he would never be able to stand up to.

IRONICALLY, Duilio would never know that he'd have been wrong about that.

After leaving the Musee Barche, Elizabeth and John B. had 'wandered lost' around Venice for some time, keeping eyes and ears open for more than just the spectacle that the last day of Carnivale offered. Occasionally they'd cross paths with a costumed figure wearing a sprig of lavender, and exchange nods and smiles and waves without conversation – that could come later. Perhaps at Campo San Luca, before the concert they'd all gather to see, hear, and disrupt as required. Meanwhile, they would stay alert for trouble as best they could.

At the fringe of the Mercerie district they'd seen at a distance a harlequin-suited figure. The lavender stood out against one of the white diamond shapes, but just as distinctive for them was the slightly awkward gait of a man whose knees were a constant source of unvoiced pain.

"How old do you think he really is, babe?" Elizabeth asked, quietly.

"Hard to say, sweetheart. I think older than he lets on, put it that way. Chronologically, at least," Stewart added with a wry smile.

"Young at heart, you mean?"

"Something like that... hey, some sort of disturbance."

He pointed a block further along from them, where a crowd was gathering. Instinctively the Australians made their way to the front of the circle that was forming.

It was forming, they discovered, around an all-too-familiar figure.

On his knees, hunched over, and rocking back and forward slowly, was Ugo Culatello. The black-and-silver striped mask lay on the ground beside him. Tears rolled down his swarthy face. He seemed oblivious to everyone around him – oblivious to everything except where he was staring, at the trembling hands he held out before him.

What was most eye-catching about those hands was the blood streaming from them, which of course was what had attracted the crowd when he'd staggered from an alleyway and collapsed to his knees.

The source of the blood wasn't hard to identify, either. The three long fingers on each hand had been removed. Swiftly and efficiently, apparently. The remaining thumb and pinkie combinations flexed slowly and reflexively, their movement being the real focus of Ugo's gaze.

Some concerned on-looker had gone to fetch some sort of policeman, but the fisherman's son would give no assistance when questioned later. He'd had a momentary glimpse of a figure in black and white before the hood of his own cloak had been pulled down over his face. A shove caught him off balance and he'd tumbled into an alley where his head cracked into a stone wall. Even with his thick cranium, he'd been momentarily dazed.

In the brief time that he was stunned he felt something cold slip around first one hand, then the other – some sort of thin wire, an officer of the *Polizia di stato* theorized aloud. Then nothing more than a sudden tug. No pain, really. But as he tried to push the cowl of his cloak away a spurt of blood hit him right in the eyes. He couldn't see – couldn't see his assailant, who obviously didn't linger to admire their work, and couldn't at first see the damage that had been done.

It was only as he wiped his face with the back of his hand as he struggled to his feet that Ugo realized what had happened. Even as he'd reeled out of the alley his knees had buckled, and he'd begun to sob helplessly.

It wasn't just blood loss causing shock, it was the impact of reality, and the oldest brother's realization of the life that lay ahead of him. No more food by the handful. No belligerent, powerful fists, either. The whimpering mound faced life as a beggar, and knew he'd get no sympathy nor support from the Venetians that he and his brothers had terrorized. If popularity was an earthquake, Ugo Culatello couldn't have raised a wobble on the froth of an overfull badly made cappuccino.

Nor, he knew, could he count on his brothers' support. He had always ruled them with an iron fist, and if he could not make such a fist, he could not compel their obedience.

Perhaps it was sad, in its way, that Ugo was incapable of seeing any prospect of anyone behaving in a way other than how he would himself. The weak were to be preyed upon. And now he was weak.

There was no service that he could offer Il Duce now, so he knew better than to hope for help there. Even if there had been a slim prospect of Delocchio financing the surgery to reattach the fingers, as a reward for services rendered, the lost digits were nowhere to be found. Some of the city's feral cat population had an unusual supplement to their diet that afternoon.

John B. and Q watched and listened, joining in the general gestures of helpless "didn't see a thing, sorry" responses to the desultory questions of the *polizia*. They'd assured the officer that they'd come upon the scene too late to have seen anything helpful, and no, they were visitors to Venice, didn't know anyone by sight, even if they hadn't all been in these wonderful costumes.

The pair walked away, sharing some *schadenfreude* satisfaction at the fate of the brutal thug. The wizard contemplated the 'wire' theory expressed by the policeman. Something thin, strong and flexible. A string from a guitar, or a lute? He remembered a casual remark of Giancarlo's: "I am not built for fighting, but I learned some tricks over the years". Was this one?

He remembered the look on the face of the silver-haired man after the incident in the *Trattoria Luciano,* and said quietly, "He shouldn't have hurt Nicola."

The saying 'the best fighter is never angry' is sometimes ascribed to Lao Tzu, but that seemed to John B. an inexact translation. 'Never hot-headed' seemed more appropriate, and certainly, in a practical sense, more accurate. He knew from his own fights over the years that he could remember. Anger could burn cold, and was often more effective that way. Fighting with a clear head was a definite advantage, and Giancarlo was among the most clear-headed individuals Stewart knew.

"Can't say I'll be shedding any tears of sympathy, whatever happened, and whoever's responsible. They did Venice, and us, a favour. That's one less for us to worry about tonight, anyway, babe," said Elizabeth with some satisfaction.

"Civic improvement, you reckon? Can't argue."

If Q expected any further comment, it didn't come. The wizard was quiet, and deep in thought as they wended a meandering route towards the Campo San Luca.

The elimination of Ugo Culatello as a potential threat was no bad thing, but the wizard was very sure that there was a far greater threat on their horizon than anything the burly brothers could offer.

.ooo.

26

THE COVERT WAR: THE MAIN EVENT

It wasn't quite six o'clock when the Allies gathered at a little *grappa* stall on the edge of the Campo San Luca. Most of them, anyway. Morton and Tadeusz had been delayed by late-arriving, big-spending customers. The liquor was served refreshingly cold, but that did little to mask its potency. The sun had almost set, but there were plenty of lights about the square.

A few small white canvas shelters like the one they were in dotted the area, but the crowds were thickest around two distinctive structures. One was the scaffolding tower that held the platform upon which, some five metres above the ground, were a pyre-to-be of sawn branches, timber and kindling, and the grotesquely painted figure of the Old Hag.

Nestled among the soon-to-be firewood, it looked almost like a sarcophagus, an ancient Egyptian relic reimagined for Venice, and decorated with coloured cloths and scarves. One of them, draped over the head of the mannequin, had been adorned with a peculiar hand-drawn symbol. It looked like a Grand Prix circuit designed by a lunatic. Barricades had been placed to keep the audience at what had been optimistically deemed a safe distance.

The other structure attracting attention was, of course, the marble pedestal which would be Leonardo Delocchio's stage.

One small area on the left of the area in front of the stage had been roped off, and twenty-one plastic chairs placed in three rows. These were for some of the Venetian 'elite' - real or self-proclaimed - who had paid handsomely for the very exclusive privilege.

On the stage itself, Dino had already set up the array of four keyboards that Il Duce would be playing at different points of the show. The welter of leads and cables which, in less capable hands could have looked like an explosion in a spaghetti factory, had instead been carefully taped to resemble a small family of thick snakes. Amplifiers and speakers were precisely set around the square to ensure the music would reach every part of the audience.

The road crew had handled Delocchio's seemingly endless, increasingly petulant demands for "little adjustments" across the afternoon, knowing there would be more to come as the swelling crowd changed the acoustics.

The star of the show himself was in one of the tents, right beside the stage. When not fussing over a keyboard or mixing desk (often undoing the careful work of his crew) he sat in the padded comfort of his oversized scooter. There he made imperious demands for whatever food and drink was his sudden whim.

The harried stage manager Nina Carina had done her best to satisfy him while trying to attend to her other responsibilities, and was frankly delighted at the arrival of the woman introduced as 'Squealer', who immediately took over what felt unpleasantly like child-minding duties. The redhead was very much used to the star's 'little ways'. Even if she seemed a little distracted, she was also in an obvious good mood, which remained unruffled by Leonardo's foibles. (She *did* like that word!)

And she did have Luigino with her to do much of the fetching and carrying while she stayed to soothe the maestro's nerves. He could hardly be called a 'runner', still hampered by the moonboot on his fractured shin, but he was still adept at pushing and forcing his way through a crowd. Not giving a damn about anyone else was an advantage.

The stage seemed like the place to be, the Allies reasoned. Il Duce Grosso was up to something, he'd made it plain that he intended to be at the centre of the Carnevale's closing event – whatever was to happen, it would surely happen there. Downing the last of the *grappa* more quickly than was perhaps wise, the group started to make their way across the square.

"I wish people wouldn't get in our way," muttered John B. Although the crowd didn't miraculously part *a la* the Red Sea, clusters of people did happen to break up at convenient moments, particularly large or intransigent tourists were distracted and moved away at the right time, or a large family would suddenly need to find a toilet just as the wizard and his companions approached.

There was a roar from the crowd as the main attraction took to the stage, waving one lugubrious hand as the other clutched a microphone.

"Thank you. Thank you all," he said in a voice that made it clear he was receiving no more than his due.

"*Feh*! Pig!" snarled Nicola, and went to dart ahead, knowing she could squirm through narrow gaps more quickly than her adult companions.

But Giancarlo laid a hand on her shoulder. "No, widget. Leave him to me, please," he said, then followed the slightly bulkier figure of Christos veering towards an area to the side of the stage.

Perhaps the disguise was increasing the latter's confidence, as he determinedly applied shoulder or elbow to anyone blocking his path.

Leonardo was promising "something magical tonight". The words struck John B. like a slap, but it was Pasqualina who caught the wizard's eye. Standing unobtrusively at the very edge of stage left, the pale woman's lips moved strangely as her hand clutched the little home-made pendant.

Delocchio made a grand sweeping gesture with both pudgy hands.

At that cue Nina Carina lit a long, fuel-soaked plait that hung down from the Old Hag's platform. A few fireworks that had been woven into the ribbons added spectacle to the flame that snaked its way up the fuse to the kindling at the base of the wooden pyre. Some sparks ignited little spot fires among the coloured fabric festooning the Old Hag.

Suddenly John B. staggered and clutched his forehead. What the hell was in that *grappa*? A voice. There was a female voice, shouting in his head. But Q was right beside him. The language – what was the language? Not English. Not Italian. Older? Yet, familiar? Something... from a dream.

The sudden, intense pain immobilised Stewart. It was all he could do to stay on his feet. Somehow, he managed to point toward the Old Hag, intuitively aware that was the source of whatever was happening.

A similar pain gripped Mario, though marginally less intense. He at least could move, and did so, reeling in the direction of the fireworks platform. Realizing the objective that the wizard indicated, and unaware of the extent of her beau's distress, Elizabeth rushed to support the gondolier. Following hard on her heels was Nicola.

Some distance away, now separated by the milling crowd, Giancarlo also grabbed at his skull. He grabbed at Christos' shoulder to support himself. The latter stopped and held up the grey man as best he could. The maestro waved a hand as if trying to shoo flies from his face.

"Not important..." he gasped. "Disrupt... Duce," he managed, and braced himself with hands on his knees.

Satisfied that at least the older man wasn't about to immediately fall over, Christos turned back to pushing his way through the nearby crowd.

The fuse lit, the fire would erupt within the minute. Leonardo awaited his moment. It was all theatre – Pasqualina had suggested it, though he'd never publicly acknowledge that – the old ritual to be tied to the new music. It would assure, she'd said, that his composition would be etched indelibly into the minds of the audience. The sound together with the spectacle, the whole borne onward by the momentum of the deepest and darkest parts of history. The deepest and darkest parts of racial memory, lurking within the old traditions. He would be unforgettable! With a satisfied smile, he played his first few dramatic introductory notes.

Everything seemed to happen at once.

The crowd roared approval at the start of the pyrotechnics and the anticipated destruction of the Old Hag. Their noise disguised from Delocchio the fact that the sound of his music suddenly ceased, so at first, he continued the surprisingly nimble dance of his fat fingers across the keys.

Even as he did, the kindling was lit, and flames began to leap up the pyre. The fabric was igniting first, but the stacked timber wouldn't take long.

Mario clung to the ladder leading up to the Old Hag's platform, trying to steady himself before climbing. He managed a few rungs, but then grasped at his head and fell backward. Even as he landed he pointed up, up at the Old Hag.

Elizabeth didn't know exactly what was going on, but she got the idea. Well, she'd run through a fire before, back on Islay. If she was quick...

She was quick enough to clamber up, and tear the strangely marked scarf off the head of the mannequin as it burned, momentarily puzzled to notice that the peculiar shape seemed to have burned itself onto the wooden box. The box that was starting to smoke. The box from which, she realized, was coming a dull pounding and muffled cries.

Throw it down from the platform? How much less dangerous would that be for whoever was trapped in there? But what other option was there? She pounded on the hot wood, to no effect. Eyes starting to stream from smoke, she tried to get her fingertips under an edge, hoping to tear off a lid, or a side, but there was no purchase.

Voices from the crowd, shouting. Some encouraging, thinking she was part of the show? Others railing, thinking she was trying to stop proceedings? Damn right she was!

Suddenly an edge of her gown caught fire, ignited by a gout of flame from a length of old branch that was part of the stack. Before she had time to panic, there was another figure crowding the platform beside her. A small figure in a red costume that shone luridly in the firelight. The flames reflected off something else, too. The blade of a sturdy knife, lifted from the distracted roadie Dino. Nicola may not live the life of a street urchin any longer, but she hadn't lost all the survival skills.

A deft slash removed the burning section of fabric, which fell onto the pyre and was quickly consumed.

"Lid... box," Elizabeth managed to rasp out through a mouthful of smoke as she slapped at the mannequin, trying to beat out small flames.

Nodding, the girl managed to insert the blade where the brunette indicated, but she didn't have the power in her hands to separate the parts of the box. Elizabeth added her own strength and leverage, but even then, feared that it wouldn't be enough – not before the fire overcame them both.

Then, success! A frenzied push from the inside, just as the knife was levered and twisted, and some of the nails gave up their grip. Shift the blade, another effort, and there was a gap. Room for fingers to grip properly, pushing and tearing. Even as it caught alight, the lid bearing the image of the Old Hag was torn from the smouldering wooden box.

A figure tumbled out in a tangle of blue and gold fabric, some of which immediately started to burn and melt. Elizabeth and Nicola frantically beat at those new flames, while pushing the stiff-limbed intended victim onto the top rungs of the ladder.

Then Mario was there. Swaying unsteadily, but he'd scaled high enough to reach up and grasp Marina. The gondolier's innate sense of balance kicked in, and he carried his load to the ground swiftly. The two rescuers were close behind, Elizabeth on the ladder, Nicola descending the scaffolding in a blur of red fabric.

No sooner had they hit the paving stones when there was a loud whoosh from above. The wood of both the box and the pyre had hit combustion point, and erupted in a great burst of flame. And the crowd roared.

The curator was in no condition to walk, let alone run. Her limbs were stiff and painful. But she still protested indignantly when the boatman and the Australian woman seized the moment of distraction amongst the crowd to carry her to the edge of the Campo.

"Undignified? Hah! Stop complaining, Historian – you are safe now," Mario panted as he lay her down with more gentleness than his words suggested he felt.

Elizabeth's throat was still wracked by smoke as she looked back toward the stage area, managing to croak out the words, "I don't think... anyone... is safe... yet..."

The tradition of burning an effigy, often of an old woman, is known in many parts of Europe. In some parts of Italy, particularly, the old wisdom has it that the direction in which the sparks of the blazing figurine fly is a divination of the season to come – good or bad. John B., his head clearing enough for him to move, looked up at the platform his beloved had just managed to vacate. He noticed that the sparks were whirling straight up and vanishing – no, not vanishing, being absorbed.

Absorbed into something black. Above the crowd, above the stage, above the burning platform. A strangely swirling amorphous black shape, barely the size of a dinner plate but pulsing and growing slowly, inexorably larger. The return of Shub-Niggurath.

The wizard ran for Il Duce's stage.

As he ran, John B. worked his left hand into the gesture that Scarlet had reminded him of. The sign of Koth, it was called. From the edge of the stage, Pasqualina saw the gesture and stared. How could he know this? What else did he know?

The wizard read from his phone. "*Imas weghaymnko quavers yewet...*" Even as he said the ancient eldritch words he sensed that there was something wrong. Well, other than the sudden apparition of an ancient powerful demon in the air above his head. Something else.

The dreadful black shape continued to grow. Stewart stared at the screen of his phone. The words were gibberish as far as he was concerned, but evidently not the right gibberish. What did he know about spells anyway? Maybe this one could only work once? A pity Scarlet wasn't here herself.

The pain had subsided, but his head was still ringing.

Leonardo, having realized that his masterpiece was no longer audible, had moved out from behind his keyboard to check the connections on some leads. Pasqualina darted out from her discreet position and grabbed the big man's shoulder. She shoved him towards Stewart, who'd pushed his way through the crowd at the front of the stage, alongside the celebrities.

"Kill the Australian!" she shouted over the mob's din.

"What? What are you talking about? Don't push me! What's happened to my music?"

"It was him! He's responsible!" the redhead shouted back, and pushed the musician again.

This shove was impelled by frustration, fury, and possibly madness. It was strong enough to push Delocchio off balance. Two staggering steps, and he suddenly ran out of stage, toppled sideways and fell into the crowd. All that saved Il Duce from serious injury were the bodies of three people he landed on. Unfortunately, one of them was John B. Stewart.

As he went to ground Stewart's skull smacked a flagstone. It added a new note to the symphony of pain in his head. That word 'symphony' spun in his mind for a moment, other words cascading from it: musical words. Clefs, crotchets, minims, quavers...

He stared at the phone he'd somehow kept hold of. The screen hadn't yet gone blank – he scrolled with his thumb to keep it alive. Quavers. He was sure the incantation he'd recited in battle with the sorceress in the South Australian desert hadn't had any English words in it. Suddenly 'quavers' stood out like a crow in a row of doves. Auto-correct! Scarlet's phone must have changed the original word and she'd missed it. But what the hell was it meant to be?

Delocchio was squirming like an angry walrus, trying to get to his feet. His shifting bulk pressed heavily on Stewart's left hand, and the pattern of pain confirmed that the hand was still maintaining the sign of Koth. The wizard's mind raced.

He started working through the alphabet, substituting letters, hoping for a spark of familiarity. Quafers? Quagers? Quahers? That was it! Somehow, in that desperate underground struggle, through a fog of pain, fear and alcohol, the words he'd uttered had etched themselves on his memory just enough to be recognized now.

Gasping for the breath that Leonardo's wriggling weight had squeezed out of him, he managed to read aloud again. "*Imas weghaymnko quahers yewet...*"

He was in no position to see, but had to hope that the black shape in the sky had stopped expanding.

Hampered by the press of well-meaning fans as much as by his own body shape, Delocchio was still flailing helplessly, but his movements did at least allow John B. to roll away and regain his feet. The wizard had suddenly developed some sympathy for the last blob of toothpaste being squeezed in its tube.

As the musician-turned-art dealer jiggled and wriggled he raved almost incoherently. From the stage, Pasqualina screamed back at him.

"You fool! You fat fool! All my careful planning! You've been my tool, my mask while I prepared the way for my true master. Months of preparation getting you to this point, and you're too clumsy to play a damned note! What use are you to me?"

Il Duce Grosso stopped squirming momentarily, and stared up at her transfixed. Someone else, using *him*? That wasn't *fair*! He shrieked in childish petulance, completely forgetting the purple-garbed Australian beside him.

"You used me?!? Nobody uses me! I'm the richest man in Venice! I could buy and sell you a thousand times over, woman! I'm not your tool, you're mine! I hired you, you're my property, to do whatever I tell you – just like all the others I keep on my payroll! *I'm* the one in charge!"

Only a little way away, the darkly clothed Signore Medici listened with considerable interest, and wrote quickly in his ever-present pocketbook.

Even through his raving, Delocchio spotted Luigino at the side of the stage.

"Get her! Get her!" the fat man cried waving a pudgy hand towards Pasqualina.

Culatello couldn't hear his boss properly, and saw only the flailing arm. He also saw at the front of the stage, attempting to climb up, the shaggy figure in the purple costume, mask now a crushed mess somehow still hanging from a string around the wizard's neck. The Australian! He and that damned woman of his were the cause of all his recent grief!

He pulled a long fishing knife from somewhere under his silver-and-black robe, and started to lunge forward, his movement awkwardly hampered by the cast on his leg. The woman he knew only as the cook was no more than an impediment to his attack. She jerked backward, away from him and the waving blade.

Then there was a new sound: part hiss, part snarl, part weird gargling cry. A bundle of dusty black fur flew, and Toscanini's claws raked deeply across Luigino's face. The thug screamed and grabbed at his feline assailant, dropping the long knife.

Addled as the cat's brain was, he still remembered, amongst all the taunts, tortures and abuse of kittenhood, precisely who it was who'd kicked him in the head. A measure of revenge at last. A final deep gouge, and he slipped from the former fisherman's hands and fled back into the crowd.

Whatever good looks Luigino may have imagined he possessed would now be permanently compromised by the scarring of his face. A single scar he may have tried to pass off as a legacy of a blade, and concocted a story to make himself seem a victim, or even a hero. Women fell for heroes. The four deep parallel lines across brow, cheek, and nose, however, were very clearly the work of an angry cat, and would never be fancifully presented as anything more glamourous.

Shrieking, he toppled right over Stewart and into the crowd. His already abused shin was trampled, the recent break made drastically worse, the moonboot inadequate to protect the bone from the crush of people still trying to give the massive maestro a wide berth. The mewling noises Luigino now made were probably more cat-like than anything Tosca produced these days.

Without Ugo or anyone else to tell him what to do, the youngest Culatello would creep into the throng, and then wait far too long to see a doctor. Infection would set in, and the foot would be amputated. In what was left of his pride he would return to the Burano haunts of his younger days, expecting to find a woman there who'd be willing to support him.

With his scarred face and clumsy wooden prosthetic foot, not to mention his surly demeanour and bad temper, he was of course 100% wrong. He did, at least, find menial work back on a fishing boat. He didn't even notice the smell by then. Luigino Culatello would go on to live a long life that he rarely enjoyed.

Ducking under the falling would-be attacker, John B. struggled onto the stage. Moving better than Luigino, he lunged to grab Pasqualina. Again, she was able to sway back out of the way, but only just. She was close enough for the wizard to catch her talisman in her hand.

The cord of his tricorn hat, now bashed into shapelessness, had snagged in his hair. He was able to grab it, and a quick slash with the razor blade that was still jammed in an edge was enough to sever the leather thong around her neck without her even noticing.

Realizing that Marina had been freed, and the Australian woman was out of reach, Squila was opening herself and her power up to Shub-Niggurath. The final option of a sacrifice – her own. She'd recognized a strange feminine power when in the Musee Barche. When the abducted Elizabeth had been brought to the Palazzo the cook had sensed that the emanations weren't quite the same, therefore both women must have something special about them.

But now neither was at hand – the best power available was that which she'd nurtured in herself for most of a lifetime. Not her first choice, she'd have preferred to be part of the fun when the Old Ones returned, Shub-Niggurath at their forefront. But she was willing to make the sacrifice. Surely her true masters would recognize and reward her loyalty somehow.

One tendril of the blackness stretched down toward her, lay on her head like the beneficence of an ebon octopus, twining almost lovingly into her red hair. She snatched up Luigino's knife and gashed her own arm. As her blood flowed out, it was as though the blackness flowed into her. Eyes like bright obsidian marbles gazed at John B.

"I know you..." came a voice, felt more than heard.

It came from Pasqualina's mouth, but also from somewhere far beyond.

The transfiguration process held Squila immobile. The wizard seized the opportunity, and wound the cord around her bleeding arm, pulling the leather tight to act as a tourniquet above the gash. The Talisman itself fell upon the open cut, even as the blood flow stopped.

The crowd still massed around Leonardo, all of them mercifully oblivious to what was happening at the side of the stage. Many were still enjoying the special effects and the fire, and presumed the music would start when this dramatic pyrotechnic display was over.

Delocchio himself was screaming in incoherent rage, his own bulk and the pressing mob keeping him from regaining his feet. He rocked and wailed like a giant baby, the nearest of the observers starting to shrink back in a kind of horror at the behaviour of the fallen superstar.

The far greater horror still threatened at the side of the stage. Dino and the road crew were staying at what they hoped was a safe distance. They knew nothing of the demonic threat, but they'd seen a knife flash, blood flowing, and the irrational behaviour of their erstwhile employer. No – not being paid well enough for this. Several of the crew slipped away into the anonymity of the crowd, shucking their silver livery as they went.

Pasqualina had dropped to her knees, and was silent. The blackness in her eyes ebbed and flowed in waves.

"Oh no, you're not dying on my watch, lady. I wish you to survive this," muttered John B., holding her face in his hands.

Leaving Marina in the care of Mario, and briefly encouraging Nicola to find and help her mentor if he needed it, Elizabeth had sidled and forced her way through the crowd and up onto the stage.

She knelt at the side of her beloved even as he stared at the strange woman who was so much more than a cook. She got there just in time to see the black tendril separate from the self-taught sorceress, a lock of red hair momentarily lifting toward the rapidly diminishing black shape above, like an inadvertant gesture of farewell.

The sparks and burning embers were no longer being drawn to that one spot, and they soared into the Venetian night sky, soaring now like free spirits.

The glossy black sheen drained from Pasqualina's eyes. At first, it was replaced only by whiteness, her eyeballs had rolled so far back in her head. Then the orbs slipped back down. But the stare was vacant.

When the Ancient One had started to occupy the vessel that was her skull, it had evidently made room for itself by burning out any intelligence there.

The former cook's mouth twisted into an incongruously happy smile. It looked like she was watching a favourite, light-hearted movie, maybe a romantic comedy, on a private screen that was just in front of her face.

Only the thin trail of drool that was starting to slip from the corner of her mouth and down her chin gave an indication of the shattered mind.

John B. slowly released his grip on her head. The redhead blinked, unseeing. Shallow breaths slipped in and out, through her nose and between the weirdly smiling lips, automatic and even. She was alive, technically, and would remain so for as long as the strictly Catholic medical professionals into whose care she was handed would permit.

Not repressing a shudder, Q grasped her beau's hands.

"Was that the... thing you met in that cavern?" she asked quietly.

The wizard nodded. "One time was more than enough. Twice – brrrr. I get what Scarlet tried to tell me once about evil having a form. That's what it feels like, and I really don't want to encounter it again."

"You beat it, though, babe."

"Funny what you can do when you don't think about it."

.ooo.

27

FINAL FLOURISHES

With the help of one of the remaining road crew, Dino had managed to get Leonardo upright, and they'd steered the big man to the area down beside the stage. They tried to get him onto the steps back up to the performance area, but the musician pushed himself away from the handrail.

"No! No! I can't possibly! Not now, not after all that carry-on!" he railed.

Nina Carina appeared nearby. "But signore! The crowd! All these people, here to see and hear you perform..."

"To hell with all of them! I don't care about them! This is about *me*! *I'm* upset!" he bellowed in response.

It was unfortunate, but appropriate, that one of the road crew had managed to reconnect the amplifiers just in time for the microphones to pick up Il Duce's roaring tantrum. It wasn't only the shocked celebrities in the highly-priced 'elite' seats who heard the revealing tirade.

The crowd reacted just as you might expect, and the 'prominent local identity' destroyed his own reputation in less than twenty words. Venetians who hadn't been at Campo San Luca heard about the outburst within days, and the Delocchio fanbase evaporated quickly. Suddenly his recordings would be flooding the second-hand stores, and they didn't sell there, either.

Oblivious to all of that, though, the fat man continued to rant and rave as he made his way back to the white canvas shelter, still within effective range of the microphones.

"How dare someone else think they can use me! That's not fair! I don't care about the crowd. They were getting my talents for free anyway. I can't be expected to behave how other people want! I have a condition! I have..."

"Yeah, yeah. I know. I know," replied John B. Stewart, contempt dripping from his voice. He leaned insolently against a stanchion of the canvas shelter, continuing, "Other people are of no importance, are they? Except as far as how much they'll grovel to you. And how much money you can screw out of them."

Even as the microphone was unplugged by Dino's trembling fingers, Il Duce glared at the wizard.

"There's nothing wrong with being rich! I'm a very wealthy man. I'm *important*. I have a *lot* of money. And it's got nothing to do with *her!*" Leonardo shouted, pointing a shaking, pudgy finger at the redhead now sitting quietly drooling on the ground beside the stage, being tended by Nina Carina until someone with more medical expertise arrived.

"Ah. Now, it's interesting to hear you say that, sir."

A new figure walked into the shelter, nodding politely to the two Australians as he passed them. It occurred to them that they'd noticed him before. The black hat and long black coat were familiar. The man slid his dark glasses down his nose slightly, and peered over the top of the smoky lenses. He clutched his black leather briefcase tightly, and didn't offer a handshake to Il Duce. He was smiling, but it wasn't a friendly expression.

"I seem to have caught you at a bad moment, Signore Delocchio. However, your moments are about to get worse, I think, and so there is no time like the present, *si*? My name is Sebastiano Medici, and I have been looking forward to speaking to you for quite some time now."

Delocchio spluttered and swore as he collapsed into the seat of his scooter. The mysterious man in black ignored any attempt at interruption, though, commencing an obviously well-prepared monologue.

A small audience quickly gathered around the shelter, while the great majority of the crowd dispersed to find bars in which to discuss the evening's surprise and compare outrage and disappointment at the fallen hero.

Marina had consented to being escorted home by the gondolier.

Christos, realizing that the work was done, had decided he'd reached his threshold of dealing with a lot of people, said a quiet goodnight to Giancarlo, and slipped unobtrusively away. But the grey maestro and his protégé were determinedly not missing the denouement, and now stood beside the Australians.

They would soon be joined by Teasy and the Blob, both grinning broadly at the little contessa's gleeful description of the reversal of Delocchio's fortune. And it was only getting better.

Medici revealed himself to be an investigator for the Italian tax department, who had long suspected the musician and art dealer of significantly, fraudulently, understating his income. The dark man read off several damning snippets of information from his pocketbook. He didn't name his sources. It was obvious to Leonardo that he'd been betrayed, by who didn't matter – as far as he was concerned, it was probably everybody! Arrest was a distinct possibility. The seizure of assets and enforced bankruptcy, more probable than possible.

When the tax investigator mentioned "income derived by the activities, legal or otherwise, of Signore Delocchio's known associates", Tadeusz remarked loudly, "I believe we may be able to assist you with your enquiries, signore."

His partner added cheerfully, "I'm quite sure we can direct you to others who can offer further corroborating evidence, sir." He handed his business card to the long-nosed investigator, who accepted it with a small bow.

With Il Duce's power clearly being broken, there seemed a very good prospect of persuading business owners who'd been victims of the Culatello brothers to come forward with their stories. Certainly, the jeweller and silversmith would be encouraging them.

Il Duce Grosso had finally gone quiet, and was sweating profusely under the gaze of Sebastiano Medici. The investigator stroked his nose thoughtfully.

"One thing intrigues me, Signore Delocchio. Actually, many things do, I admit, but one in particular that is perhaps pertinent to my enquiries, and your financial situation. I have found no early evidence of your activities. Or even your existence. You seem to have appeared here in Venice, indeed Italy, almost miraculously, a little over ten years ago. What is your country of origin, sir?"

Leonardo inflated his ample chest, his stomach going along for the ride.

"I am a citizen of the world!" he exclaimed with characteristic pomposity.

"As are we all, sir," replied Medici with impeccable calm. "But you are now a resident of Venice, and that brings with it certain responsibilities. Particularly financial ones. If you are to remain such a resident."

The art dealer tried to maintain what he hoped was an expression of suitable outrage, while inwardly his mind raced. The "if" that the unpleasant government official just mentioned...

"I have a reputation for being charitable, you know. But perhaps I could consider the option of emigration..." he began.

"Charity with other people's money doesn't count for much, surely, Inspector?" asked Elizabeth.

"Indeed, signorina," agreed Medici. "And I would not use the term 'emigration'. I think 'deportation' would be more appropriate. Your assets would, of course, be forfeit in any case."

Very slowly, the 'pillar of the community' said, "I... do have family... in Australia, I believe..."

Indeed, he did. He'd been born in a rural town and raised mostly in a Sydney boarding school. If he was to be sent back, he'd be sure to set up in another part of the country. He stared at Elizabeth, the most recent object of his carnal desire. The women in Australia did have their charms. Even stripped of his assets, he could start scheming anew, somewhere where nobody knew or recognized him.

"Of course, I doubt that they would be aware of me," he continued. "But with a little enterprise and determination, a man may yet make his fortune."

"Forge your own path, you reckon?" said Elizabeth with a laugh, snapping a photo of the startled fraudster.

"I'm hardly an expert on social media," John B. admitted, "I do reckon, though, that you don't look like a bloke who could fade into anonymity."

"*Feh* – not hard to recognize this one!" agreed Nicola, her mentor smiling quietly behind her.

With a winsome smile and a squeeze of her darling's hand – not the painful one – Elizabeth said, "Y'know babe, over the years you and I worked in Canberra, I'm *sure* that you and I made some useful contacts in our Department, and others. Folks who'd be *more* than happy to work with Signore Medici, and keep a close eye on this character. Whatever he might choose to call himself," she added shrewdly.

Delocchio looked even more uncomfortable. Maybe bankruptcy in Italy wasn't such a bad option. His current Venetian activities may be compromised (he didn't yet know his 'network' of hired help had disintegrated), but he could start again, somewhere else...

The polite smile of the tax inspector hadn't slipped. He gestured towards the Australians, as though to acknowledge their offer. "My own Department will be, as you suggest, 'keeping an eye on' our friend's activities. I will be taking a particular interest myself. Should he retain his liberty, which is by no means assured."

John B. stood watching thoughtfully while Medici ventured more questions, now getting mostly monosyllabic responses. The man in black continued to take notes, though, and made a quick call to enlist the attendance of members of the *Guardia di Finanza*. Signore Delocchio would be taken into custody, purely as a precaution.

The wizard spun his battered tricorn hat on the end of its cord, and pondered where and how the fallen idol may have obtained some of the 'starting capital' for his activities. Not from conventional sources, or Medici would presumably have traced and mentioned them. Not favours from friends old or new, either. Leonardo was almost the archetype of 'does not play well with others'.

Stewart patted the fat man's knee, provoking a nervous twitch (it would have been a jump from a lighter fellow), and said, "Tough news about the tax office, mate." He lowered his voice. "I wish that your other creditors catch up with you, too."

Il Duce Grosso looked up in alarm. There was another storied merchant of Venice who'd been threatened with the forfeit of a pound of flesh. The art dealer had plenty of pounds to spare if it came to that, but the expression on his face suggested that those creditors were numerous, and at least some could be as ruthless as he was. Even the walls of a jail cell would not be adequate protection, he suddenly realized.

The taxman turned to face Elizabeth and said mildly, "I understand you have some property that Signore Delocchio had expressed some interest in. May I recommend to you the choice of a more reputable investor? If required, I could furnish you with some names of people who's probity I would be much more confident of."

"That would be... appreciated, signore," the brunette replied.

Medici immediately wrote three names and phone numbers on a page of his little notebook. His memory was clearly prodigious, despite the affectation of frequent note-taking. He tore out the page and handed it to Elizabeth, offering a smile and a nod to her and her beau.

"*Molto grazie*, Signore Medici," said John B. on behalf of them both.

The wizard gave an exaggerated final bow to Delocchio and walked from the white shelter, arm in arm with his beloved Q, with Nicola close by his other side. Bouncing out from where he'd been hiding, Toscanini gave a satisfied gurgling mew and fell into step beside his young mistress.

Holding hands and smiling, Tadeusz and Morton joined them as they departed.

Only Giancarlo remained, briefly. He smiled down at his one-time collaborator, who'd effectively stolen his work (and, more importantly, the work of others whose friendship the grey maestro valued).

"I wish you luck, Leonardo," he said evenly, then with a nod to Sebastiano Medici, followed the others out.

Slowing slightly for the grey man to catch up, John B. casually remarked, "Of course, there's more than one kind of luck, isn't there?"

LaGrigio's smile was broad as his fingers entwined with Nicola's. "Oh yes, my friend. Indeed!"

THE DISAPPOINTING FINALE to the Carnivale merited some space in the newspaper, although as more than one writer observed, the occasion was traditionally a celebration of chaos, and that had certainly been delivered.

More column inches were devoted to the fall from grace of the "previously highly-regarded S. Delocchio". Suddenly he was as reviled as he'd been lauded. His 'public spiritedness' was sneered at as deception, his 'generosity' dismissed as fraudulent fabrication. Even his creative genius was openly questioned – how much of "his" music had the fat man really played, critics wondered?

One of Medici's suggested investors proved to be an excellent choice. A more than satisfactory sum was deposited in Elizabeth's Swiss account, and the buyer very promptly collected many of the old coins from the Musee Barche. Some, however, at the Australian's insistence, were to remain the property of the museum.

Three days after the end of Carnevale a large manila envelope was delivered by courier to Manovalo 219. Addressed to Signorina Elizabeth, it contained a brief but sincere note of thanks from Marina DeNucci. It also contained a sheaf of foolscap papers.

Handwritten in flawless cursive script, they contained the translation of Antonio Zeno's correspondence about his journeys with Henry St. Clair. This was not the somewhat sanitized, redacted version which had seen publication. This appeared to be a direct translation of the original documents, rendered into English with a greater care for accuracy than elegance of expression.

"Oh! Oh – this will be useful, I think," said the aspiring authoress.

The wizard smiled at the delight in his beloved's voice. "I hope so, sweetheart," he replied. "You deserve it, jumping into the fire the way you did."

"You'd have done exactly the same, babe, if you'd been closer."

"But I wasn't. Thank you."

There was a small celebratory dinner that evening in the *Trattoria Luciano*. Luciano had installed an electric piano for his guests' enjoyment, and sacrificed some table space to clear a small dance floor.

After their superb main course, the music had begun. Christos and Robi had brought guitars, naturally, and were strumming the rhythm accompaniment for Nicola, who'd been allowed free rein on the keyboard. Tadeusz and Morton danced close and contentedly, more liberated than even they had suspected by the lifting of the threat of the Culatello brothers and their boss. Mario danced playfully with one of Luciano's waitresses who he had, figuratively and literally, swept off her feet.

The 'little contessa' was absorbed in her stirring rendition of *In The Hall Of The Mountain King*, with a variety of clever embellishments to Grieg's original music. Hardly a typical dance tune, but her audience didn't care.

Her mentor watched proudly, and said quietly to the Australians at the table with him, "She will outlive Giancarlo LaGrigio, I sincerely hope, but I take great comfort in knowing that the music she creates will live even longer. I look forward to knowing it."

"You'll live on in that music, you mean?" asked Q, puzzled.

Giancarlo only smiled, seemingly lost in thought as he watched Nicola play.

John B. wore a similarly thoughtful smile as he said, "Your relationship with Nicola is intriguing, my friend. I wonder if it could thrive as it has, anywhere else but in Venice?"

"Possibly, or possibly not, you're right. Especially in this era. Yes, I'm aware of appearances. I appreciate your respect, and your efforts to be understanding, Elizabeth."

The brunette smiled a little awkwardly as the maestro continued. "If it helps, let me explain that I neither have, nor seek, any experience of sharing my life with someone on the other side of such an age gap. I've lived a long life, my friends, and I've never known anyone quite like my widget. In her own time, she'll run free. But I want to be the safe place that she could run back to if necessary. If not 'always', for as long as possible. Sometimes I feel that she is the best thing that ever happened to me. I'd like for that to be mutual."

There was no gainsaying that sentiment, and smiles of genuine affection were exchanged between the three.

Sometime later, after one of Luciano's more extravagant dessert concoctions had been enjoyed, a message arrived on John B.'s mobile phone.

"It's Scarlet," he explained. "It must be quite early morning down where she is. I sent a text earlier, filling her in, as best I could, on what had happened. She was relieved, she reckons, but never in doubt. Nice of her to say so. Oh, and sweetheart – you and I are invited to an Outback wedding next month!"

"Well! There's a change to the travel plans! Not that I mind, I'm just surprised by the suddenness. But I'm starting to realize that nothing about Charlotte Burke should surprise me."

Stewart blinked innocently. "Plans? We had plans?" he asked.

At the mention of a wedding, Morton had to suppress an embarrassed start. He discreetly nudged his partner, who in turn delicately kicked John B.'s shin without attracting attention. The Australian managed to read TZ's peculiar facial gestures and reached under the table to accept the small parcel surreptitiously handed to him. Tadeusz had been waiting for a signal from his partner, and had assumed there was a plan to his timing. The reality was that between the food, the music, the dancing and the overall mood of celebration, the Blob had simply forgotten.

The wizard cleared his throat, and tapped a spoon against his wine glass to call for silence around the table. He stood up, unusually self-conscious.

"Um... can I just have your attention for a moment, please, folks? First up, I want to thank you all. For your company, your support, your friendship. I realise that not all of you really quite understand what we were up against, or what happened – believe me, you're better off that way. The important thing is, we came through it okay, and the Silver Duke and his *stronzi* mates won't be causing any more trouble. Not for us, you, or anyone else close to us, I reckon. And that couldn't have happened without all of you. Speaking of close, I want to acknowledge the person closest to me. Closer than I thought anyone would ever be."

He looked down into a pair of extraordinary green eyes gazing up at him, glistening, and continued.

"Whatever I do, whatever I face, is easier and better for knowing that I'm loved, and I love in return. I'm not much on formality and ceremony, I must admit. Pretty lady, this isn't a proposal, but it's a public affirmation of how I feel..."

"How *we* feel, babe."

"Thank you, pretty lady." He held out his hand, in which nestled a small package wrapped in purple silk, tied with a sea green ribbon. Tadeusz Zybysko was perceptive as well as romantic.

Elizabeth didn't pick up the parcel – she unwrapped it where it lay on his palm. As she lifted the lid of a small box she gasped, her brilliant green eyes widening. Nestling in the box were a pair of rings. An amethyst and a turquoise, both old stones but newly and exquisitely recut and polished to bring out the best of their colours, had been set in matching rose gold. The twin designs owed a lot to both Viking art and older, Celtic knotwork.

"Oh. Wow," was all she softly said as she drew the two treasures out of their nest.

Without another word John B. took the turquoise ring from her, and slid it onto the ring finger of her left hand. Elizabeth returned the action with the amethyst ring, slipping it onto his left hand. She looked up, smiling at everyone around the table.

"Public affirmation. I love this man," she said.

"And I love you," he replied, his own gaze not leaving her face.

Their friends burst into spontaneous applause as the two Australians kissed.

Laughing, Nicola said, "Lizbetta, it did not need to be said!" She reached to squeeze the brunette's shoulder. "But it is good that you said so, *si?*"

Sometimes things aren't what they seem. But importantly, sometimes they are.

Sometimes the mask is the real face.

- FINITO -

NEXT:

Out in the Mediterranean Sea, ancient and powerful forces are gathering. The final battle in a war as old as history, with the future of humanity as the prize. And John B. Stewart and Elizabeth McKew are at the very centre of it.

The unlikely wizard and his beloved find their own secrets revealed as his magical power is called on like never before. The oldest of enemies threaten to tear them apart, just when they, and the world, need each other most. Each must decide where they stand as ruthless forces of the past fight for the destiny of mankind.

THE ANCESTORS OF ATHENATOS
- The Ninth Book of Dubious Magic

THE DUBIOUS MAGIC BOOKS:

The Wizard of Waramanga

The Carvings of Cobbemarmoo

The Mad Machines of Mundara

The Warriors of Wiwo'ole

The Spirits of Sron Dubh

The Sailors of Svalgsay

The Treasure of Tepatamwa

Visit *www.meredian.store*